Charles Albert Lidgey

Wagner

Charles Albert Lidgey

Wagner

ISBN/EAN: 9783337385705

Printed in Europe, USA, Canada, Australia, Japan

Cover: Foto ©Andreas Hilbeck / pixelio.de

More available books at **www.hansebooks.com**

Wagner

By

Charles A. Lidgey

With
Illustrations and Portraits

London : J. M. Dent & Co.
New York : E. P. Dutton & Co.
1899

Preface

IT is probably safe to say that there has lived no more discussed a musician than Richard Wagner. For this reason I have purposely omitted any attempt at a Bibliography. The number of books, articles, and pamphlets that have been written about him and his works is legion, and anything like a representative list would have swollen this volume to unreasonable proportions. Amongst the more important biographical workers there should, however, be mentioned the names of Glasenapp, Tappert, Gasperini, Dannreuther (in Grove's " Dictionary of Music "), and Chamberlain, while Wagnerian students owe a debt of gratitude to the excellent translated work which has from time to time been accomplished by Ashton Ellis, H. and F. Corder, and Alfred Forman. For similar reasons I was compelled to abandon the idea of supplying the various *motifs* in musical notation. To give only a few would have served no useful purpose ; to give them in detail would

v

Preface

have necessitated some three hundred examples. I have therefore endeavoured to present to the reader as comprehensive a view as possible of an artist whose many-sided versatility is unique—a man whose life is a shining example of pluck in the face of difficulties. I have in conclusion to express my grateful thanks to Professor August Wilhelmj for the kindness which has enabled me to present to the public some hitherto unpublished photographs and manuscripts.

THE AUTHOR.

1, STONE BUILDINGS,
LINCOLN'S INN, W.C.

Contents

vii

Contents

art—" Eine Faust Overture "—Sketches for " The Flying
Dutchman "—Pillet's dishonourable conduct—Writes
" Der fliegende Holländer " in seven weeks—Studies in
history and legend—A holiday at Teplitz—Sketches for
" Tannhäuser "—Returns to Dresden—Successful pro-
duction of " Rienzi "—Production of " Der fliegende
Holländer "—Lukewarm attitude of the public—Becomes
joint Hofcapellmeister to the Court orchestra—Other
conducting work—" Das Liebesmahl der Apostel "—
Wagner as a conductor—Completes " Tannhäuser "—
Assists at Weber's re-interment at Dresden—Sketches
for " Lohengrin " and " Die Meistersinger "—First performance of " Tannhäuser "—Hostile press criticism—
Completes " Lohengrin "—" Jesus von Nazareth "—
" Die Wibelungen, Weltgeschichte aus der Sage "—
" Der Nibelungen Mythus als Entwurf zu einem Drama "
—" Siegfried's Tod "—His art theories—The Revolution
of '49—His part therein—Escapes to Weimar to avoid
arrest—Liszt gets him away to Paris—Eventually reaches
and becomes a citizen of Zurich   17

CHAPTER III

Life in Zurich—His friends there—Liszt—Literary work—
" Die Kunst und die Revolution "—" Das Kunstwerk
der Zukunft "—" Kunst und Klima "—" Das Judenthum
in der Musik "—" Oper und Drama "—Production of
" Lohengrin " at Weimar—Poem of " Der Ring des
Nibelungen " printed—Completes " Das Rheingold "—
Second visit to London, as conductor of the Philhar-
monic Concerts—Hostile English critics—Completes
" Die Walküre "—Commences " Siegfried "—Lays it
aside in favour of " Tristan und Isolde "—Leaves Zurich
—Visits Venice and Lyons and eventually reaches Paris

viii

Contents

CHAPTER IV

Contents

x

Contents

CHAPTER VII

Contents

xii

Contents

List of Illustrations

xv

Wagner

CHAPTER I

His birth—His father's death and mother's second marriage—
Ludwig Geyer—Removal of the family to Dresden—Visits
to the theatre with his stepfather—Death of Geyer—Early
school days—Return of the family to Leipzig—Early musical
studies—School and University life at Leipzig—Studies in
mediæval legend—Composes a Symphony—" Die Hochzeit "—
Becomes chorus-master at Würzburg—" Die Feen "—Returns
to Leipzig—Rejection of " Die Feen " by the theatre—Becomes
director of the theatre at Magdeburg—Wilhelmine Schröder-
Devrient—" Das Liebesverbot "—Its first performance a fiasco
—Returns to Leipzig—Rejection of " Das Liebesverbot " by
the theatres at that city and Berlin—Is appointed conductor at
the Schauspielhaus at Königsberg—Marries Minna Planer—
Sketches for " Die hohe Braut " ignored by Scribe—Becomes
First Music-director at the new theatre in Riga—His work
there—Commencement of " Rienzi "—Sets out for Paris.

THE early portion of the nineteenth century was notable
in the annals of music. It witnessed the development
of the heaven-sent genius of the mighty   *His birth*
Beethoven ; it fostered the youthful promise
of Weber, Spohr, Rossini, Auber, Berlioz, Chopin,

Wagner

Schumann, Mendelssohn, and Liszt; and it saw, on the 22nd of May, 1813, the birth of Wilhelm Richard Wagner. His father, Carl Friedrich Wilhelm Wagner, was a man of culture and refinement. Holding a position officially described as "Actuarius bei den Stadtgerichten," and involving clerical duties in the city police courts, he spent his leisure time in the study of poetry, and other artistic pursuits, and was especially partial to amateur theatricals. At the age of twenty-eight—he was born in 1770—he had married Johanna Rosina Bertz, a native of Weissenfels, who shared her husband's artistic leanings; and by her he had nine children, of whom Richard was the youngest.

The child's early days were spent in troubled times. In October, 1813, came the battle of Leipzig, and his father did not long survive that event, dying in the following *His father's* month from a fever brought on, without *death and* doubt, by the fearful condition of the place *mother's* after the struggle. The widow was left *second* in great distress. Of private means she had *marriage* little or none, and the pension to which she became entitled through her husband's death was but small. It is not strange, therefore, to find that in 1815 she married again.

Her second husband, Ludwig Geyer, deserves more than a passing word, because there can be *Ludwig* little doubt that it was association with him *Geyer* which implanted so strong a love of the stage in his small stepson, however much the lad may

2

The house in which Wagner was born

Early Artistic Surroundings

have owed his genius to heredity. Geyer was a man of many and varied artistic attainments ; a painter of note, a singer whom Weber liked to hear in his operas, a playwright whose comedies obtained a fair amount of success, and an actor whose popularity was then assured. At the time of his marriage he was engaged at the Königsl.-Sächs-Hoftheater at Dresden, and thither the family soon removed. Here it *Visits to* was little Richard's greatest delight to be *the theatre* allowed to accompany his stepfather to rehearsals, and the impressions there received were no doubt deepened by the conversation of the artistic friends who formed Geyer's favourite home circle.

Geyer wished, so Wagner himself says, to make a painter of him, but the boy's genius did not lie in that direction. Before Geyer's death, in 1821, Wagner had learned to play some few little airs upon the piano, " Üb immer Treu und Redlich- *Death of* keit," and the then newly published " Jung- *Geyer* fernkranz " of Weber ; and his playing of these to Geyer on his death-bed elicited from the latter the remark, " Has he, perchance, a talent for music ? " But, at this early period, there was implanted in Wagner the love of the drama and everything connected therewith, which was the key-note of his life's work. Even in his later days music was but one of the means he employed in the endeavour to create a perfect art in which dramatic action was ever the dominant feature ; and the child's surroundings in

3

Wagner

Dresden, and his constant association with people and things theatrical, must have had much to do with the bent his mind ultimately assumed.

After his stepfather's death he was sent to the Kreuzschule in Dresden, where he soon became the favourite pupil of Professor Sillig. He evinced a great *Early school days* liking for Greek, and his musical studies made little or no progress. A tutor gave him some lessons on the piano, but he proved a sorry pupil, and was never more than an indifferent performer. Music to him was then a secondary consideration, but he plunged with avidity into Greek, Latin, Mythology, and Ancient History, translating the first twelve books of the Odyssey out of school hours. He began writing verses, and when he was only eleven years old a poem on the death of a schoolfellow was published as being the best the school could produce. Fired with this success, he " promptly determined to become a poet "—a characteristic instance of his impetuous nature—commencing a study of Apel's works, and planning various tragedies in the Greek style. Shakespeare, also, was not neglected ; he made a metrical translation of Romeo's monologue, and spent two years over the elaboration of a tragedy which was a mixture, more or less, of " Hamlet " and " King Lear." This production was a curious affair ; he introduced some two and forty personages at the commencement, but the slaughter which ensued was so tremendous that it necessitated the resurrection of many

Early Musical Studies

of the principals in the character of ghosts to bring the play to any sort of issue. The writing of this elaborate work was interrupted by the removal of the family from Dresden to Leipzig. Pecuniary difficulties and the enforced acceptance by his eldest sister Rosalie of an engagement at a theatre in the latter town were the cause of the change.

Return of the family to Leipzig

In 1828 young Wagner was sent to the Nicolai-schule at Leipzig, and, to his great mortification, was placed in the third form. At Dresden his position had been in the second, and he immediately became disgusted with all forms of philological study. This circumstance proved, perhaps, the turning-point of his life. He varied his work on his tragedy by attending the concerts at the Gewandhaus, and there heard for the first time—Beethoven. The impression produced on him he declared to be "overpowering," and nothing would satisfy him but an accompaniment to his tragedy of music such as that of "Egmont." He also fully believed himself capable of writing it. He borrowed from a circulating library a copy of Logier's "Method of Thorough-Bass," and in secrecy

Early musical studies

and solitude composed a quartet, a sonata, and an aria. The family were then apprised that he considered he was destined to be a musician. The announcement was received with some incredulity; for not only had the discovery of the manuscript of the tragedy led to a suspicion that his studies at school had been

5

Wagner

neglected, but there existed no proofs of any preliminary work at the subject—not even the ability to play upon an instrument. The boy's enthusiasm, however, prevailed, and a master, Gottlieb Müller by name, was engaged. But dry technical study was not to Wagner's liking, and poor Müller had an experience the reverse of amiable with his hot-headed young pupil, the result being that the lessons were soon discontinued.

About this time, at the age of sixteen, he left the Nicolaischule and joined the Thomasschule, but settling down to regular work was an impossibility. He made the acquaintance of Hoffmann's works, and *Studies in mediæval legend* the perusal of the story of the Meistersinger (or Minnesinger) at Wartburg and the "Meistersinger Martin der Küfer von Nürnberg" in all likelihood first implanted in him the love of mediæval legend which was to bring forth such striking results in after-years. Tieck's "Tannhäuser" was also eagerly read. Inspired by the mysticism of these authors, his ideas of musical expression took larger forms. Nothing but the full orchestra would satisfy him, and he composed an Overture in B flat, $\frac{6}{8}$ time, in which the persistent reiteration at every fourth bar of a *fortissimo* thud on the drum excited the mild derision of the audience when it was performed under Heinrich Dorn at the theatre as an entr'acte. A more important fancy was the projection of a pastoral play suggested by

6

His only Symphony

Goethe's " Laune des Verliebten," inasmuch as the conception entailed the composition of both words *and* music ; but this came to nothing, being abandoned perhaps in favour of a new idol—politics, into which he threw himself with the greatest enthusiasm, the excited political atmosphere of the time adding fuel to the fire.

In 1830 he left school and matriculated at the Leipzig University, not with the idea of studying for any profession, but in order to attend lectures on philosophy and æsthetics. Student-life, however, proved too fascinating, and he gave himself up to all its excesses, to the neglect of music and everything else. But his strength of character soon reasserted itself, and he resolved to master counterpoint. To this end he placed himself under the cantor of the Thomasschule, Theodor Weinlig, and such was the rapidity of his progress that in less than six months he was able to solve the driest problems in that dry study. Mozart and Beethoven were his models at this period, particularly the former ; and he composed a Sonata, a Polonaise for four hands, and a Fantasia, marked by simplicity both of matter and treatment. The next year witnessed him pursuing his studies with diligence, and writing a couple of overtures upon the Beethoven model. In 1832, another overture was composed and also his only completed Symphony. The latter work was first *Composes a* brought to a hearing in London a few years *Symphony* ago by Mr. Henschel at one of his Symphony Concerts,

7

and is interesting as evincing a power of terse and vigorous use of thematic material, remarkable in one so young ; it shows, however, none of the marvellous precocity which distinguished the early efforts of a Mendelssohn.

The Symphony completed, he set out for Vienna, being anxious for a glimpse of that famed city of music. To his disgust, "Zampa" held the field, and he departed in wrath. Stopping at Prague, he made the acquaintance of Dionys Weber, the director of the Conservatorium at that city, who took a fancy to him and performed several of his compositions, including the Symphony, at the Conservatorium. During his stay he was seized with a desire to write a libretto for an opera, and composed a *"Die* tragic story which he named "Die Hoch-*Hochzeit"* zeit." On his return to Leipzig he at once · began writing the music, but the subject found no favour in his sister's eyes, and the book was promptly destroyed. The Symphony was also performed at a Gewandhaus concert, and met with an encouraging reception.

Young Wagner by this time had fully resolved to embrace music as a profession. He entered upon it with advantages which have fallen to the lot of few of the world's greatest musicians. His early years had been spent in the quenching of a thirst for culture and literature, remarkable in itself, and far-reaching in its ultimate effects. His study of the finest tragedies of the Greeks resulted in the evolution of the theories

8

His Character

embodied in "The Art Work of the Future;" his love of mythology found its ultimate satisfaction in the re-incarnation of the old Sagas; his fearless desire for truth led him to put forth his greatest powers, even in the times of his darkest need, towards the realization of all that was true and noble in his art. There was nothing small about Richard Wagner. Even in his boyish days his mind was occupied with the study of masterpieces, whether of music or literature; his aims were ever towards high ideals. The range of his reading was wide; his sympathy far-reaching; his enthusiasm intense; his reverence for genius deep-rooted. During the family's residence at Dresden, Weber was a constant visitor, and the great composer excited feelings nearly akin to awe in the breast of little Richard. Later on, Wagner was enabled to give practical testimony to the esteem and regard in which he held Weber's memory; and the care and solicitude with which he carried out the arrangements for the removal of the body of the dead master from London to his beloved Dresden are touching proof of the warmth and depth of his affection. And when to all these qualities we add that spirit of sturdy self-reliance, which, under certain circumstances, appeared to the world at large rather as aggressive com- *Becomes* bativeness, we see the man as he was when, *chorus-* at the age of twenty, he settled down to *master at* active work as chorus-master at the theatre *Würzburg* at Würzburg, with the by no means princely salary of ten florins a month.

9

Wagner

This appointment he owed chiefly to his elder brother Albert, a man fourteen years his senior, the father of the well-known singer, Johanna Wagner. Albert Wagner was a personage at the little theatre—being stage manager as well as principal tenor. The duties of this new post were not arduous, and Richard's indomitable energy soon led him again into composition. The subject of a play by a Venetian playwright, Carlo Gozzi, entitled "La Donna Serpente," had attracted him, and by the end of the year (1833) he had completed the words and music of an opera in three acts, which he *"Die Feen"* named "Die Feen." This work contains many passages of marked beauty, and was a real advance upon his earlier efforts. There is also to be found in it a forecast of the strong dramatic individuality which impressed itself so markedly in later years upon his versions of the old Sagas in the "Ring des Nibelungen," "Tristan und Isolde," and "Parsifal." But the music contains no trace of the Wagner of the future; he himself says that Beethoven, Weber, and Marschner were his models, and their influence is sufficiently apparent in the score. Besides the work that the composition of the opera involved, he found time to write additional music for some of his brother's *rôles*, and to assist in the doings of the Musikverein, where some of his compositions were performed.

Early in 1834 he returned to Leipzig, and encountered the first of the long series of disappointments which would have damped the ardour of most men. He had

Schröder-Devrient

admirers who had influence with the press, and his sister Rosalie had a certain power at the theatre; through their agency he obtained an introduction to one Ringelhardt, at that time the director. Ringelhardt accepted "Die Feen;" but the stage manager, Hauser, took a dislike to it, and it was laid aside. *Returns to Leipzig* Wagner felt the disappointment keenly, the more so as his earlier associations with his native town had seemed to indicate that the sweets of success were within his grasp. He left Leipzig, and shortly afterwards became the director of the theatre at Magdeburg. During his stay in his native city, however, an event had happened which led his thoughts into new channels as regards the possibilities *Becomes director of Magdeburg theatre* of music. For the first time in his life he heard a really good singer—Wilhelmine Schröder-Devrient, and the impression she made upon him was deep and lasting. She subsequently became one of his most intimate *Wilhelmine Schröder-Devrient* friends. Her singing, notwithstanding the triviality of the opera in which she appeared (Bellini's "Montecchi e Capuletti"), ·impressed him with the importance of vocal melody—"song," as he himself a year or two later insisted upon with some warmth. A performance of "Masaniello" shortly afterwards turned his thoughts in the direction of the value of action and scenic effect, and he set to work, soon after his arrival in Magdeburg, to write in the light of his

Wagner

new convictions. The result was an opera in two acts, "Das Liebesverbot," based upon Shakespeare's "Measure for Measure," in which the influence of his new models was patent. In Magde-burg he remained till the spring of 1836.

"Das Lie-besverbot"

He soon established himself on a friendly footing both with the artistes and the public. He introduced many improvements in the stage manage-ment, and at rehearsals was ever on the alert to secure attention to detail and perfection of *ensemble*. He wrote much also; an overture to "Columbus" (a play by Apel), music for the celebration of New Year's Day, 1835, songs to a fantastic farce, "Der Berggeist," and other compositions poured from his active brain, in addition to the opera upon which he worked constantly.

This congenial life, however, was not to last long. The theatre was assisted by a small subvention from the Court of Saxony, and the management was in the hands of a committee; but, notwithstanding this help, the director—Bethmann by name—laboured under a condi-tion of chronic impecuniosity, and in the early part of 1836 matters reached a crisis. In 1835 Wagner had undertaken a tour in search of fresh artistes, and had been promised a benefit by Bethmann in return for this extra service. In the early part of 1836 the company was in a high state of dissatisfaction : some of the prin-cipals had even threatened to leave. But, as the benefit was to assume the shape of a performance of "Das

" Das Liebesverbot "

Liebesverbot," for Wagner's sake they consented to remain. By superhuman exertions on the composer's part the rehearsals were got into some sort of order, but Bethmann claimed the proceeds of the first performance for his own pocket, on the ground that the expenses of the production warranted the change of arrangements. The first representation attracted a crowded *Its first* house, but proved a lamentable fiasco ; even *perform-* worse results attended the second attempt, *ance a* inasmuch as the audience was of the most *fiasco* attenuated description, two singers quarrelled and came to blows, the prima donna became hysterical, and the performance had to be put off—indefinitely, as it happened, for the company was broken up the next day.

This untoward incident left Wagner in sad straits ; he was almost penniless, and in debt besides. In the hope of getting " Das Liebesverbot " accepted at the theatre, he returned to Leipzig, and offered it to Ringelhardt, expressing the diplomatic wish that that worthy's daughter might be entrusted with the principal part.   But his diplomacy availed him nothing.   Ringel- hardt seems to have been hard to please in *Rejection of* the matter of *libretti*, and, having already *" Das Lie-* shelved " Die Feen," found himself unable *besverbot "* to allow his daughter to appear in a piece *by Leipzig* " of such frivolous tendency " as the new *and Berlin* opera.   The Königstädter Theater at *theatres* Berlin, whither he next turned his steps, also declined the work, and Wagner was at the end of his resources

13

Wagner

when he left that city for Königsberg. Here he found friends, some of his old associates at Magdeburg having obtained engagements at the theatre. Amongst them was his special friend Wilhelmina (otherwise Minna) Planer, with whom acquaintance ripened into love ; and *Marries Minna Planer* on November 24, 1836, they were married, Wagner having then been appointed conductor at the Schauspielhaus after successfully directing a series of concerts. At Königsberg he remained till 1838. No great musical activity seems to have marked the period, his chief work being an overture on the subject of " Rule Britannia."

But a desire was growing on him to write an opera on a more extended scale than anything he had yet attempted. With a well-known librettist he thought he would have a greater chance of success, and he accordingly sent sketches to Scribe of an opera, to extend to four acts and to be entitled " Die hohe Braut." The Parisian took no notice—a circumstance perhaps not unnatural. Wagner's ill-luck in the matter of his directors pursued him. The official at Königsberg likewise became bankrupt, and again Wagner had to seek employment in other directions. His old friend Heinrich Dorn, who had produced his first overture, *Work at Riga* here stood him in good stead, and through his influence Wagner obtained the appointment of First Music-director at the new theatre in Riga under the directorship of Karl von Holtei. Thither he removed in 1838, and did much

14

excellent work. His indefatigability at rehearsals was such as to draw remarks from Holtei expressive of wonder if not of admiration; he gave concerts during the winter season; he rehearsed Méhul's "Joseph" with enthusiasm; he had a benefit at the theatre; and he managed to save money. This latter fact was of the utmost importance to him.

Always conscientious, he was oppressed by the sense of the debts he had contracted at Königsberg; and money was more needful than ever for another important reason. He had conceived "Rienzi;" nay, more, he had completed the libretto and written the first two acts of the music. But the provincial stage possessed resources too limited for the production of a work on such a scale as Wagner had conceived this. Paris was the place which must see the fulfilment of his ideals, and, his engagement having terminated, to Paris he resolved to go. In the summer of 1839 he accordingly left Riga. He first went to Königsberg and paid his debts. Thence he went on to Pillau, and, accompanied by his wife and a favourite Newfoundland dog, took passage in a sailing ship *en route* for Paris.

Commencement of "Rienzi"

Sets out for Paris

With this departure ended an epoch both in his life and in his artistic career. Although "Rienzi" was finished subsequently, its conception belonged entirely to the period when he worked on established models, when the "opera," as distinct from that form of his own

Wagner

creation, the "music drama," was the medium through which he expressed his thoughts. Thrown into constant contact with the practical work of the stage, his assimilation of the conventions then existing is not to be wondered at, although even in "Rienzi" it is easy to trace the desire to expand the limited possibilities of "grand opera." Henceforth his work was to be untrammelled by connection with the tradition almost inseparable from the conductor's desk, and his mind was to be free to evolve his own ideal of what a true drama should be. He never resumed official connection with the theatre, although in his early days in Paris it was not from lack of trying, for any means of livelihood would then have been eagerly welcomed. But the experience gained in the provincial theatres was to prove of the greatest value. His knowledge of the resources of the orchestra was immensely increased; his grasp of dramatic situation widened. And, what was more valuable still, the reverses and disappointments he experienced served but to strengthen his character, and to enable him to face without flinching the far greater trials that lay before him. The foundation had been laid of that indomitable spirit of self-reliance which in after-years led him to conceive, and write the greater part of, the "Ring des Nibelungen," because he believed it to be good, without even the hope of ever seeing it performed. His knowledge of human nature had been enlarged; the enthusiastic boy had become an earnest man.

CHAPTER II

THE voyage from Pillau upon which Wagner embarked in July, 1839, was one which he had good cause to remember. A series of appalling storms overtook the unfortunate sailing vessel he had selected for the journey, and more than

A stormy voyage

17   C

Wagner

once shipwreck seemed inevitable. Fortunately, such a disaster was avoided, but it was not till after three and a half weeks of misery that London was reached. Wagner was greatly impressed with the majesty of the terrible elemental conflicts of which he had been an unwilling spectator, and the legend of the *The "Fly-* "Flying Dutchman" had naturally recurred *ing Dutch-* to his mind. Always eager for information, *man"* he questioned the sailors about it, and found that their superstition tallied with his own reading.

In London he and his wife rested some eight days, first staying a night at the Hoop and Horseshoe, No. 10, Queen Street, Tower Hill, and then taking up their quarters at the King's Arms boarding house in Great *His stay* Compton Street, Soho. Wagner's annoy-*in London* ances did not end with the voyage, for the dog was lost, and his owner suffered much anguish of mind until the animal was happily recovered. The time in London was otherwise pleasantly spent. The aspect of the town and the Houses of Parliament interested the young musician, he says; but *Crosses to* of the theatres he saw nothing. Having re-*Boulogne* covered from the fatigues of the journey, the couple proceeded to Boulogne, where they remained *Meyerbeer* four weeks. It was here that he made the acquaintance of Meyerbeer, and arrived at a certain degree of intimacy with him. Meyerbeer professed great interest in the young aspirant for fame, and gave him letters of introduction to the directors of

18

Wagner in Paris

the Opéra and the Théâtre de la Renaissance, to his own agent, M. Gouin, and to Schlesinger, the music publisher and proprietor of the powerful *Revue et Gazette Musicale*.

Wagner has often been very severely criticised, having regard to this Boulogne episode, for what are termed his subsequent strictures on Meyerbeer. He has been held up to execration as a model of base ingratitude, a man devoid of feelings almost of common honour. The criticism must be noticed in passing, and will be dealt with later on. It is enough to remark here that Wagner's displeasure was directed against the *artist* and not the *man* in "Das Judenthum in der Musik"—a distinction which makes all the difference.

It was in September that Paris was eventually reached, and Wagner established himself and his wife in lodgings in the Rue de la Tonellerie. It was claimed for the house that it had witnessed the birth of Molière, and it was situated in an out-of- *Arrives in* the-way and dingy quarter in keeping with *Paris* its new tenant's humble means. Wagner lost no time in making himself known to the personages to whom Meyerbeer's introductions had been directed; but he soon found that although those personages *Ill success* were excessively polite, matters progressed *with the* no further. Pillet, the director of the *theatrical* Opéra, proved a complete stumbling-block *directors* so far as the production of "Rienzi" was concerned; and, although arrangements were made for the translation of "Das Liebesverbot" by a French librettist, and some of the music was tried and found acceptable by the management of the " Renaissance," the director, as was customary with Wagner, became bankrupt, and the arrangements were necessarily abandoned. Always sanguine, Wagner had, as soon as the negotiations seemed to be satisfactory, migrated to more expensive rooms in the Rue du Helder, and by an unfortunate coincidence it was on the very day of his removal that the director failed. A discouraging omen.

These reverses were but the shadows of a dark future. Even the Boulevard theatres would have none of him. He did make a beginning on a vaudeville of Dumanoir, *His early struggles* " La Descente de la Courtille ; " but the music was declared impossible by the singers, and greeted with derision. He tried to get an engagement as *choriste* at a still smaller theatre, but the conductor declared he had no voice, which was, indeed, fairly accurate criticism. His struggles to make both ends meet at this period were painful. Song-writing was next attempted. He set a French version of " Die beiden Grenadiere " to music, introducing the " Marseillaise " at the close, as Schumann did—a difficult song, which met with little or no success. " Mignonne," a little gem in its way, found its way into a periodical, its composer receiving but a few francs for it ; " Dors mon enfant " and " Attente," its contemporaries, did not appear in print till some two years later in Lewald's *Europa ;* " Mignonne " being republished at the same time in the same journal.

His Wife's Devotion

Amidst all the darkness there was, however, still some light for the man's artistic nature, and it was furnished by the concerts at the Conservatoire. The capacity for taking infinite pains was then, as now, a *The con-* feature of French orchestral performances ; *certs at the* we read of the 9th Symphony of Beethoven *Conserva-* being rehearsed for three years before it was *toire* performed in public ! And the perfection of *ensemble* thus attained was noted by the unknown young artist who was so constant and attentive a listener, and its importance more and more borne in upon him, especially as at the opera and in the salon the *virtuoso* was then supreme.

At this period Wagner was out of tune with the world. The stars at the opera annoyed him ; Rubini's "sempiternal shake" was torture to him ; we are reminded of Berlioz in the vehement desire he expressed for purity in art. Even Liszt, who was destined to be his truest friend and champion, presented himself to his view as a mere charlatan, a man "who would play a Fantaisie sur le Diable to an assemblage of angels !"

The iron had entered into Wagner's soul, and he was beginning to learn the lesson that the true artist is out of place amongst the giddy and fashionable throng which men call "the World." His greatest com- *His wife's* fort was the touching devotion of his wife, *devotion* and, although in later years lack of mutual sympathy drove them asunder, Wagner, up to the time of her death, always spoke of her with affection. The union was unfortunate. Minna Wagner had not the power to understand her husband's genius : it is hardly to be wondered at—few people then had. But to her love for him, and her real and tender solicitude in his weary Paris days, we have his own testimony. Let that suffice. He had his small circle of friends, too ; men of literature, music, and art ; Lehr, a student of languages ; Anders, devoted to Beethoven ; Kietz, the painter—many a happy hour was spent in their congenial society.

The dominant note of his character at this time was, nevertheless, one of revolt : revolt against the prostitution of art to the ends of individual display and personal *His revolt* aggrandizement. He was beginning to *against the* realize his own powers, and to recognize his *debased* destiny in the artistic world. For there can *condition* be no doubt that no one ever has estimated, *of Art* or, indeed, ever will estimate, the true value of Wagner's art better than he did himself. He knew his work was good ; with the unfailing insight of genius he was his own severest critic ; and, in the days when success seemed impossible, he never relaxed his efforts, but strove manfully on to express that of which the expression seemed to be a duty both to himself and mankind at large. He has often been chidden for vanity and arrogance ; it would be more just to praise the singlemindedness which led him to uphold his ideals in the teeth of opposition well-nigh fanatic in its venom.

The first result of this mental struggle was the magnificent overture known as "Eine Faust Overture."

Early Struggles

Inspired by the performance of Beethoven's 9th Symphony, in the winter of 1839, Wagner for the first time shook off the trammels of convention, and poured forth his whole soul into the pages of one of the finest of purely orchestral works. The composer's very heart seems laid bare; the storm and turmoil of his troubled existence, *"Eine Faust Overture"* the pure rays of hope shining through the struggle, the peaceful ending after the strife—every bar of the music seems to show us Wagner, the man as he was. The overture, however, with the exception of a trial performance in Dresden in 1844, does not seem to have seen the light till the publication of a revised version in 1855.

In the summer of 1840 Meyerbeer was in Paris. Wagner sought him and obtained a personal introduction to Pillet, who again manifested extreme politeness. Matters seemed more likely to progress on this occasion, for Pillet listened to the proposed plot of "The Flying Dutchman," and suggested that sketches should be prepared. The names of French *Sketches for " The Flying Dutchman"* librettists were even discussed. Wagner, well pleased at this, set to work. He consulted Heine with regard to his proposed treatment of the legend, inasmuch as he wished to adopt Heine's ending as set forth in the "Memoiren des Herrn von Schnabelewopski." The sketches were completed and left in Pillet's hands as accepted. Shortly afterwards, to Wagner's utter amazement, Pillet coolly suggested that he knew of a composer

to whom he had promised a good libretto, and that the
" Dutchman " seemed to satisfy all the necessary requirements.   All the satisfaction Wagner could get in answer
to his indignant protests was a promise that the matter
should remain in abeyance for a time.

Meanwhile he was getting further into temporal
difficulties.   He had been reduced to doing hack work for
Schlesinger, the publisher, transcribing anything and
everything for the piano—even for the cornet !—revising
proofs, and suchlike drudgery.   He had, however, managed
to finish " Rienzi," and, seeing that there was no chance
of its production in Paris, sent the score to Dresden in
the hope that it might meet a better fate in a centre
where he was not unknown.   He could no longer
afford to continue living in the Rue du Helder, and in
the spring of 1841 was compelled to sub-let his rooms
and remove to the suburb of Meudon.   Essay-writing
for the *Gazette Musicale* further eked out his small
resources, one of his contributions, " Das Ende eines
deutschen Musikers in Paris," being obviously to a
certain extent an autobiography.

About this time occurred the only performance of
one of his works during the first Paris period, the overture
to " Columbus " being played at one of
Pillet's dis- Schlesinger's concerts.   In the mean time
honourable nothing had been heard from Pillet.   The
conduct crowning point of his misfortune, however, soon   arrived ;   Pillet   calmly   announced   that
he   had   given   the   sketches   of   the   " Dutchman "   to

"Der fliegende Holländer"

another composer, and offered their author five hundred francs as compensation ! Wagner had perforce to submit to this abominable treatment. Meyerbeer had left Paris ; he had no powerful friends to bring Pillet to book ; his own remonstrances—and we may be sure they lacked nothing in vehemence—were fruitless. But, nothing daunted, he accepted the five hundred francs, and in *seven weeks* wrote the libretto and composed the whole of the music of "Der fliegende Holländer" with the exception of the overture. That had to be postponed for a couple of months, in order that he might complete the miserable hack work he *Writes the "Hollän-der" in seven weeks* had on hand, his sole regular means of subsistence. In writing the "Holländer" he hoped to appeal to the German spirit, but the managers at Munich and Leipzig at first refused it as unfit for Germany. His lack of success with the directors, however, only spurred him on to fresh efforts. He began reading diligently, ever on the look-out for subjects suited to dramatic treatment. He actually projected one libretto, "Die Sarazener," based on an episode in the conquest of Apulia and Sicily by Manfred, son of the Emperor Friedrich II., but this was ultimately abandoned.

Up to this time historical subjects had attracted him strongly, but by a lucky accident he lit upon a copy of the Volksbuch version of the legend of Tannhäuser, and read it with avidity. The chance perusal of this volume revived an old love. The time and place served to

Wagner

intensify the recollection of his boyish days and of the beloved Fatherland. For Wagner was ever intensely German, and the misery he had undergone in his fruitless

Studies in history and legend

struggle for fame in the French capital had wakened a longing to return to his own country, to appeal to his own countrymen. And here seemed his opportunity ; to make that appeal through the medium of their own folk-legend. The idea fastened upon him. In the light of added years and experience he found beauties in the old legend which even the " mystical coquetry and frivolous Catholicism " of Tieck's poem failed to hide. He plunged eagerly into the study of such books as the " Sängerkrieg," " Loherangrin " (in a MS. copy of the " Wartburgkrieg "), and Wolfram von Eschenbach's " Parzival " and " Titurel," endeavouring as far as possible to trace each legend to its source, and make himself its master.

Whilst he was thus engaged, the news arrived that " Rienzi " had been accepted for production in Dresden, and in 1842 he turned his back upon inhospitable Paris,

A holiday at Teplitz

and set out for Teplitz in the Bohemian Hills, there to enjoy a brief holiday before proceeding to Dresden for rehearsals. At the risk of repetition, the importance to Wagner's artistic career of this stay in Paris cannot be too much insisted on ; he insists upon it himself. His ideals became purified by his sordid surroundings, and the beginning was made of his titanic struggle for truth

26

Success of " Rienzi "

in art. Even those who admire him least must admit that, having put his hand to the plough, he never looked back.

The time at Teplitz was passed in making sketches for the new opera which was to be the immediate result of his recent researches—" Tannhäuser ; " and in July, 1842, he arrived in Dresden. The contrast of his reception to his Paris experience was striking. The tenor, Tichatschek, was enthusiastic ; his idolized Schröder-Devrient was to sing Adriano's music ; and moreover he found in Fischer the chorus-master not only an enthusiast, but a devoted friend to whom he became deeply attached, and to whose memory, on his death, he paid a warm and sincere tribute in an article in the *Neue Zeitschrift* of December 2, 1859, entitled " Dem Andenken meines theuren Fischer " (to the memory of my beloved Fischer.) The performance on the 20th of October was a huge success—so much so, that although it lasted from 6 p.m. till midnight, the singers would not hear of any cuts being made. Other performances were given, and Wagner was the idol of the hour. He appeared at a soirée given by Sophie Schröder (Madame Schröder-Devrient's mother), and was asked by an old friend, Laube, with whom he had held political disputations in his boyhood, for an autobiographical sketch for the *Zeitung für die elegante Welt* ; " a request which elicited the " Autobiographische Skizze," full of engaging candour.

Sketches for " Tannhäuser "

Returns to Dresden

Successful production of " Rienzi "

27

Wagner

After the success of "Rienzi," the directors of the theatre were eager to produce "Der fliegende Holländer," and, after a somewhat hasty preparation, it was per-

Production of " Der fliegende Hol- länder "

formed on January 2, 1843, under Wagner's own conductorship. The performance proved somewhat of a check to the tide of his triumphal progress. He had placed great reliance on the subject as being one calculated to appeal to a German audience, but the style of the new work was absolutely novel to its hearers, and left them in a state of bewilderment. There were no impressive *ensembles* as in " Rienzi ; " the tinsel of that opera was lacking ; and notwithstanding the efforts of Schröder-Devrient as Senta, which drew from Schumann's *Zeitschrift* very warm encomiums, the attitude of the public was lukewarm.

At this time there was a vacancy in the post of joint Hofcapellmeister to the Court orchestra, and Wagner entered into a competition for it, with success. A journey

Becomes joint Hofcapell- meister to the Court orchestra

to Berlin with a view to the production at the Royal Prussian Opera of " Rienzi " and " Der fliegende Holländer," undertaken whilst awaiting the decision of the adjudi- cators, led to no result. He was formally installed in his new position on February 2, and also obtained other conducting work in connection with the "Liedertafel," and the "Männergesangfest." For the latter, a male voice chorus festival held in July, 1843, he composed "Das Liebesmahl der Apostel" (The

28

Wagner as a Conductor

Love-feast of the Apostles), a descriptive musical setting of the story of the Pentecostal Supper. The composition was, however, but a *pièce d'occasion*, and, though containing some clever effects, possesses comparatively little interest.

" Das Liebesmahl der Apostel"

His tenure of the office of Hofcapell-meister was not a success. The truth was that he was unsuited for official life, and the duties of the post soon became irksome to him. He had undertaken it in response to pressure. The salary was constant, which meant much to him then, and his wife and friends, including the intendant of the theatre, had all brought their influence to bear upon him. But the work was heavy, and his ideas of what art should be differed from the preconceived notions of those in authority. To add to his discomfort, intrigues were set on foot against him, which reached a culminating point two years later when "Tannhäuser" was first performed. Still, his work was of high merit. He insisted as he had done at Riga on the utmost attention to details of phrasing and *nuance*. Mozart, Weber, Beethoven, Gluck—all received equally loving care at his hands, and the Pensionsconcerte under his direction became famous. As a conductor, indeed, he was

Wagner as a conductor

worthy to rank among the finest the world has produced. Intimate knowledge of the scores be interpreted, exact appreciation of the effect desired by the composer, added to the personal magnetism without which all other gifts count for little, enabled him to get results from his orchestra such as only the most highly gifted conductors can obtain.

Wagner now commenced to work hard on the score of "Tannhäuser." Throughout the year 1844 he was constantly occupied with it, revising and retouching with the greatest care. He was conscious that he was now carrying his theories a step farther, and desired the new work to leave his hands as perfect as he could make it. "Tannhäuser" in a sense is a production of a transition period, but, examined closely, it will be found to be constructed on the lines of the "music-drama" and not of the "opera." The music is evolved from the action, and the "leit-motif" begins to acquire more significance than in "Der fliegende Holländer." The concerted music is not inserted from the point of view of mere musical effect, but as the natural complement to the exigency of the dramatic situation. The theories which were subsequently to be embodied in "Oper und Drama" were beginning to assume more concrete form.

Completes "Tann-häuser"

Towards the end of this year Wagner was enabled to perform an act which must have afforded him a melancholy pleasure. Weber had died in London in 1826, and been buried there. A movement was set on foot for bringing the remains back to Dresden, where the deceased musician had been Kapellmeister for some years. Wagner threw himself heart and soul into the scheme, took charge of all the musical arrangements,

Assists at Weber's re-interment at Dresden

Failure of "Tannhäuser"

and himself composed a funeral march on *motifs* from the dead master's " Euryanthe " which was not the least impressive feature of a touching ceremony. *Sketches* In the spring of 1845 he allowed himself *for " Lo-* what he was pleased to term a holiday—in *hengrin "* other words, a respite from his official duties ; *and " Die* for he returned from Teplitz, whither he *Meister-* again betook himself, with sketches for two *singer "* new operas, "Lohengrin " and " Die Meistersinger."

On his return " Tannhäuser " was put into rehearsal, and on October 19 was performed for the first time. Tichatschek was the Tannhäuser, Schröder-Devrient the Venus, and Johanna Wagner the Elisa- *First per-* beth. The performance provoked a storm *formance* of criticism. The hostility of the news- *of " Tann-* paper criticisms was almost extraordinary. *häuser "* The subject was abused as being distressing, and the music violently attacked because—it was not sufficiently cheerful ! The wonderfully beautiful third Act was found to be dull ; the poetry of the finale passed unnoticed save to elicit a regret *Hostile* that Tannhäuser had not married Elisa- *press* beth ! Schumann alone saw the beauties *criticism* of the work and the promise it gave of still greater things to follow.

The only effect this tornado of abuse had upon Wagner was to make him more firmly resolved than ever to make the public regard his views of art even as he did himself. So far from being discouraged, he was

31

spurred on to redoubled energy.   In this respect his critics did him good rather than harm, but there can be little doubt that the unfair opposition be encountered had much to do with the aggressive tone of his later literary writings.   In private life he was lovable and amiable.   In his attitude to the public he felt himself to be a sort of Ishmael.   A more accommodating man would have passed through life without a tenth of the opposition which beset Wagner's path in his early days. But this opposition was the only possible result of the uncompromising attitude he adopted.   In this respect he has often been misunderstood.   His desire for truth, as he felt and knew it to exist, was the mainspring of his actions, not a desire to advance his own opinions simply because they were his own.   And not to recognize this fact is to entirely misapprehend both the man and the artist.

The failure of " Tannhäuser " led to disastrous consequences.   A contract he had entered into with a publishing firm in Dresden (C. F. Meser) involved him in heavy loss, and his distaste for official work, coupled with the troubled state of the political atmosphere and the treatment he had received from the press, aroused a spirit of revolution within him.   He began to associate with agitators.   This step gave fresh opportunities to his enemies, of which they were not slow to avail themselves, and he soon found that theatrical managers in other towns were beginning to eye him askance. Nevertheless he worked steadily at " Lohengrin " throughout 1847, although he felt that the work would

" Lohengrin "

have even less chance of success than " Tannhäuser," in the state into which the musical taste of Dresden had then fallen. The public were attracted only by the lighter forms of opera, and he knew that in "Lohengrin" he had made an advance upon anything which he had previously written. The influence of his detractors, he discovered, had made itself widely felt. A performance of " Rienzi " had been arranged for the King of Prussia's birthday on October 5 (1847). But on his arrival in Berlin the press attacks were renewed and the performance postponed ; and, when it did take place, the expected royalties were conspicuous by their absence, and Meyerbeer, somewhat markedly, had left the city.

Matters in Dresden were now nearing a crisis, soon to culminate in the Revolution of '49. There was too much political excitement in the air to allow of much interest on the part of the public in matters artistic, and any chance of the production *Completes* of "Lohengrin" was out of the question. *"Lohen-* It was finished, however, in the early part *grin"* of 1848, and Wagner immediately began casting about for fresh subjects. His mental activity at this period was enormous. In addition to composition, he found time to pen an elaborate scheme for the foundation of a truly National Theatre ; and his endeavours to find a new subject for dramatic treatment not only entailed great research, but resulted, moreover, in the production of four works of considerable importance. The first was a sketch, ".Jesus von Nazareth," which was

Wagner

laid aside, but is of great interest as containing the germ of the idea of " Parsifal." The second, an essay entitled " Die Wibelungen, Weltgeschichte aus der Sage," was

Dramatic and historical sketches the result of his researches into the history of Barbarossa—the last effort he made towards finding subjects for drama in history. The other two were far more important, a prose version of the myth of the Nibelungen entitled " Der Nibelungen Mythus als Entwurf zu einem Drama," and " Siegfried's Tod," consisting of a prologue and three acts written in verse.

The production of these last two works marks the beginning of a new era in Wagner's life. Hitherto his mind had wandered hither and thither over the widest range of subjects—religion, philosophy, history, legend—with no definite result. The study of the " Siegfried " myth brought him the conviction that at last he had discovered the secret of the new drama which he believed himself destined to create ; that the theme of that drama must be the great elemental truths

His art theories of *human nature*, the inmost heart of mankind—the Folk—and not of the isolated individual. Stripped of the quasi-philosophical terminology by which the meaning of his writings is often partially obscured, Wagner's theory was simply this : The spoken word, even when accompanied by appropriate action, can best but appeal to the intellect ; something additional is required to arouse the emotional side of human nature. That something is music. The perfect

34

The Revolution of '49

drama must be a combination of factors which appeal both to the intellect *and* the emotions ; and since music can only appeal to that which is common to all human nature, it follows that the only subjects fit for true drama are those which (to use his own words) are "purely human, freed from all convention, all historic formality, all that is particularistic and accidental." Henceforward we find him directing the whole of his energy to the reform of the abuses which had crept into art, more than ever strenuously opposing all that savoured of charlatanism, fighting the battle of "art for art's sake" in the face of desperate odds. And he retained his high ideals to the end. The success which attended his efforts at last, instead of spoiling him, inspired the creation of the fitting crown to his life's work—the noble "Parsifal."

Wagner at this period was, as we have seen, filled with the spirit of revolt. It is probable that politics, as such, did not interest him to any very large extent ; but, to his mind, the interests of art were inextricably mixed up with the social and political system, and that system, in its corrupt state, he held responsible for the low ebb to which art had sunk. The part he *The Revo-* took in the events which led up to the Revo- *lution of* lution does not appear to have been very con- *'49. His* siderable ; a couple of speeches, one of them *part* delivered at the "Vaterlandsverein" club— *therein* an organization of conspicuous tendency—are the most of which there is any record. But they were sufficient to bring down the displeasure of the authorities, regard

Wagner

being had to his official position, and on the outbreak of the Revolution in May, 1849, he was privately warned that his absence would be a wise precaution towards ensuring his safety. Profiting by the hint, Wagner

Escapes to Weimar to avoid arrest managed to slip away quietly to Weimar; none too soon, as it turned out, for his friend, August Roeckel, was seized and spent many years in prison. He found Liszt at Weimar engaged in rehearsing "Tannhäuser;" his stay there, however, was destined to be short. News soon arrived that efforts would be made to effect his arrest as a "politically dangerous individual;" but Liszt was equal to the emer-

Liszt gets him away to Paris gency, and procuring him a passport, got him away safely *en route* for Paris, himself accompanying him as far as Eisenach. Wagner arrived in Paris with feelings of great content. Liszt had considered that he might now be able to obtain some hold on the Paris public; he himself was burning with his new theories, and desirous of publishing a series of articles on "the prospects of art under the Revolution." He soon found, however, that the publishers looked askance at his enthusiastic proposals; music also offered no opening, so he betook himself to Zurich in June.

Becomes a citizen of Zurich He was influenced in this selection, no doubt, by the fact that several of his Dresden friends had fled thither after the troubled events of May, and having resolved to settle down there, at all events for a time, he sent for his wife, who soon joined him. In October he became a citizen of the town.

36

CHAPTER III

Life in Zurich—His friends there—Liszt—Literary work—" Die
Kunst und die Revolution "—" Das Kunstwerk der Zukunft "
—" Kunst und Klima "—" Das Judenthum in der Musik "—
" Oper und Drama "—Production of " Lohengrin " at Weimar
—Poem of " Der Ring des Nibelungen " printed—Completes
" Das Rheingold "—Second visit to London, as conductor of
the Philharmonic Concerts—Hostile English critics—Completes " Die Walküre "—Commences " Siegfried "—Lays it
aside in favour of " Tristan und Isolde "—Leaves Zurich—
Visits Venice and Lyons and eventually reaches Paris—Gives
concerts there—Public opinion divided—Production of " Tannhäuser " through the influence of the Princess Metternich—Its
failure owing to the Jockey Club cabal—Permission given him
to return to Germany—Leaves Paris and goes to Biebrich-am-
Rhein—Commences " Die Meistersinger "—Visits Leipzig,
where the overture to " Die Meistersinger " was performed—
—Settles at Penzing near Vienna—" Tristan " put into rehearsal but withdrawn—Renewed press attacks—Leaves Vienna
—Invitation to Munich from King Ludwig II.—Settles there
and writes the " Huldigungsmarsch " and the essay " Ueber
Staat und Religion "—First performances of " Tristan "—His
relations with the king—The latter's protection withdrawn
through the influence of Wagner's enemies—Leaves Munich
and at last settles down at Triebschen.

WAGNER's period of exile was destined to be protracted ;
not until 1861 did he obtain permission to revisit Germany. His residence in Zurich lasted till 1859, and
during that period there is little to chronicle save the

37

record of his literary and musical production. In this respect, however, the ten years spent in Zurich were the most important in his life. Generous friends came

Life in Zurich

to his assistance at the outset, and through their aid he was placed in a position which enabled him to pursue his work freed from pecuniary responsibilities. The first of these friends was a pianoforte teacher named Wilhelm Baumgartner, also

His friends there

Jakob Sulzer, first Staatschreiber; another was an Englishwoman, Madame Laussot (*née* Taylor), the wife of a French merchant, who, though personally unknown to Wagner, afforded him substantial pecuniary help; while later, Frau Julie Ritter, from 1851 to 1856, made provision for a fixed annual sum to be paid to him, and a merchant named Wesendonck in the latter year placed a villa at his disposal, and in other ways gave him considerable assistance.

Besides these there was his greatest friend, Franz Liszt. The friendship of these two men was in every way remarkable. The one was rich, powerful, at the head

Liszt

of musical Europe; the other poor, unrecognized, comparatively unknown. But Liszt had perceived Wagner's genius, and it became one of the chief aims of his existence to assist and befriend him in every possible way. Few men ever found such a nobly disinterested champion as Wagner found in Liszt. By performances of Wagner's works at the Grand Ducal Theatre at Weimar, performances, moreover, which were notable for the utmost sympathy and insight; by

Franz Liszt

Literary Work

his writings on Wagner's art-work, which displayed the profoundest acquaintance with the true nature of the end Wagner had in view; by his unwearied advocacy of Wagner's interests amongst the sovereigns of the German states; by the material aid he so constantly and generously gave, Liszt proved himself one of Nature's truest noblemen, and it is to Wagner's infinite credit that no one could have spoken in more sincere and grateful terms of a friend than he did. The correspondence between the two shows that Wagner regarded Liszt in the light of a saviour; in the light of that beautiful friendship he felt inspired, knowing that, whatever the world might think, there was one man at any rate who could appreciate and understand him.

It was characteristic of the man, that, having conceived it to be his mission to give forth his views on the art of the future to the world, there should be no pause in his labour until he had completed the task he had taken in hand. Until 1853 *Literary work* musical composition was neglected, his whole time being feverishly devoted to the formulation and exposition of his theories. "Die Kunst und die Revolution" (Art and the Revolution) was the first work to issue from his pen, followed in quick succession by "Das Kunstwerk der Zukunft" (The Art-Work of the Future), "Kunst und Klima" (Art and Climate), and "Das Judenthum in der Musik" (Judaism in Music); these were all completed by the end of 1850. For details of his literary work, the reader

Wagner

is referred to the Appendix ; it is sufficient to note here that 1852 saw what was practically the concluding word on the subject in "Oper und Drama" (Opera and Drama), a masterly summary of his views, written, moreover, with greater freedom from the somewhat pedantic phraseology which often renders his meaning difficult to follow in the earlier works.

Although not actually engaged this while in musical composition, his connection with matters musical was still kept up. The conductors at the theatre were Carl Ritter, a son of the Frau Julie Ritter previously mentioned, and Hans von Bülow, both men of great ability, and Wagner occasionally superintended performances. Here again his wonderful power over the orchestra asserted itself, and it is perhaps not too much to say that he was the founder of the school of conducting which has produced such masters as Von Bülow, Richter, Anton Seidl, Mottl, and our own countryman, H. J. Wood. He conducted also some orchestral concerts, and lectured on musical drama, reading his own *Production* poem of "Siegfried's Tod" by way of illus- *of "Lohen-* tration. He also had the satisfaction of *grin" at* learning that Liszt had produced "Lohen- *Weimar* grin" at Weimar (August 28, 1850), where it had been most favourably received by the artistic and critical audience which Liszt's influence had been able to attract.

In 1853 music again began to absorb his attention. In the early part of the year, the poem of "Der Ring

40

Wagner in London

des Nibelungen " (conceived in 1851, as he writes to his friend Uhlig) was printed for private circulation. The genesis of the poem is interesting; it was written backwards. Wagner found that much explanation was necessary to render many of the incidents in "Siegfried's Tod" intelligible; and, further, that to carry out his dramatic plan narration by itself was insufficient, action was necessary. Consequently "Siegfried," Die Walküre," and "Das Rheingold" came into being, each prefatory to and explanatory of the poem to which, in point of time only, it was sequential. Soon after the poem was completed, and during a brief holiday at Spezzia, the musical germs of "Das Rheingold" took possession of him during a sleepless night. The work proceeded rapidly. "Das Rheingold" was finished in May, 1854; in June he was already engaged upon "Die Walküre," the composition of which was completed, save the orchestration, during the ensuing winter. The completion of the work was delayed through two causes.

Poem of "Der Ring" printed

Completes "Das Rhein-gold"

In February, 1855, his attention was diverted by the performances of "Tannhäuser" which were given during that month at Zurich, and the necessary rehearsals. In March he paid his second visit to England. The Philharmonic Society (then known as the Old Philharmonic to distinguish it from its rival the New Philharmonic Society, long since defunct), was in sore need of a

Second visit to London

41

conductor. No Englishman was, or at any rate was considered, competent for the post. Of foreign musicians of repute, the choice seemed to lie between Spohr and Berlioz; but the latter had been secured by the rival Society, and the former's engagements did not permit his acceptance of the offer. In their emergency the directors bethought themselves of Wagner, and negotiations, commenced in the January by the visit to him of Mr. Anderson, one of the directors, resulted in an engagement to conduct eight concerts during the months of March, April, May, and June.

The announcement of this engagement provoked much opposition in the English press, headed chiefly by Davison of the *Times* and *Musical World* and Chorley of the

Hostile English critics

Athenæum. To those two gentlemen Wagner and all his works were anathema, and it was a singular irony of fate that Davison's successor should have been Francis Hueffer, the man to whom belief in Wagner was almost a musical religion. Wagner's first interview with the band at rehearsal was amusing. The "Leonora" Overture No. 3 was taken in hand, but so listless and tame was the commencement that Wagner laid down his *bâton* in amazement, scarcely able to believe his ears. It seemed impossible that this could be the famous Philharmonic orchestra, and so he told them. His personality added weight to his words—he was always popular with his orchestra—and there was no further trouble. The programmes of these eight concerts contained much

" Die Walküre "

excellent music ; but it is interesting to note Wagner's emphatic protest against their excessive length—two symphonies, two overtures, a concerto, and two or three vocal pieces being considered by no means an excessive allowance for a single concert !

In his spare time he continued to work hard on the orchestration of " Die Walküre," and, having made the acquaintance of Karl Klindworth, entrusted him with the task of preparing the pianoforte scores of the " Ring," an undertaking carried out with the greatest skill. He enjoyed much congenial society also, meeting, amongst others, Ferdinand Praeger and Edouard Roeckel, a brother of the August who had paid so dearly for his participation in the Revolution at Dresden. Edward Roeckel, a pupil of Hummel and a fine pianist, had settled in Bath as a teacher of the pianoforte, and was the means of introducing Wagner to that peculiarly English institution—a whitebait dinner at Greenwich. Whilst in London, Wagner occupied lodgings at 31, Milton Street, Dorset Square, Marylebone, and 22, Portland Terrace, Regent's Park.

On his return to Zurich the orchestration of " Die Walküre " was rapidly advanced, and was eventually completed in the early part of 1856. His health, which had never been robust, gave *Completes* way in the spring, and in May he suffered *" Die* acutely from an attack of erysipelas. This *Walküre "* entailed a somewhat protracted rest, which was enlivened in November by a long visit paid to him at St. Gallen

43

Wagner

by Liszt. The chief object of interest to the two friends must naturally have been the "Ring," and later we find Liszt speaking of it in the most enthusiastic terms. In the spring of 1857 he was at work again, and the full score of Act I. of "Siegfried" was completed and that of Act II. nearly so.

Commences "Siegfried"

A chance incident then caused the work to be laid aside. After all, Wagner was but human. He had worked steadily for four years at the "Ring," and the more he worked the less did it seem possible that he would ever see the realization of his ideas on the stage. He longed to witness the performance of a new work ; moreover, he wanted money. The friends who had assisted him, with the best of good intentions, perhaps not unnaturally could not understand his nature, and proffered advice ; and he felt that at all risks he must regain his independence. At this juncture an agent arrived at Zurich professing to be the bearer of a commission from the Emperor of Brazil to compose an opera for the theatre at Rio Janeiro. The commission, of course, fell through, but it resulted in Wagner's immediately commencing upon "Tristan und Isolde :" the poem and the music to the first Act were completed the same winter. A spirit of unrest was now growing upon him. His sense of isolation depressed him. In 1859 he learned that an application for pardon had been refused by the King of Saxony. He was possessed by a terrifying

"Tristan und Isolde"

Concerts in Paris

fear that his epitaph would have to be "Too Late;"
he felt that the conditions his well-meaning friends
hinted at would become unendurable. In
the early months of 1859 he left Zurich
and once more became a wanderer. His
first halting-place was Venice, where the second Act
of "Tristan" was completed in March.
August found him at Lyons, where the
third Act was finished. By September
he had once more made his way to Paris.

*Leaves
Zurich*

*Eventu-
ally reaches
Paris*

One of his first acts was to call upon M. Carvalho with
a view to getting "Tannhäuser" produced at the Théâtre
Lyrique. Carvalho seemed inclined to undertake the
production, and a day was fixed for a trial of the music.
But Wagner, at best, was a poor pianist, and, in his excitement, poured forth such an extraordinary medley of
thumping, gesticulating, and shouting, that the director,
at the conclusion, murmured some polite platitudes and
withdrew. Wagner's troubles now recommenced. He
was resolved that he would be heard,
and arranged for three orchestral and
choral concerts at the Théâtre Impérial
Italien in January and February, 1860, the programme, which was the same at each concert, being
made up of excerpts from "Der fliegende
Holländer," "Tristan," "Tannhäuser," and
"Lohengrin." The performances divided
Paris into camps. A large following became
enthusiastic; the opposition was quite as strong and

*Gives con-
certs there*

*Public
opinion
divided*

determined. Financially, the result was a loss of some 10,000 francs.

The "Letter to Hector Berlioz," published in the *Presse Théâtrale* of February 26, 1860, in reply to a feuilleton by that critic-musician in the *Journal des Debats* of February 9, is a most temperate reply on Wagner's part to his detractors. The term "Music of the Future" was ever being hurled at him as a reproach ; even the gifted Berlioz had fallen into the error of assuming that Wagner's aim was "either to give out well-worn saws as something new, or to insanely attempt to make out a case for something idiotic ; " and he had again to explain that his essay on "The Art-Work of the Future" lent no colour whatever to the "stupid and malicious misunderstanding" which had led to the invention by Professor Bischoff of Cologne of the derisory term "Music of the Future," but was simply an endeavour to show that, as applied to Drama, Poetry had definite limits of power to excite the emotion which could only be exceeded by the aid of Music, and that consequently true Drama needed Music for its consummation.

A journey to Brussels in March and the organization of two concerts in the Belgian capital resulted in further pecuniary disaster, and Wagner had to part with a large portion of the fees he had received from Messrs. Schott and Co. for the copyright of the "Ring." His state of mind at this time was pitiable. That he should be compelled to "sell" his art to obtain the means of livelihood filled him with a sense of loathing. His real nature

" Tannhäuser " in Paris

was so simple that it was easily misundertood. Art was
to him the essence of all that was noble and beautiful
—a thing to be kept holy and unsullied; his whole aim
was to bring forth work that should satisfy his highest
ideals : his enemies saw in this conscientiousness nothing
but overweening vanity.

A ray of hope was nevertheless at hand to dispel the
gloom for a time, though, as events turned out, his hour
of triumph was to be short-lived. At the instance of
the Princess Metternich the Emperor com- *Production
manded the performance of " Tannhäuser " of " Tann-
at the opera. Preparations were made on häuser"*
the most sumptuous scale; Wagner was
given practically *carte blanche* in every respect. The
chance of his life seemed at hand, and he threw himself
into the work of rehearsals with untiring energy ; there
were no fewer than 164. So much importance did he
attach to the production that he re-wrote the opening
scene, sacrificing his preconceived form to the Parisian
desire for something in the nature of a ballet ; and he published a prose translation of the poems of " Der fliegende
Holländer," " Tannhäuser," " Lohengrin," and " Tristan," prefaced by a lengthy exposition of his views, for
which he adopted, by way of title, the very phrase, "Music
of the Future," whereby his opponents had sought to pour
ridicule upon him. The rehearsals did not progress
smoothly. The conductor was none other than Dietsch,
to whom Pillet had given Wagner's sketches of the "Flying Dutchman " in 1841 ; it is hardly to be wondered

Wagner

at that Wagner's relations with him ended in open rupture, a circumstance all the more unfortunate as Wagner was unable to get rid of him. The production took place on March 13, 1861. What happened is a matter of history; probably no more disgraceful scene *Its failure* was ever witnessed in a theatre. An *owing to the* organized opposition by the Jockey Club, *Jockey Club* whose members found themselves deprived *cabal* of their favourite form of entertainment, the ballet, proved so intractable that Wagner withdrew the work after the third representation.

In spite of his disasters, Wagner's personality made him many friends, and he speaks of his recollections of the time as not unpleasant. Villot, the keeper of the Imperial Museum, to whom Wagner dedicated his "Music of the Future;" Nuitter and Edouard Roche, who translated "Tannhäuser;" poets, like Vacquerie and d'Aurevilly; artists, such as Bataille and Morin; authors, like Léon Leroy and Charles de Lorbac; politicians, like Jules Ferry, Emile Ollivier, and Challemel Lacour; journalists, like Théophile Gautier, Ernest Reyer, Catulle Mendès, and Jules Janin; Gasperini and Champfleury, who subsequently wrote valuably upon him—the *élite* of literary and artistic Paris were his friends, and helped to compensate him for the indignities he suffered at the hands of a prejudiced and ignorant cabal. But the failure of "Tannhäuser" left him in evil case—his remuneration was to have been a fee for each performance—and he might have starved but for the generosity

48

Return to Germany

of Mme. Marie von Muchanoff, who, although not herself wealthy, came to his aid when he was at his wits' end to obtain the simple means of existence.

The influence of the Princess Metternich had, however, been sufficient to obtain for him permission to return to the German states other than Saxony (this final ban was removed in March, 1861), and he soon availed himself of his new liberty to visit Vienna. His *Permission to return to Germany* delight may be imagined when, in that city, he heard his "Lohengrin" for the first time. So moved by its reception was he that, at the conclusion, he was impelled to utter a few words of thanks to the audience and artists.

Another pleasing event happened in August, namely, a visit to Weimar, where Liszt organized a reception in his honour which was attended by a host of prominent musicians. In the autumn Wagner returned to Paris. The subject of "Die Meistersinger," which had attracted his attention sixteen years previously, now engrossed it, and the winter was occupied in finishing the poem, which was printed for private circulation in the following year. In February, 1862, he left Paris and settled down at the little town of Biebrich-am-Rhein to write the music. Whilst there he was visited by a lad of sixteen, who subsequently became one of his great friends, and took an active share in the production of the "Ring" and "Parsifal"—

Commences "Die Meistersinger" at Biebrich

Wagner

—the great violinist Wilhelmj. In the winter he
left Biebrich for Vienna, and on the way
conducted the overture to the "Meistersinger" at a Gewandhaus concert at Leipzig, where its beauties obtained instant
recognition. Having arrived at Vienna
he took a small house in one of the suburbs, Penzing,

*Visits
Leipzig*

*Settles at
Penzing*

Disappointments

and entered into negotiations for the performance of
" Tristan."

The directors of the theatre deemed that, after the
success which had attended the production of " Der
fliegende Holländer," " Tannhäuser," and " Lohengrin,"
a new work from Wagner's pen might prove an attrac-
tion. " Tristan " was accordingly put *"Tristan"*
into rehearsal. But disappointment was *put into re-*
again in store. The theatre was corrupt: *hearsal but*
the press more so. All the old intrigues *withdrawn*
burst forth anew, and the public, having exhausted the
novelty of Wagner's appearance, evinced no desire for
further acquaintance with him or his works. The
tenor, Ander, either could not or would not sing the
music ; Wagner was not allowed to engage Schnorr,
who subsequently created the part, and after numerous
rehearsals, variously put at 57 and 77, had taken place, the
performance was abandoned. Wagner tried Karlsruhe
and Prague without success ; even Liszt's influence at Weimar failed to lead to rehearsals, much less a performance.

The old monetary troubles began to press on him
again. For, although his early works were at that time
fairly popular in Germany, the fees paid to the composer
were excessively small ; and he was informed by the
management at Dresden, where " Tannhäuser " and
the " Holländer " enjoyed public favour, that, as these
operas had been produced during the period of his
Kapellmeistership, he was entitled to no fees, it being
the duty of a Hofcapellmeister in Saxony to produce

Wagner

an opera once a year! It is satisfactory to learn that
Wagner was subsequently enabled by the success of
"Die Meistersinger" to force this grasping management to its knees. He was now reduced to giving
concerts to eke out a subsistence. Two were given in
Vienna, and during 1863 Prague, St. Petersburg, Mos-
cow, Pesth, Karlsruhe, Löwenberg, and Breslau were
visited in turn. A certain amount of money was made
by these tours, but his affairs nevertheless went from
bad to worse. His enemies attributed
Renewed press attacks this to the "sybaritic existence" he led;
luxury worthy of Oriental potentates was
ascribed to him. But, even granting that
some of the stories of extravagance were true, he was
to be pitied rather than condemned. He was not a
man who cared for ordinary success; such little vanities
as he possessed were childlike in their simplicity. What
his whole soul craved for was *appreciation*; his only
longing was to be *understood*. In Vienna he was alone
in every sense. His wife had returned to her family in
Dresden, her health having given way during the stormy
conclusion of their life in Paris; the art life of the
giddy capital had nothing in common with his high and
earnest aims. His health was bad; his cherished "Ring"
he hardly then expected to live to complete, much less
to see performed; black despair had fastened on him.
Let those who would lift the finger of scorn pause to
consider whether, under such conditions, they would
have exhibited one-tenth of the moral courage that

52

King Ludwig II.

Richard Wagner showed. At last the crisis came; he felt he could endure this state of things no longer, and would abandon a public career for ever. He accepted an invitation to a country house in Swit- *Leaves* zerland, and turned his back upon inhos- *Vienna* pitable Vienna.

And now a remarkable thing happened. Wagner had passed through Munich, and wandered on to Stuttgart. Thither he was followed by the secretary of King Ludwig II. of Bavaria, with an invitation *Invitation* to Munich, there to finish his work. *to Munich* The young king had been led to this by *from King* a study of Wagner's works. Gifted with *Ludwig II.* singular refinement and high ideals, he was immeasurably struck with the force of Wagner's views, not only on art, but also upon religion, philosophy, and the state. Instead of the ravings of a democrat he found the thoughtful utterances of a man who had a high ideal of monarchy; for it must be remembered that Wagner's ideas of revolution were concerned not with the destruction of institutions which exist simply because they exist, but with the regeneration of the human race, the restoration of that primitive condition in which man's actions were dictated by the instincts of the highest form of human love— veneration for the head of the family, the father, in place of which had sprung up the fear begotten by the commands of the State. King Ludwig was a dreamer, albeit a dreamer of the beautiful, and but ill adapted to the cares of a kingdom; the sad end of "the mad

53

king " is too well known to need repetition. But to Wagner he came as a friend sent from Heaven. It seemed to the storm-tossed man that at last his great longing for sympathy was to be fulfilled. Even Liszt had not been able to enter completely into his views outside the pale of music, but in the king Wagner found a man capable of entering into his whole artistic aims with the readiest sympathy and understanding. He was

Settles at Munich granted a small allowance of £100 a year from the privy purse, and became naturalized as a Bavarian subject. His first act was the composition of the "Huldigungsmarsch" (March of Homage) as a sort of thank-offering to his royal benefactor, soon followed by a masterly essay, "Ueber Staat und Religion" (Concerning the State and Religion), written at the king's request. In the autumn his stipend was increased, a little house on the outskirts of Munich being moreover placed at his disposal ; and he was commissioned to finish the "Ring." Further favours were heaped upon him. In January, 1865, Semper the architect was instructed to prepare plans for the erection of a new theatre in Munich

First perform- ances of " Tristan " under Wagner's superintendence ; four performances of "Tristan" were given under the conductorship of Von Bülow, the composer supervising ; and the king, in July, closed the old Conservatorium in order that his favourite's ideas for a new music school might assume definite shape in conformity with an elaborate scheme which had long been dear to Wagner's heart.

Driven from Munich

There can be no doubt that Wagner's purpose throughout the whole of his intercourse with Ludwig II. was single-minded and sincere ; there can be as little doubt that had the king possessed as much discretion as enthusiasm the lamentable *His rela-* results of Wagner's stay in Munich might *tions with* have been averted. Wagner's influence *the king* over him was supreme. A less scrupulous man might easily have used such an influence to his own ends ; all that Wagner obtained was a bare existence and a small house rent free ! Nevertheless, the opposition and vituperation he met with exceeded even his past experience. Pressure of such strength was brought to bear upon the king that he was compelled to withdraw his protection, and residence at *The latter's* Munich became an impossibility. Poor *protection* Wagner was indeed to be pitied. All his *withdrawn* hopes were again dashed to the ground, and his misfortunes had been increased by the death, three weeks after the final performance of " Tristan," of the tenor, Ludwig Schnorr von Carolsfeld. A fine actor, with a magnificent voice, the poet-composer declared that without him " Tristan " was impossible. His cup was full to overflowing when he left Munich in *Leaves* December, and the realization of his dreams *Munich* seemed farther off than ever. His first *Settles at* move was to Vevey ; thence he went *Triebschen* on to Geneva ; and ultimately he settled down at Triebschen, near Lucerne, where he remained till 1872.

CHAPTER IV

THE past few years had been spent by Wagner amidst surroundings that had rendered composition to a large extent impossible. Triebschen brought him a much-needed rest. Another change soon occurred in his life. On

Life at Triebschen

56

His Second Marriage

January 25, 1866, his wife died. As has been already shown, the marriage had proved unfortunate, and since 1861 they had lived apart, although this had been partly brought about by her delicate health and consequent inability to sustain the fatigues of continued change of residence. Soon *Death of his wife* after Minna's death, Cosima, the wife of Von Bülow and daughter of Liszt, left her husband in favour of Wagner. In 1870 they were married. *Marries* Further dwelling upon this question is *Cosima von* outside the biographer's province. It is *Bülow* sufficient to state that in his second mar- *(née Liszt)* riage Wagner found a wife who could understand and sympathize with him, and that he bears frequent testimony in his letters to his love for and devotion to her. The matter can well rest here, with the added reflection that the beautiful "Siegfried Idyll," composed as a surprise for his wife after the birth of his son Siegfried, accurately mirrors his happiness and peace of mind during these Triebschen days.

He now resumed work on "Die Meistersinger" and finished it in 1867. Leisure was also found for a series of articles on "Deutsche Kunst und Deutsche Politik" (German Art and German Politics) which *Completes* appeared in the *Süddeutsche Presse.* In the *"Die* following year he paid his last visit to *Meister-* Munich to superintend the final rehearsals *singer"* of "Die Meistersinger." The performances were directed by Von Bülow, who secured an admirable

Wagner

rendering of the work; the two men ever remained fast friends. Returning to Triebschen he turned his attention again to the "Ring," and in 1869 completed

Completes "Sieg- fried" "Siegfried," which had lain neglected for twelve years. Literary work during this year was represented by an essay, "Ueber das Dirigiren" (On Conducting), in the *Neue Zeitschrift für Musik*. The Munich Hof-theater in this year witnessed the first performances of

First per- formance of "Das Rheingold" at Munich "Das Rheingold" and in the succeeding year "Die Walküre;" but Wagner took no part in them and they had little success. The Meister was then absorbed in the composition of "Die Götterdämmerung," the Vorspiel and first Act being finished by June, 1870. In September the profoundly thoughtful essay on "Beethoven" was published.

If the chronicle of these few years seems bald, the reader must blame Wagner himself, and not his bio-grapher. The period of calm retirement must have been a more than welcome relief after the strenuous life in Paris, Vienna, and Munich. But it was not in Wagner's nature to remain quiet for long. The outbreak of the Franco-German War fired his veins,

"Kaiser- marsch" and incited him to poetry and prose; to music also, as witness the "Kaisermarsch." His attitude at this time led to his being hated by the French; only recently has he been forgiven. But this hatred was the result of misunderstanding.

Bayreuth

Wagner was intensely German. He looked upon the war as a means of creating a united Germany, and thereafter a united German people, a German Folk, and a German Art. The fact that the antagonist happened to be France was immaterial. Badly as he had been treated in Paris, no mean motive of petty vengeance inspired his words ; they would have been uttered, of whatever nationality the foe might have been. As the hostilities proceeded and his country's arms were ever and again victorious, his restlessness increased. The realization of his dreams seemed at hand ; the moment had arrived when he must be in a position to proclaim his aims far and wide to the German people. The first necessity was the building of a theatre in *Idea of a* which the "Ring" could be adequately *national* staged. He set out to find a suitable *Festival* spot for its erection, visited many places, *Theatre* and ultimately lighted upon Bayreuth in May, 1871. Bayreuth seemed to fulfil all his requirements, and the next step was the sensible one of obtaining the advice and assistance of practical men. He enlisted the sympathy of Friedrich Feustel, a rich banker, and Adolph von Gross, another influential resident, and to them unfolded his scheme. Through their influence he obtained from the municipality a free grant of land for the site of the theatre and a house for him- *Removal to* self ; and on the 9th of November, at *Bayreuth* Feustel's house, the historic decision was arrived at that at Bayreuth the Festival Theatre should

59

Wagner

be built. By the following April the family had left Triebschen and settled at Bayreuth.

On the 22nd of May, 1872—his birthday—Wagner laid the foundation stone of the new theatre. The site for the building was eminently well chosen, at the top of a small hill commanding beautiful views. The *Commence-* audience comprised over 400 leading musi-*ment of* cians of Germany, and at the conclusion *building the* of the ceremony he made a characteristic *theatre* speech setting forth the objects of his undertaking. He destined Bayreuth to be a centre for German art, a place where German musicians led by a German master would leave the vain allurements of a degraded, pleasure-seeking art, to pass to the true fulfilment of their high vocation. For he believed that during the past century German art had undergone unexampled development, and that all that was needed was for him "to unveil the edifice, which, though long unknown, had long stood ready in the German mind; to tear off its false robes and leave the ragged envelope to moulder away in the breeze, and its last shreds to be absorbed in the vapours of a new and purer artistic atmosphere." Disillusionment was, alas, to come, and it broke his heart. The ceremony of laying the foundation stone was followed by a concert, at which the "Kaisermarsch" and Beethoven's 9th Symphony were performed under Wagner's direction. The rendering of the latter work is said to have been the finest it has ever received; certainly such an orchestra of virtuosos

Wagner Societies

(Wilhelmj leading) has seldom been assembled, and the chorus was made up from the best three choral associations in the empire.

The estimated cost was 300,000 thalers (equal to £45,000), and it had been decided (by the advice of Tausig the pianist, one of the few friends who had stood by Wagner in Vienna) to issue a thousand bonds of 300 thalers each, payment of the money to be spread over some years if necessary. Wagner's intention was to give three performances of the "Ring" cycle at the first Festival, each performance extending over four evenings. There was to be no payment for admission ; only those invited and the holders of bonds (*Patronen*) would be allowed to be present, but it was to be permitted to divide each bond into three, so that one person might attend each of the three performances. Tausig was a man of immense energy and resource, and his early death at the age of thirty in 1871, soon after he had started the *Patronen* scheme, was a great loss to Wagner. Only a small proportion of the money had been subscribed when the foundation stone was laid, and two years after their issue only 240 of the bonds (*Patronatscheine*) had been taken up. Soon after Tausig's death, however, the happy notion had occurred to Emil Hecker of Mannheim to form "Wagner Societies," through whose exertions money might be raised by subscriptions, concerts, and so forth, and Hecker himself founded the first at Mannheim. The

Tausig's Patronen scheme

Wagner Societies

idea proved a success, and not only in Germany, but throughout Europe and even in Egypt and the United States, these societies took root and flourished. The Khedive of Egypt subscribed 10,000 marks ; the society in London gave ten orchestral concerts in the years 1873 and 1874. Wagner himself worked with all his energy. He gave concerts in various towns in Germany and in Vienna, and co-operated with Liszt in one at Pesth. These brought in some £10,000. Another £1000 was paid to him to compose a Festival March for the Centennial ·Exhibition at Philadelphia. All this went to the fund. But, otherwise, the apathy displayed by the Germans was amazing. Wagner's music by this time had become extraordinarily popular. Yet to an appeal for aid in the undertaking, of which 4000 copies were sent to various booksellers and musical dealers throughout Germany, not a single response was received, save the signatures of a few Göttingen students for a few thalers apiece !

Seeing that the theatres had made large profits out of Wagner's works, *without paying him any royalties*, an appeal to them to give benefit performances for the fund *Poor re-* did not seem unreasonable. Of eighty-one *sponse to* theatres written to, however, three declined, *appeals for* and the remaining seventy-eight had not *funds* even the courtesy to reply ! That the public would have willingly invested money on Wagner as a commercial speculation was proved by the fact that over 200,000 thalers (£30,000) were readily subscribed to

The Bayreuth Object

a company calling itself "Wagneriana" which endeavoured to induce Wagner to give the festival plays in
Berlin; it had taken more than two years of hard work
to collect less than half that sum for the Bayreuth project. And yet it could scarcely be alleged that the latter
was undertaken in a manner likely to suggest financial
mistrust, the council of administration being headed by
Friedrich Feustel, a rich and well-known banker of
Southern Germany, and completed by Adolph von Gross
of Bayreuth, Dr. von Muncker, the Bürgermeister of
that town, Emil Heckel of Mannheim, and Friedrich
Schoen of Worms, all men of integrity and ability. London
and Chicago also made tempting offers, but Wagner
refused them all. The noble disinterestedness of the
man was never so apparent as at this time. He might
easily have become rich; but he would not sell himself
for money. The temptation must have been cruelly
strong.

The "Ring" was the darling work of his heart, and
he had but to say the word to secure its representation
with all the perfection even he could desire. But that
was not Richard Wagner. His own words *His object*
are eloquent : "My object is to arouse the *—Desire to*
dormant powers of the Germans; this is *elevate the*
almost more important than the success of *German*
my undertaking in itself." Let those who *race*
will fasten on that little word "almost," and try to read
into the sentence another so-called instance of Wagner's
vanity and egotism; the words sum up the tragedy of

63

Wagner

his life, the tragedy of a noble man misunderstood by the very men he lived only to raise to higher and purer ideals.   The inception of the Bayreuth Festival Theatre was dictated by no mean motives of self-aggrandizement or even self-glorification.   Wagner by no means considered himself the arch-priest of the art he advocated ; in a pregnant footnote to " Oper und Drama " he makes it unmistakably clear that he regarded himself but as a beginner.   But he did feel, and feel with all the intensity of a true priest, that his efforts might result in the awakening of the slumbering German nation to a sense of artistic truth, in the dawning of an era when from the silent hill of Bayreuth there might radiate an influence which should unite a new Germany in one loving bond of artistic brotherhood.   He believed that all that was wanted was the force of example, and he knew, too, that he alone was the man who was ready to set it.   The fire, he believed, had been kindled ; the flame only wanted fanning to become a beacon light to the world.   That is the meaning of that word " almost."   And instead—

Temporary failure of the scheme in 1874 he found that so little interest had been taken in his scheme that he had to declare the undertaking at an end, with the theatre left incomplete ; a result entirely attributable to the undisguised enmity of the press.   This was the final blow to Wagner's hopes, and he never recovered from it.   His own subsequent success mattered little ; the apathy of his countrymen cut him to the quick.   Bayreuth nowadays is looked upon as

64

The Festival Theatre

" the fashionable thing to do ; " few of its visitants pause
to consider the meaning of what they see. Fewer still
recognize it for what it really is—at once the realization
and the tomb of the life-work of a genius. Wagner's
ideal of Art has not yet been attained.

Fortunately he had been dissuaded by his friends from
publicly announcing the deplorable response which had
been made to his appeals, and help was at hand. King
Ludwig again came to his assistance. Al-   *King
though he had been forced to withdraw his   *Ludwig II.*
protection, the king's interest in his friend   *saves the*
had never waned, and during Wagner's stay   *under-*
at Triebschen he was more than once visited   *taking*
by the young monarch incognito. And now the king
gave practical evidence of his sympathy with the project
by advancing the required funds out of his private purse
on the security of the unissued *Patronat-*   *" Die Göt-*
scheine. The building operations were re-   *terdämme-*
sumed, and by 1875 had so far progressed   *rung" com-*
as to permit of rehearsals taking place, the   *pleted*
" Götterdämmerung " having been finished in the
preceding year.

The Festival Theatre itself differs so entirely in
construction from any other playhouse that a somewhat detailed description is necessary. It   *Description*
must be remembered that Wagner's idea   *of the*
was that all performances were to be given   *Bayreuth*
free. Consequently the auditorium is de-   *Theatre*
signed in such a manner as to secure, as far as possible,

to each person as good an opportunity for seeing and hearing as his neighbour. There are therefore no galleries, no arbitrary divisions into boxes, stalls or pit; the seats are all disposed on an inclined plane stretching upwards from the stage and spreading out in slightly fan-shaped fashion. At the extreme back of the auditorium are nine boxes known as the Royal Boxes, and now reserved for royalty and Madame Wagner's guests; above these is a gallery containing some 200 seats, generally allotted to the *personnel* of the theatre. The auditorium proper contains 1344 seats. The stage is very large, and so constructed that an entire scene may, with equal facility, be bodily raised into the roof, lowered into the basement, or removed to either wing. The orchestra is disposed underneath the stage so that it is completely hidden from the view of the audience, but in such a manner that the conductor has not only the band but the whole of the stage under complete control. During the performance the auditorium is completely darkened, so that there is nothing to distract the spectator's attention from the little world temporarily represented on the stage. The magical effect of such music as the prelude to the "Rheingold" or to "Parsifal," rising, as it were, from the infinite, can only be realized by actual experience; description is impossible. Illusion is further heightened by means of a double proscenium, whereby the division of the stage from the audience is accentuated. The acoustic properties of the theatre are excellent, a more than remarkable

The First Festival

circumstance considering that it was entirely of Wagner's own design. Indeed Semper, himself one of the finest architects of his time, remarked that the fact of Wagner being a great musician had resulted in the loss to the world of a great architect. Considerable doubt was originally felt by some as to the results that would ensue from the sunk orchestra, but experience has proved that Wagner's theory was sound. The occasion of its first test led to a touching incident. The experiment was made with the magnificent "Walhall" theme, and Wagner was so affected that he burst into tears.

Throughout July and August, 1875, rehearsals in the incomplete theatre proceeded apace. Later in the year Wagner went to Vienna and there superintended rehearsals of "Tannhäuser" and "Lohen- *Rehearsals* grin," which were performed in the *for the first* November and December to enthusiastic *Festival* audiences. In the early part of the next *commenced* year there was very serious doubt in Wagner's mind whether the festival performances should take place. The number of *Patronate* instead of 1300 was only 400 ; his original plans had been completely nullified. It was nevertheless determined that the performances should be given. The rehearsals re-commenced on June 3. As far as the artistes were concerned, they one and all thoroughly entered into the spirit in which its originator desired his scheme to be carried out ; leisure and emolument were freely sacrificed by all, and no stone was left unturned to make the enterprise a thoroughly artistic success. Each artist who joined the little band had to engage to give his or her services for three full months, and not until August 6th, after two months of hard work, did the full rehearsals commence. The public were admitted to some of these, at first without payment. But this led to a scene almost of riot, and the management subsequently charged for admission, a step which brought nearly £1000 to the fund. King Ludwig was present at them all.

On August 13, 1876, the performances commenced. The first cycle lasted from the 13th to the 16th ; the second, from the 20th to the 23rd ; and the third, and last,

First perform- ance of " Der Ring " from the 27th to the 30th. The names of the original members of the cast are en- graved on a marble slab in the peristyle of the theatre ; the reader will find them in the Appendix, and there recognize many that have since become familiar in Wagnerian drama, first and foremost being that of the great conductor, Hans Richter. Through the kindness of Professor Wilhelmj, who led the orchestra on the occasion, I am enabled to reproduce a most interesting document, hitherto unpublished, namely, Wagner's own autograph list of the band. To the same source, I am indebted for the Bayreuth medal. This was designed by Semper, and is carried out in bronze. It was originally intended that one should be presented to each artiste whose performance was worthy of special distinction ; but this led to considerable heart- burnings, and the idea was ultimately abandoned. Only

68

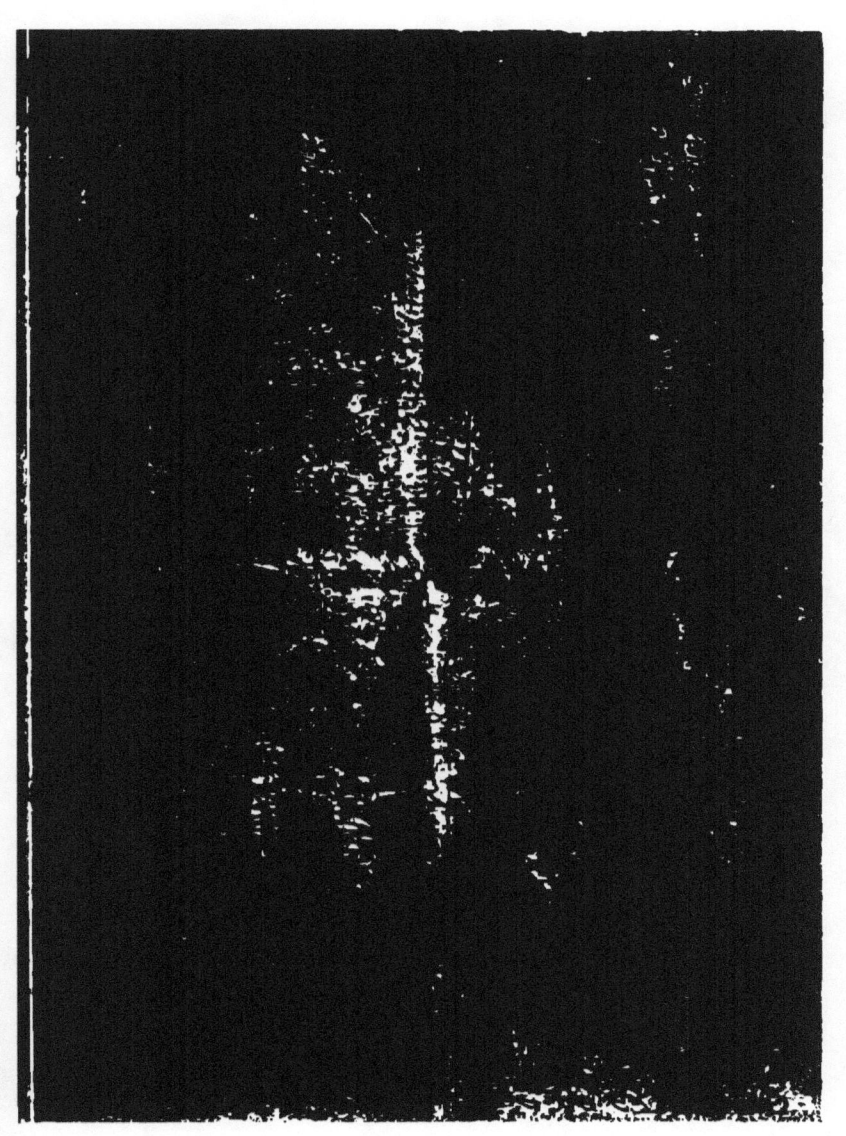

AUTOGRAPH LIST OF THE ORCHESTRA AT THE FIRST PERFORMANCE OF "DER RING DES NIBELUNGEN"
(IN THE POSSESSION OF PROFESSOR WILHELMJ).

Wagner Concerts

some eight were struck, Wilhelmj, Richter, and Niemann being amongst the recipients. The festival was in every way an artistic success, but the financial issue was disastrous. There was a deficit of £7500, and as the liabilities of the *Patronen* had been fully discharged by their original sub- *A loss of £7500* scriptions, there was no reserve fund to fall back upon, and the loss had to be borne by Wagner alone.

England, however, had shown great interest in the scheme, and Wilhelmj advised that a series of concerts conducted by Wagner himself would be profitable. Once again the man's indomitable pluck asserted itself. In spite of ill-health he determined to make the effort, and arrived in London in April, 1877, remaining there till June 4. A series of six concerts con- *The* taining large excerpts from his works, took *Wagner* place between May 7 and 19, at the Albert *Festival at* Hall, conducted by Wagner and his faithful *the Albert* henchman Richter. Everything that was *Hall,* possible to present Wagner's music in the *London* best light was done; the orchestra numbered 170, with Wilhelmj as leader, and many of the principals at Bayreuth in the preceding year were present as soloists. This "Wagner Festival," as it was called, came very near to involving Wagner in further loss; *"Parsi-* as it was, there was only a very bare margin *fal" poem* after paying expenses. Two further con- *completed* certs, however, given on May 28 and 29, at reduced prices and with more "popular" programmes, resulted in Wagner's being able to secure some £700 for the Bayreuth funds. During his stay in London he read the MS. of his recently finished poem of "Parsifal" to some friends at the house of Mr. Edward Dannreuther; in December it was published.

With his return to Germany began the closing scenes of Wagner's life, and the few years that remained to him brought him some measure of consolation for all he had endured. He was happy in his home-life, he was conscious, too, that his ideas on art had taken root and were bearing fruit—in small measure, it was true, but still there was sufficient evidence that he had not toiled in vain; he had lived, moreover, to witness the performance of his "Ring" in the theatre he had worked and longed for through many weary years of disappointment and misfortune. But there was one thing lacking—the awakening of his beloved Germany to the new art-life which, in 1870, he had so ardently anticipated as the inevitable outcome of events that would, he believed, unite all Germans into one great brotherhood.

Wagner has often been regarded as half a century in advance of his age. In some respects this is true; if popularity be any proof of a proposition, the supporters of this theory may point complacently enough to the power which his name exercises in modern days to fill theatre and concert-hall. But, so far as the man himself is concerned, it would be far more true to say that he came into the world many centuries too late. The Germany

His Ideals

of his ideals had nothing in common with the nation
which the Franco-Prussian War united into an Empire
for purposes purely of State. Wagner's ideal German
was Hans Sachs, the type of all that is noble
and self-sacrificing in human nature. He *His ideals*
found modern German character far more *of German nationality*
nearly associated with that of an Alberich;
there is no place for the simple German burgher
in the Germany of to-day. Call him an idealist, a
dreamer, what you will—Wagner was an honest, true
man. His letters to Liszt show at times an almost
fierce contempt of personal success; he counted his life
well spent if only he could induce his own countrymen
to regard Art as something by which mankind could be
brought to the leading of a truer and more beautiful life.
A dream, perhaps; but a noble dream. In this respect
Bayreuth became the tomb of his hopes.

Plans were laid for the holding of another Festival in
1877, and a new *Patronat* suggested. But the ridicule of
the press had again done its work. Having obtained admission to the performances of the previous year *A second*
under cover of the *Patronatscheine*, the critics *Festival*
succeeded in frightening away the timid; *perforce*
the idea of another Festival had perforce *abandoned*
to be abandoned, and with it Wagner's scheme for
establishing at Bayreuth an institution "for training
singers, musicians and conductors to qualify themselves
for the correct and intelligent performance of works
of the true German school." Not only that, Wagner

Wagner

was compelled to part with the " Ring" itself; the work of his life had to pass into the hands of an agent—costumes, scenery, and all. This was the result of Wagner's attempt to uplift his nation!

Henceforth, till 1882, he lived in retirement, and devoted himself to the composition of the music to *The "Bay-* "Parsifal" and to the writing of various *reuther* articles for the *Bayreuther Blätter*. This in-*Blätter"* teresting journal, edited by Von Wolzogen, first appeared in January, 1878, and was published by and for the Wagner·Verein with the object of spreading Wagnerian propaganda. The strain of his *Ill-health* early battles now began to tell upon him, and his health became so broken that, from 1879, he was compelled to winter in South Italy. The sketches of the music to the first Act of "Parsifal" were finished in the spring of 1878, those of the second *Completes* Act in October of the same year; while *"Parsi-* the April of 1879 saw the skeleton of *fal"* the whole work completed. The preceding Christmas had witnessed the performance of the prelude at Bayreuth by the Meiningen orchestra under the conductorship of Von Bülow. On January 13, 1882, the full score received its final touches at Palermo.

For six years the Festival Theatre had remained closed. During that time, however, money had accumulated, and musical Europe was in a state of excitement to hear the latest—and, as it proved, the last—work from the

His Death

Meister's pen. Performances of "Parsifal" were rendered possible, and during July and August, 1882, sixteen representations were given, the last being conducted by Wagner personally. Immense success attended them. The profoundly beautiful music-drama made the deepest impression, accentuated possibly by the greater concentration exhibited in it than in the "Ring." *Production of "Parsifal" at Bayreuth* "Parsifal" came as the saviour of Bayreuth, but its author was not to witness another performance of the crown of his life's work. He retired to Venice for the winter, and there spent his leisure in writing articles for the *Bayreuther Blätter*, in which he took much interest. His health also was good enough to permit of his superintending rehearsals for and conducting his juvenile symphony at the Liceo Marcello on Christmas Eve.

But the end was near. His heart had become seriously affected, although he had been kept in ignorance of the fact by his doctor. On February 13, 1883, he was playing on the piano, at his beautiful house on the Grand Canal at Venice (the Palazzo Ven-Cramini), *Death at Venice* the first scene from the "Rheingold." He rose to take his daily outing in his gondola, but was overcome by a sudden faintness. By evening the overworked heart had ceased to beat—Richard Wagner was dead.

He was buried on the 18th in the grounds of his

Wagner

own house at Bayreuth—Wahnfried—to the strains of

Interred at the touching funeral music from his own
Bayreuth "Götterdämmerung."   His faithful dog
"Russ" lies near him. No elaborate monu-
ment marks his resting-place : but from the little
ivy-covered grave, with its plain unlettered stone,
there   will   ring   to   all   time   the
strong, noble message of the
man who sleeps his last
sleep within—"Der
Glaube lebt"
—"Faith
lives."

CHAPTER V

THE quotation which concludes the preceding chapter (from " Parsifal ") strikes the key-note of Wagner's character. Faith in human nature—and particularly the human nature of the German race— inspired his life-work. Of his influence on music, even at the present day, there can be no question ; whether the ideas to which music took a secondary place in his purview will be as fruitful, time alone can prove. In writing a biography of most of the world's greatest musicians, the development of their musical nature is, as a general rule,

His faith in human nature

75

all that calls for criticism or even remark. But with Wagner the case is wholly different, and the relations he bore to Art, in its wider sense, must be understood before any idea can be formed of his musical personality. His entire intellectual life was based on two main principles—Faith and Love; upon the former his whole personal hopes were built; through the latter he hoped that the ultimate regeneration of the human race might be effected. His views on politics, philosophy, religion, and art were all inspired by and tinged with these two great articles of his belief, and no just estimate of his character can be formed if this be lost sight of.

To the casual observer Wagner was a man who compelled attention, although about middle height, and of not otherwise commanding presence. But his eyes, as

Personal character- istics
many know, were singularly expressive, and his voice full and rich. In calm moods those eyes, by their limpidity and depth, betokened a grave and thoughtful soul lurking behind; that voice, in its sonorous cadence, produced a pleasant sense of harmony in the listener. But when roused, the eyes flashed fire; the voice became as the rushing of mighty waters—the whole man was transformed. And no better idea could be given of Wagner's real nature. The one side of his character was calm, self-reliant, strong in the love of all that was noble and beautiful; the other, by which he has more generally been judged, aggressive, self-defensive, polemical in the assertion of what he deemed to be the truth.

Schopenhauer

The ways of his life were cast in stormy places; his whole existence was one long struggle; even the day of his death was clouded by disillusion. Small wonder, then, that he shrank into himself, and appeared to the outer world only in the guise which his opponents had thrust upon him. His pride forbade any other course. He could not dig in the same fields as those to whose every canon of a prostituted art he was opposed with the whole vehemence of his nature; to beg from them was even more repugnant. Over and over again in his writings he protests against the way in which he was persistently misrepresented. "I am only an artist!" he exclaims; and this is the second proposition to be borne in mind in studying his life.

In a few words, Wagner's life was the outcome of a faith that humanity could be led towards the highest ideals only by the agency of Love, and that no one could better further that consummation than the true Artist. Stated thus baldly, the proposition hardly seems to require proof; but it must be remembered that the solution of the simplest thesis may escape the most profound philosopher, and Schopenhauer alone has propounded a philosophy that at all tallies with that which pervaded Wagner's nature. *Wagner and Schopenhauer* And even here there is the fundamental difference, that while Schopenhauer arrives at his conclusions with regard to Art incidentally, as part of a complete system of philosophy, Wagner deals with all the great problems of life from the point of view not

Wagner

of a philosopher, but an artist—and his philosophy always comes back to that standpoint. With Wagner Art is the absolute term in the equation of Life. Life should be beautiful, and that end cannot be attained or even approached without the assistance of the most perfect products of Art. His writings were not the ephemeral products of a redundant intelligence; they were the ripened fruit of long periods of germination, and in them we may perceive the gradual evolution which characterizes his whole work, and the habit of introspection which led him to minutely analyze each successively developed phase of thought.

It has already been pointed out that Wagner in his early days was devoted to the classics. A boy of thirteen does not ordinarily translate the first twelve books of the *His mental activity* *Odyssey* out of school hours by way of amusement! All through his life this mental activity was predominant; his thirst for knowledge was only equalled by the rapidity with which he slaked it. Consequently his range of subjects was enormous, and his grasp of them conspicuous, albeit invariably tinged with his own individual point of view.

The first potent influence with which he came into contact was the atmosphere of the stage; the visits he *Early connection with the stage* paid with his stepfather to the Dresden Theatre were indelibly impressed upon his memory, and were the origin of his earliest dramatic efforts. After his stepfather's death his attention became more turned to music;

His Impulsiveness

but even in those early days his impressionable nature received an impetus from without, and the first subject to attract him was politics. The Revolution of July, 1829, caused him to neglect music and, indeed, almost everything else, in order that he might throw himself into his new craze. And he had then reached the mature age of sixteen ! The fact that he did so is, nevertheless, wholly characteristic. Throughout his life we find him apparently yielding to momen- *His impul-siveness* tary impulse. It is often alleged against him that he was inconsistent ; but a more careful study of his writings will show that the apparent inconsistencies which, without doubt, are to be found, were really due to the courage with which he did not hesitate to confess previous errors. His youthful excursions into the domain of politics naturally led to no result ; they were soon forgotten, and the subject did not attract him again until late in the forties. In fact, until about the year 1840 there was nothing in Wagner's life to suggest the independence of mind which he was after-wards so strikingly to evince. His existence was that of many another hardworking and struggling musician, enduring much privation, but still greedily drinking in all that offered itself in the way of good music, and doing his best to follow in the steps of the models which seemed to him worthy of copying. Mental problems troubled him but little in those early days, and the " Autobiographical Sketch " which he wrote in 1842 is a mere record of events, with no attempt at psychological analysis.

Wagner

But there was nevertheless working within him a spirit of revolt against the conditions under which he found art labouring at that period. This spirit had found utterance in the feuilletons, "A Pilgrimage to Beethoven" and "The End of a Musician in Paris," written with autobiographical reference during the dreary years of his first stay in Paris, and supplemented by the "Freudenfeuer" (Bonfire) articles which were shortly afterwards published in Lewald's *Europa* magazine.

From this period dates Wagner's complete artistic development. Hitherto he had been but groping in the dark; trying to find subjects suitable for "opera-texts," subjects lending themselves to brilliant spectacle and sonorous musical effect. His writings had not been the result of an inner impulse to publish abroad a firmly developed creed; they had been dictated merely as one of the few means open to him to earn a few francs. His mind was a species of chaos at this time. His studies of German legend had just been commenced, and he had been fascinated by them without being able satisfactorily to account for the phenomenon. It was in this mood that he returned to Dresden in 1842, and entered upon the prosaic duties of joint conductor of the Court orchestra.

Dresden was to be the scene of Wagner's first and only appearance as a politician: he soon saw himself that he was quite unsuited for practical politics. The part that he actually played in 1848 and 1849 was insignificant enough, but it had the effect of procuring his exile, and furnishing him with a text for much

Politics

literary matter. He left no mark on the political history of his time, because he was unable to understand his countrymen—the secret, indeed, of all his failures. Wagner did not understand men. The *His failure* petty spirit of self-interest was so foreign to *as a poli-* his nature that he failed to recognize it in *tician and* others. If a thing was wrong, he argued, *its cause* it was wrong, and should be denounced; expediency was a term which had no place in his vocabulary. But even a successful revolutionist owes much to its judicious recognition, and every great statesman's success has been attributable to ability to seize on the need of the moment.

Wagner, however, regarded life from the standpoint of a poet. He had already found out, since his composition of the "Flying Dutchman," that he had within him the powers of a poet, and not "a mere concocter of opera-texts." Springing up within him he felt a Necessity—a Need to reach the inmost essence of human nature, "whereto the desire which reaches forth to farthest distance turns back at last, for its only possible appeasement." This Necessity was accentuated by the period in which its inception took place—was perhaps even originated by it. The debased estate into which art had fallen both in Paris and Dresden had led him into profound speculation as to its cause. In Politics as such he took little interest; but it seemed to him that the condition of things in matters artistic which he so much deplored was directly the outcome of the causes which inspired political unrest in those troubled days,

Wagner

and it was therefore his duty, *as an artist*, to lift up his voice also in protest.

What, then, was his standpoint? Not what one would expect to find in an ordinary revolutionist, not the sort of vapouring in which the typical Socialist or Anarchist delights—but a firm declaration in Mon-

His idea of revolution archy as the ideal principle of government, a faith in God to discover the right law. These were the tenets of Wagner the Revolutionist! Both propositions were expanded by him; both expansions need examination. Wagner believed in Kingship as the fundamental principle of government; but in this belief his desire for revolution was retrogressive, and coupled with a strong qualification. The king

A supreme king ruling directly over a free people must be supreme, but he must rule, first, *directly*, secondly, *over a free people*. Wagner's ideal of life was the Family. In the family the father is head, his supremacy is unquestioned, all the other members render him implicit obedience. Why? Because all are united by the supreme bond of Love. Their actions are dictated by no selfish spirit, no self-interest mars the happy union; each member is free, and his obedience (which is dictated only by Love) to the head of the little community necessarily results in the mutual well-being, seeing that it is prompted by the one dominant feeling of community of interest. In such a family the individual has perfect freedom, insomuch as his every action is prompted by love for the common weal.

Political Ideals

But the modern State is a complete subversion of this ideal; its principle is that each individual member requires protection from his neighbour. The State assumes to itself the *rôle* of father in the family, but the obedience it exacts is based upon fear and not upon love. Even in obeying its laws, the individual is not prompted by love of the State, nor by love of order; he merely complies with a prescribed course of conduct whose ultimate aim is to ensure *his own* security. His existence is now governed by considerations which are purely selfish, and this selfishness enters into all his actions. Forced by the State into a definite groove as regards the ordinary routine of life, his individuality expands only within that groove, and becomes self-centred instead of all-embracing. Hence there arises an aristocracy, who, having no direct political responsibility either to the king or the people, are free to enrich themselves by any means, and at whosesoever cost they are able. Therefore, in an ideal society, such as Wagner dreamt of, there can be no intermediary between the king and the people. The king would be supreme; all his energies in his people's interest would spring from love for their welfare: the people, being absolutely free, would of their own free will render him obedience, but an obedience inspired by the recognition of him as the first of a free and contented people. Amongst that people there would be no distinctions; but they would form a republic with the king as "first and truest of all Republicans." And, that no petty jealousies might exist, the kingship should be hereditary; no petty intrigues should result in the acquisition of that exalted office. Freed from all trammels of jealousy and self-seeking would the king hold his great trust. His example, said Wagner in his celebrated speech at the Vaterlandverein club in 1848, would be "the most beautiful application of the words of Christ: Whosoever will be chief among you, let him be your servant. For in serving the freedom of all, he will make humanity conscious of the incomparable, divine import of the conception of Freedom."

Wagner was no Socialist. In this same speech he denounced, with all the vehemence of which he was capable, the "most insipid and senseless of all doctrines, called communism." His ideals were based *Wagner and Socialism* upon something far higher than "the mathematically equal division of property and earnings;" they were founded upon "the right of free human dignity." And when the Germany he dreamed of should have arisen regenerated, a new and free race, its sons would carry its influence into new and distant lands—not as the Spaniards, to whom the New World was but a "priests' slaughter-house;" nor as the English, to whom it was "a trades-man's till"—but with the message of freedom to the oppressed, "in German fashion, and nobly." Wagner's revolution was not to be a merely political one, but a regeneration of mankind. The power of money would be abolished, human activity would take its place; and

Religious Views

then God would find the *laws* for applying their new-found principles in life.

In this last sentence may be found his attitude towards religion, and it is very significant to find it incorporated in the speech above mentioned alongside of his views on the ideal republic. Wagner has often been accused of downright immorality of ideas. It has been a favourite weapon in the armoury of the adversary, fortified by exaggerated insistence on the finale to the first Act of " Walküre," where the words " Bride and sister be to thy brother " are placed in the mouth of Siegmund. The criticism is only worth noticing in order to draw attention to the pitiless punishment which follows the doomed pair, and which it is so convenient to overlook. It is impossible to study Wagner's works without being struck by the singularly deep religious feeling by which they are pervaded. The broad basis of his religion was the emancipation of the human race : this was his conception of "the fulfilment of the pure doctrine of Christ." To him the doctrine that Jesus preached was Love ; and in his earnest desire to arrive at the rock of truth in religion, life and art, we cannot wonder that he felt little or no sympathy with those who seemed to him to have obscured that precious truth with clouds of arbitrary and ostentatious dogma designed to further the worldly interests of priesthood. These are matters of individual opinion, but we must at least allow that Wagner's convictions were sincere, and that

His deep religious feeling

he is not alone in them. It is sufficient for the present purpose to recognize that his political views did not dim his earnest belief that such an ideal society as he pictured could not be brought into existence without the support of a strong religious basis, " the right of men as decreed by God "—" the fulfilment of the pure doctrine of Christ." These are not the words of the atheist.

Such, then, was the part that Wagner played in politics ; for these opinions he suffered exile for twelve years. His entrance into the political arena had been prompted solely by the conviction that the future of art was dependent upon a better order of things. After the failure of " Tannhäuser " in 1845, he wrote that he saw but one single possibility before him—to induce the public to understand and participate in his aims as an artist. It would have been easy enough for the composer of " Rienzi " to have tickled the public ear with operas such as it loved, had he been so minded ; but Wagner's ideals were not to be satisfied by the creation of what were to him meaningless nothings. He was then beginning to thresh out the theories with which his name will always be associated, and this excursion into politics was the first active step in the process. It was to him essential that the public taste should be purified, and to that end a necessary preliminary was the destruction of a corrupt government and a luxuriously selfish aristocracy, as being two of the greatest obstacles to the artistic development of a free nation. He believed that art was the birthright of the people—the

Art and the Folk

Folk. By them it had been originated ; from them it had been snatched by the luxurious few. What religion was to the future, art should be to the present. Henceforth Wagner's mission was to restore *Art the* to the German people their lost heritage ; *birthright* to show them what they had let slip away *of the Folk* and how to regain it ; to unite all Germans into a great nation through the instrumentality of Art.

Once he had settled down at Zurich Wagner lost no time in accomplishing his self-imposed task. He felt that if he were to be the pioneer of this mighty enterprise he must first assure his own position. The literary works which followed one another in such quick succession were primarily inspired by the desire to probe the whole theory of art to its utmost limits. The task was not congenial, but he felt it was necessary to establish the proposition at whose solution he had intuitively arrived. It is more than possible to believe that Wagner would have composed all his later music-dramas in the form in which they now exist had such works as " The Art-Work of the Future " and " Opera and Drama " never been written —that his artistic instinct would have led him to adopt the same form of musico-dramatic expression without the intermediate process of exhaustive analysis which diverted his thoughts from music from 1849 to 1853. However that may be, the fact remains that he himself looked upon these five years as the seed-time of the harvest of his later life, and the manner of all his later works as attributable to this protracted literary labour.

87

Wagner

The first of the Zurich essays was "Die Kunst und die Revolution" (Art and Revolution), written at the end of 1849 with the events of the Dresden troubles *"Die* fresh in his memory. Almost in the first *Kunst und* line he proclaims his text—that the artistic *die Revolu-* development of the whole of Europe found *tion"* its starting-point with the Greeks; and shows that their god Apollo was the fullest expression of the fair, strong manhood of freedom which was their ideal—not the Apollo, the soft companion of the Muses—but the Apollo of Æschylus, beautiful, but strong, with all the traits of energetic earnestness, the fulfiller of the will of Zeus. This was the *The* god whose deeds the Athenians loved to *Drama the* honour with dance and choric song amidst *highest* the sumptuous surroundings of their exqui- *form of* site architecture; and, when to all this the *Art* tragic poet added his expression of noble thoughts in the language of dignified poetry, then was born into the world the highest conceivable form of Art, the DRAMA.

To the representation of this Drama came the sons of Greece in their thousands and tens of thousands, there to witness the image of themselves, the significance of their own actions, summed up in the presentment to their eager consciousness of their own gods and heroes. It was the Drama of Human Nature, this art of a strong, free people, strong in their individuality, stronger in their communion; it was the outward expression of

Decay of Drama

their religion. To this Drama the advent of the Roman Empire was annihilation. Henceforth there existed the reign of slavery, and true art can exist only amongst a free people. " Art," says Wagner, " is pleasure in itself, in existence, in com- munity." But the Roman dominion of the world brought in its train feelings of " self-con- tempt, disgust with existence, horror of community." Such feelings were utterly repugnant to the joy of exist- ence which welled within the soul of the ancient Greek ; his freedom had been succeeded by deepest degradation.

Decay of the Drama

Whither, then, could man turn to find expression for the sorrowful existence which had now become his heritage ? To Philosophy, and later to Christianity. Philosophy could but en- deavour to make the human being con- tented with his lot ; it could offer no scheme for its amelioration : and Christianity " adjusts the ills of an honourless, useless, and sorrowful existence of mankind on earth by the miraculous love of God."

Philosophy and Chris- tianity

The position that Wagner takes up in this essay with regard to Christianity seems, at first sight, curiously in- consistent. It is, apparently, singular to find the man who in the previous year had exhorted his hearers to be mindful of " the beautiful example of Christ," now declaring that, according to Christian doctrine, " the poor wretch who, in the enjoyment of his natural powers, made this life his own possession, must suffer after death the eternal torments of hell ! "—that " naught was

Wagner

required of mankind but faith "—that " the *undeserved Grace* of God was alone to set it free."

The explanation seems to lie in the fact that this was practically Wagner's first venture in serious literature, and, moreover, that he was arguing his case entirely as a special pleader. The closer reasoning that marks his later works is absent from this, which indeed is but a rapid summary of the considerations which had led him to a discontent none the less sincere because he had not yet adequately accounted for it to his own satisfaction. His diatribes were directed not so much against Christianity itself as against *dogma*. He saw

His impa-tience of dogma

how much so-called religion was but an empty sham, a comfortable spiritual emollient ; and, in his impetuous haste, he fierily denounced the selfish spirit which aims at its own individual welfare at the expense of the common good of humanity at large. It was *hypocrisy* which he hated— the hypocrisy which led the Church to avail herself of the Renaissance of Art, while secretly confessing that the revelations of beauty to which that Renaissance gave birth were the direct offspring of the pagan Art of Greece. His ideal of humanity was that it should be free and *happy*. Christianity, *i.e.* the Christianity of history, assumed that man on earth was imprisoned as in a loathsome dungeon. Wagner could not, from the nature of things, sympathize with a dogma which could only " sacrifice to its God on the altar of renunciation," which could only derive its artistic inspiration from the

His Creed

essence of an abstract spirit (Geist), and which condemned the physical beauty of Nature as "an incarnation of the devil." This was the fanaticism which revolted his soul : Puritanism was of necessity foreign to him. His own creed is best summed up in his own words—"Let us therefore erect the *His own creed* altar of the future, in Life as in the living Art, to the two sublimest teachers of mankind : *Jesus, who suffered for all men ; and Apollo, who raised them to their joyous dignity !*"

It will therefore be seen that, up to this point, Wagner had laid down two propositions : First, that true Art originated with the Greeks ; secondly, that their downfall marked the commencement of the retrograde movement which, in spite of the so-called *"The holy-* Renaissance, had continued up to his own *noble god of* day. But a further cause had contributed *'five per* to artistic decay—"the holy-noble god of *cent.'"* 'five per cent.'" The Greek Hermes, embodiment of the thought of Zeus, had been transformed into the Roman Mercury, the god of commerce. Instead of being the common property of a free people, Art had become the luxury of the moneyed few—the enervated aristocracy who had grown rich by preying on the very men whose birthright they had stolen along with their freedom.

And here occurs a conspicuous instance of the justice of Wagner's reasoning. To what does he attribute the evils he deplores ? Not to the Roman ascendency, not to the Church's influence ; but to those very Greeks

Wagner

whose artistic life was to him the model of all that was fairest and most beautiful. He recognized that the secret of degeneration was to be found in the *Slave*. By sheer force of contrast the existence of the slave proved that the noble attributes of Grecian manhood could alone be lasting blessings when they were "the common attributes of all mankind." And the history of two thousand years had been one long record of retrogression. The identity of the free man had become merged in that of the slave; and the few who were seeming exceptions to the sad rule owed their position solely to the power which the so-called civilization of a later growth had enabled them to turn into an instrument of oppression. Culture was now the prerogative of the rich; and thus, instead of ennobling the human race, had become the means of its further debasement, insomuch that it served but to farther accentuate the arbitrary class distinctions which were the historical result of the old Greek system of slavery. Art had become an article of commerce. The artist, instead of seeking his only reward in the public approbation of a noble work nobly performed, had become a mere "journeyman" to whom money was the only goal. And so, Art, instead of being an integral part of the beauty of life, became to those who practised it but an irksome toil, a daily drudgery, with no ulterior aim beyond the satisfaction of the needs or lusts of existence.

Therefore was Wagner's voice uplifted for the purification of the Augean stable. Since Art could not exist

Social Revolution

under such conditions, let them be abolished ; let man arise in his might and proclaim Revolution—a Revolution which should release the down-trodden *Revolution* forces of Nature, and restore to the pinnacle *of social* to which he had been elevated in ancient *conditions* Greece the *strong, fair man !* Then would *imperative* flourish "the mightiest of all art-establishments—the Theatre," to which admission would be *free*, and wherein would be enacted the true Drama, the reflection of the Life of the Community ; it would be the care of that Community to ensure that the artists were placed in such a position that commercial enterprise should have no voice in that Theatre's economy. This was the first step which Wagner deemed imperative for the production of the Art-Work of the Future.

Having thus determined the conditions under which alone Art could flourish, Wagner next turned his attention to a careful analysis of the product which would be the natural result of those conditions. His *" Das* conclusions are to be found in the thought- *Kunstwerk* ful essay, "Das Kunstwerk der Zukunft" *der Zu-* (The Art-Work of the Future), which *kunft"* was the immediate successor of "Art and Revolution." This essay contains some of Wagner's most pregnant thoughts ; it is certainly one of the most difficult of all his writings. The difficulties are caused, to no inconsiderable extent, by the fact that he largely *Feuerbach* adopts the terminology of the philosopher Feuerbach, with whose writings he was, moreover, very imperfectly acquainted at the time. In a letter written about this period, he regrets that he had only been able to peruse one of Feuerbach's early works. Notwithstanding the fact that his meaning is often obscured by the endeavour to express original thoughts within the limits of a terminology by no means suited to their due expansion, the "Art-Work of the Future" is in all respects remarkable.

It has often been said that Wagner's philosophy was borrowed from Schopenhauer. It is true that Schopen-

Schopen-hauer

hauer's tenets appealed strongly to him —when he became acquainted with them; but this essay, written at a time when that philosopher's writings were absolutely unknown to him, conclusively proves that Wagner's ideas were evolved from his own brain, and is a conspicuous instance of two great minds arriving at a similar result by different channels. Wagner had already found out for himself that the true artistic incentive was Necessity, the Need which alone was the source of life, and to which the Intellect was of secondary importance. His views, as embodied in this and subsequent writings, demand treatment at some little length.

WAGNER AND HIS SON.

CHAPTER VI

As Man is to Nature so is Art to Man—The Necessity of Nature
—Art the portrayal of Life—True Art-Work must be born of
Necessity—and therefore of the Folk, who alone act from
Necessity—Man's twofold nature, outer and inner—Dance,
Tone, and Poetry alone belong to purely human Art-Work—
Their union, as exemplified in the Drama, the perfect Art—
The Art of Dance, *i.e.* the Mimetic Art—Its decadence when
divorced from Tone and Poetry—The Art of Tone—The
" sea of Harmony "—Its separation from Rhythm—Its de-
generation into a mechanical exercise—The Aria—Reunion
with Rhythm—The " harmonized dance "—The Symphony—
Haydn, Mozart, and Beethoven—The Choral Symphony a
recognition that Poetry as well as Tone is essential to the
Art-work of the Future—The Art of Poetry—Its decadence
into a toneless, written dialect—The literary drama—Comedy
the vehicle for the actor's virtuosity, instead of a representation
of Life—The Oratorio—The " French-confectionery opera "
—The plastic arts, Architecture, Sculpture, and Painting—
Decline of Architecture before the ascendency of the Utilitarian
—Sculpture can only indicate a passing phase of the poetry of
motion—Painting, and its recognition of Nature in the portrayal of Landscape—The Art-Work of the Future—The
fellowship of artists—His belief in the German race—" Judaism
in Music "—His criticism of Meyerbeer—The Jew must fail
as an artist because he belongs not to the Folk.

WAGNER's main proposition is that the relationship
of Art to Man stands on precisely the same footing as
that of Man to Nature.

95

Wagner

Nature's countless forms are evolved without caprice or arbitrary aim; they are the result of an immutable law—Necessity—dictated by an inner natural need.

The Necessity of Nature

Necessity is the vital principle of Life. This Necessity is recognizable by man by observation of the harmony of Nature's phenomena; once their harmonious connection is disturbed, the result seems to be governed not by Necessity but by Caprice. When Man severed his connection with *unconscious* Nature and became a *conscious* being, he evolved the faculty of Thought; and with the birth of Thought arose Error, the earliest utterance of Consciousness. Error arose from attributing Nature's phenomena to arbitrary disconnected forces, in other words to Caprice, instead of to their true origin—the harmonious instinctive energy which is Necessity.

To lay this error, and to fathom the underlying principle of Necessity in Nature, is the function of Knowledge. Through Knowledge Man recognizes his own community with Nature, sees in his own life the portraiture in brief of Nature, and unconscious Nature in her turn attains, as it were, in Man her consciousness. The instrument by which this knowledge is attained is Science—Science whose highest achievement it is to set right the arbitrary concepts of the human brain, to discover the Necessity of Nature, to learn the secret of Life. Science is but finite; its highest goal is the discovery of the Necessity which governs Nature. But Life is the result of that Necessity; is unending. The

96

The Folk

portrayal of this Life which through Science man has learned to know is—Art. The Artist may originally set about his work in a spirit arbitrary, selective or meditative; but only when his choice is born from pure Necessity— when he finds himself again in the subject of *Art the portrayal of Life* his choice, as perfected man finds his true self in Nature— only then is Art-Work a self-conditioned and immediate entity. (These last few words are practically Wagner's own.) This must be the Art-Work of the Future.

If Thought were the dominant feature of Life, could it divert the vital impulse from the great Necessity of absolute life-needs, Life itself would be dethroned and swallowed up in Science, Error would reign unchecked. But the errors that have arisen through misdirected Thought and arbitrary speculation are counteracted by *True Art-Work must be born of Necessity* the workings of a vital force, and that force is—*the Folk.* The Folk is the community of all those men "*who feel a common and collective Want*"—a Want so strong, so overmastering, that it becomes a *Need.* Only such a Need, so collectively felt, can call for satisfaction as a *Necessity*, and therefore it is "*the Folk alone that acts according to Necessity's behests,*" for the *common* Need is the only true Need. Where there is no true Need, the satisfaction of desire is but Luxury, the egoistic bar to the assuagement of real Want.

The Folk itself is all-powerful, in it dwells the innate force of Life. In the satisfaction of its Need it has

Wagner

invented Speech; to it Religion and the State owe their existence. It need not even *know* what it wills; for a common and necessary Need will inevitably produce the Deed as its consequential fruition. The Folk can turn the *Willed not* into the *Non-existing;* it is the arbiter of human life. Thought arose only when Man, in his severance from unconscious Nature, first recognized his inner life-need as the common life-need of his *Species,* as distinguished from Nature with her myriad ramifications. But if Thought be mistaken for the progenitor of the Folk instead of its offspring, if the end be mistaken for the beginning, then Culture alone will become the object of a spurious Necessity—Culture which, Wagner declares, finds its utterance in *Fashion.* And Fashion, which would arrogate to itself the genesis of Art, cannot from the nature of things invent; for invention is but a finding out of Nature's secrets, and they are hidden from those who are not in sympathy with her. Fashion is but an arbitrary attempt to interfere with Nature, and is therefore the antithesis of true Art, of which Nature is the fountain-head. It therefore follows that since true Art-Work can only be born of Necessity, and the Folk alone act according to Necessity, to that great *Folk* alone can we look for the Art-Work of the Future. Only from Life itself can Art obtain either matter or form.

Having thus determined the essentials of Art-Work, Wagner proceeds by a natural process of evolution to determine how those essentials are to be satisfied. Man's nature, he postulates, is twofold—the outer and the

Dance, Tone, and Poetry

inner.   To the former the faculty of vision makes appeal, to the latter the sense of hearing.   By gesture, by expression, man is able to communicate to his fellows his inner emotions, and the eye, besides, gives him the power of distinguishing surrounding objects.   But the inner man can find *direct* communication only through the medium of his voice's Tone.   *Tone*, by itself, can only express general feelings, and those but vaguely ; in *Speech* alone is to be found the capacity for the condensation which brings to the inner consciousness distinct and definite understanding. Speech of itself is unemotional, a diamond in a dark room ; only by the flashing light of Tone can its hidden beauties be brought to light, its full significance revealed.

Man's twofold nature

It follows, therefore, that the chief varieties of human Art are those which appeal to both sides of human nature, the outer and the inner ; and they are Dance,* Tone, and Poetry.   Only these three belong to *purely human* Art, and their union was complete in the earliest form of Art-Work—the Lyric, and its loftier completion, the Drama.   That union was the embodiment of perfect Art ; independent yet interdependent, each form gained additional beauty through loving alliance.   And in this they were symbolical of human life.

Dance, Tone, and Poetry

Their union in the Drama

* By the term *Dance* Wagner always means what may best be described as the " poetry of motion ; " it is not confined to choreographic art, but is a generic term including all beauty of gesture.

99

Wagner

Man's greatest life-need is Love; he appeases that need by taking from Nature; he pays Nature's debt by giving Love to others. Only in community is Life's highest fulfilment attained. And as with Man's complete nature, so it is with his separate faculties and senses. Each is limited by strictly defined bounds, but through Love these boundaries become merged in each other, and the Freedom of *loving* community is the result— the freedom of all man's faculties—the All-Faculty. And so no single Art, dependent for its existence on one single faculty, an Art-*variety* in effect, can be free; there can only be true freedom when all these varieties are lovingly blended into one perfect whole.

The Art of DANCE—the *mimetic* Art—is the most realistic of all the arts. The material from which it is shaped is man himself—and not one single portion of

The Art of Dance

him, but the whole. The more complex is man's emotion, the more manifold are the transitions of gesture by which that emotion is expressed. In the ordering of the movements by which man strives to make his emotions intelligible to others is to be found the Speech of Motion—*Rhythm*, whereby Dance becomes an art. Rhythm itself is, however, dependable on a sense other than that of Seeing; the law of measure depends upon the sense of Hearing. The rhythmic sense was originally imparted to the dancer by a series of sounds recurring at definite intervals, such as the clapping of hands, or the striking of a sonorous body. Hence it came to pass that

The Art of Dance

Rhythm became indelibly associated with Tone ; for the movement of the dancer between the rhythmic beats is constant, continuing ; and a continuing undercurrent of Tone became essential to sustain and complement the emotion expressed by the gestures of the dancer. And as the human voice is the living flesh covering the skeleton of Tone, and Speech, as it were, the bone and muscle of that voice, its Rhythm—so it comes to pass that in Speech (the Rhythm of Tone), Dance through Tone (its own Rhythm) wins its highest satisfaction. And therefore Dance, Tone, and Poetry are each complementary of the other, and in their union is the perfect *Lyric Art-Work ;* for each branch fulfils its own function, not striving egoistically to borrow from its fellow, but rather giving place to its fellow when its own powers are unequal to the task in hand.

But when divorced from her sisters, Dance lost her high estate. First casting aside Poesy, she then treated Tone, not as an enhancement of the emotion she would express, but simply as a tool wherewith to supply herself with a guiding measure of rhythm. Dance thus lost her individu- *Its decadence* ality ; such shreds as remained to her were only to be found in the national dances of the Folk, fashioned as they were by common instinct. She became an imitator, instead of an inventor, trying to find novelty in borrowing piecemeal from whatever source offered itself, having in her isolation lost that Necessity which is the only true mother of invention. In her last extreme she even attempted by means of Pantomime to express that to which Speech alone is adequate, a performance only understandable by its spectators through the medium of an explanatory programme! Thus fared the first of the three lost sisters.

TONE is the organ of the heart; the art of tone is its conscious speech. Through Tone, Dance and Poetry are led to a mutual understanding; to the former she brings

The Art of Tone

The " sea of Har- mony "

Rhythm, to the latter Melody. Rhythm and Melody are the shores of the ocean of Tone, that immeasurable expanse of waters which makes up the sea of *Harmony*. In a fine passage Wagner describes the Greek setting sail on that mighty depth, never letting either coast line fade from his sight, softly plying his rhythmic oars, now to the measure of the wood-nymphs' dance, anon to the solemn cadence of the sacred hymns whose solemn import floated down from the temple on the mountain-top. But in Christian art the voyager, guided by desire for egoistic bliss only, left the friendly strands, and, in faith in the *word* alone, steered his frail bark with his eyes fixed on Heaven—a Heaven which presently shut in the whole horizon, but which, in spite of all his efforts, he could never reach. And, to that striver after the unattainable, the ocean of Tone became a weary turmoil of waters, now surging, now falling, but ever unappeased in its fruitless effort to obtain satisfaction from out its inmost self alone.

Thus Wagner pictured Tone divorced from her sisters

The Art of Tone

Dance and Poetry. Robbed of her rhythm by the secession of Dance, Tone could draw from Poetry only her *word*; and, as that *word* became more and more yielding to Tone's embrace, and more and more invertebrate, Tone became once more driven back upon herself, and *Its separation from Rhythm* impelled to shape herself from out her own inexhaustible depths. Hence Harmony was evolved from Tone—Harmony which is all-enduring because it knows not time (which is of the essence of rhythm), which has neither beginning nor end, which is but a constant shifting, a yearning, a dying without having achieved any object. So long as the *word* could exercise its power, it set the limits of the beginning and ending of Tone.

But when the word became merely an *adjunct*, then the endlessness of Tone craved for finite limits; for the human mind cannot grasp the illimitable, and consequently was left unsatisfied by mere Harmony. Tone therefore invoked other aid—rhythmic devices—the resources of Counterpoint— *Its degeneration into a mechanical exercise* by which her fluid breadths were rendered capable of condensation, her unstable periods brought to a more certain conclusion. But the impetus she thus sought was not born of her necessity, it was the satisfying of a merely artificial desire. The problems and devices with which she now concerned herself appealed to the *Intellect*, not to the *Heart*; with this new era music began to become simply the vehicle of the mathematical speculator. Such a state of things naturally in due time

called for relief; and as Dance in her extremity turned
to the dances of the Folk for inspiration, so did Tone turn
to the tunes of the Folk.

But she did not even then seek the aid of the *entire*
artistic man, but only of a part of him—the *singing* man.
Merely the melodic Tune did she extract, to which she
The Aria joined words meaning less as they were un-
suggested by it. The folk-tune degenerated
into the *aria*, the opportunity for the display of the vocal
agility of the singer. The human voice, the noblest of
all tone producers, lost all its distinctive power of utterance, and sank from its high office of uttering the noblest
aspirations of the heart, to the level of a mere instrument.

Side by side with this debasement, the history of Tone
nevertheless showed a struggle to regain what it had
lost. Deprived of the assistance of the word, which
Reunion had become the appanage of the Intellect
with rather than the Heart, finding no rest in
Rhythm the eternal boundlessness of Harmony, Tone
fell back upon the only resource left, the
rhythm which Dance had endeavoured to arrogate to
herself. As Dance had been driven to join hands once
more with Tone, so Tone had to renew
The "har- her alliance with her erstwhile despised
monized sister Dance. To the instruments devised
dance" by Dance to assist in marking her rhythm,
Tone lent the aid of her combinative powers of Harmony,
and the *harmonized dance* became the tap-root whence
sprang the towering tree of the Symphony. Haydn,

Beethoven's Choral Symphony

Mozart, Beethoven — with each grew stronger and stronger the offspring of the natural and happy union. The innocent gaiety of Haydn—the song-like melodies of Mozart—the "new speech" of Beethoven—these were the successive *The Symphony* phases which marked the development of Tone in her re-found approach towards completeness. Two of the Graces had redeemed their mutual error, and now only awaited, with loving embrace, the third.

To Wagner, Beethoven represented the fulfilment, not only of what had already been achieved, but of all that was *possible* in the domain of absolute music. With unerring instinct the great tone poet had followed up the varied springs of emotion, until in his colossal 9th Symphony he had set himself to exhaust the limits of the sea of sound, "to find the land which needs must lie beyond the waste of waters." And in the end, to satisfy his inner yearning, to express all that he meant that Symphony to reveal, he joined Speech to Tone and cried, "Rejoice ! Breast to breast, *The Choral* ye mortal millions ! This one kiss to all *Symphony* the world !" Only by the aid of poesy could the message of his crowning work be fully conveyed—that was the meaning to Wagner of the *Choral Symphony*. To him it was no mere species of art-variety—a symphony with a chorus—it was Beethoven's tacit acknowledgment of the limitation of absolute music, the confession that Poetry as well as Tone was essential to the Art-Work of the Future.

Wagner

POETRY—the last of the three sisters—was originally absolutely dependent for expression on Dance and Tone ; Orpheus had to compel the attention of the brutes by
The Art of Poetry the music of his voice and the beauty of his gestures before they could be attuned to duly listen to the message he had to tell them. The old Epics of the Folk, too, were *recited*, with all the added grace of tone and action, and hence arose the desire in the mind of the many which Tragedy rose to satisfy. Going back again to the Greeks, Wagner holds that it was the desire of the Folk for actuality, for *deeds* visible to the eye, that led to the establishment of the Stage, and seeks to strengthen his argument by citing the fact that the Theatre was established what time Pisistratus was engaged upon the editing and publication of Homer in literary form.

Modern criticism would not, perhaps, allow Wagner's premises ; the labours of Pisistratus are open to doubt : but he is certainly accurate in insisting, as he does, upon
Its decadence the *communal* aspect of Greek tragedy. It was essentially a popular festival, and its decline, its extinguishment beneath the mocking laughter of Aristophanes, dates from the decay of the Folk. Thereafter, Poetry, no longer able to appeal to the ear, was compelled to dumbly address herself to the eye, to become a toneless, written dialect. Poetry sank to the level of description, and, cut apart from warm, full-blooded Life, became the mere conveyance of Thought, the handmaiden of Science and Philosophy.

The Drama

But inasmuch as the consummation of Science and Philosophy—indeed, of all knowledge—lies in that which comprehends both Man and Nature, that is, Life—for the limit of Knowledge, which is finite, is infinite Life—so can that consummation be reached only in that which is drawn from Life itself—the Art-Work made up of the perfect union of the Arts derived from that Life—the DRAMA.

Drama is the outcome of a longing to impart, and it is also the outcome of a longing to receive. But if true drama is to exist, it must spring from a common impulse, must appeal to a common interest; it must originate with the Folk. The drama thus produced must of necessity appeal to all, for it is the expression of their joint Need. Thus the earliest dramatic efforts sprang from the expression by one of a *fellowship of players*, themselves part of the great Folk, of the common impulse towards dramatic effort felt in the little band. Such fellowships existed at the end of the Middle Ages; Shakespeare's dramas were constructed out of the inmost nature of the Folk for his fellow-players. But when the dramatic poet, instead of giving utterance to artistic impulse, sought rather to *dominate* it, to assert his own individuality instead of answering the Need of the Folk, then the fate befel him which must befal all those who endeavour to turn machines into actual living men. Such work awoke no responsive echo in its auditors, and the would-be dramatic poet, finding the portals of the stage thus closed to him, had to content himself with the bookseller's counter. Thus arose the *literary* drama, in which the dramatist exalted his own personal views

The literary drama

at the expense of the actual living Truth of Life. And, as with the dramatist, so with the actor. As the former endeavoured to see *himself* alone upon the stage, so did the latter seek escape from the bonds of artistic community in order to exalt his own importance in the eyes of a thoughtless public. Thus the art of the actor degenerated into mere virtuosity—the comedy became but the setting for the antics of the comedian. And so, dramatic art-poetry destined for such performers must needs either clash with the idiosyncrasies of the player, or become their abject slave.

Dance, Tone, Poetry. Only in accordance with the natural laws of Love, of *self-offering* for the common good for Love's sake, is true Art-Work possible. As Man's love for Woman passes over through her into the Child, the result of their union, and in this loving trinity finds its ultimate perfection, so must the three individual art-varieties find their consummation by *giving* themselves to each other, not by selfish striving to steal that which is not of their own essence. For what had been the result of the attempt by each variety to borrow from the other instead of enlisting its aid on terms of equality? Tone had been compelled to engulf the Word, and in Catholic music had treated it with scant reverence, superimposing it arbitrarily on top of her restless and rhythmless harmony. Protestant

Oratorio and Opera

church music, while handling the Word with more vigour, sought, as in the "Passion-music," to make it a vehicle for the expression of action rather than feeling, with a consequent leaning towards ecclesiastical drama.

From the holding aloof of Poetry from Tone arose what Wagner terms that "unnatural abortion" the *Oratorio*, which would give itself the airs of the Drama, "but only precisely in so far as it might still preserve to *Music* the unquestioned right of being the chief concern." Music *The Oratorio* asked from Poetry merely a "heap of stones," with which she might deal as her fancy dictated. But, in her arrogance, Music had committed a greater enormity still in attempting to dominate Dance as well as Poetry in *Opera*. They in turn rebelled, and the result was —chaos—the reign of the three in their most egoistic and antagonistic forms. So much music, so many minutes' ballet, so much dialogue as might be conveniently necessary to fill up the intervals not otherwise engaged ! On this plan were manufactured what our critic terms the "French-confectionery- operas." And he considered his insistence on the perfect union of the three varieties as all-necessary more than proved by the *The " French- confec- tionery- opera "* fact that the examples given to the world by Gluck and Mozart of the highest capabilities of music, had had no effect whatever on the operatic art of his own day.

Wagner

Before endeavouring to solve the problem of the nature of the Art-Work of the Future, Wagner briefly

The plastic arts

reviews the nature of the so-called *plastic* arts, Architecture, Sculpture, and Painting.

Among the Greeks, Architecture was first employed in aid of and in homage to the religious feeling of human nature. The Temple, its first expression, gave place to the Theatre, as the Lyrist was

Decline of Architecture

supplanted by the Tragedian. In each case it was the communal instinct which produced the result, the instinct of the Folk—

the Necessity for the most beautiful setting possible wherein to focus the altar or the stage. The private homes of that Folk gave free accommodation for hospitality, although there was absent from them the domineering influence of selfish personal luxury. But with the decline of the Folk there entered the age of egoism. The individual no longer sacrificed to the gods in common with his fellows, but bowed himself before Plutus, god of riches. Public life sank to the mere expression of this universal egoism, and the Beautiful retired abashed before the advance of the Utilitarian. And hence Architecture became imitative and not inventive, for only *need* can evoke invention, and, with individualism supreme, there can be no common need.

Sculpture dated from the time when the Greek had

Sculpture

sunk into luxury. No longer rejoicing in the noble love of man for man, the love even more noble than that of man for woman, he had

110

Sculpture and Painting

retired within his own four walls; Spartan simplicity had given place to selfish extravagance, and instead of finding his highest joy in the living, soulful Drama, Man employed the hireling Sculpture to beautify his palaces with his own counterfeit presentment in lifeless stone. No longer did he look for that presentment in the Tragedy enacted before him in his thousands; and consequently the living, beautiful Man, with the rich variety of his movements, became in sculpture but a creature of one single pose from which the endless possibilities of motion had to be inferred by a species of anatomical deduction. The possibility of this imitation having once been discovered, the learning of the craft became an easy matter; and therefore, even in the days when the beauteous Greek man had vanished from real life, the modern impulse to reproduce was able to fall back upon the relics of the past and find its impetus therein. But in its essence Sculpture must be *unnecessary*; for the very cause of its existence is annulled when "*actual life shall itself be fair of body*." At best it can only be a poor substitute for that which it has endeavoured to copy—the poetry of motion.

Painting, in its *artistic* evolution, also first attained significance with the decay of Tragedy—the Human Art-Work—in endeavouring to reproduce *Painting* the warmth of life of those representations then paling into obscurity. The Artist could, by means of painting, recall the bygone scenes as a portrait recalls its prototype; and Art itself became an

111

object of art, and art that *can be learned* came into existence. This art, too, needed no *Necessity* for its inception; it could be pursued under any circumstances: but it was the result of isolated self-appeasement, which is Culture. The artistic beginnings of painting therefore had their origin in a spirit of retrospection, in which, at first, the presentation of Man alone played the prominent part. To the Greek, Nature was always subordinate to Man; she was regarded only as a necessary background for the god in human shape to whose control she was subject. And this error was accentuated under the Byzantine empire; philosophy only aggravated the breach which the "anthropomorphis of Nature" had created.

But when the harmony of Nature's phenomena began to be appreciated, when the impulse which led to these discoveries overflowed in the Renaissance of Art, Painting acquired fresh impetus; and, though cramped at first by the unloveliness of Life, which threw her back upon her own invention and the traditions of art-history in her attempt to depict the historic, she nevertheless owed her salvation to her difficulty. She was driven to the study of the Nature she had now learned to recognize; she acquired the feeling for *Landscape*. So that, at last, Man in painting exchanged places with Nature and became her foil instead of she his. Undisfigured Nature asserted herself, and the painter, finding, in her, exhaustless subjects, and therefore an inexhaustible capacity, became more and more attracted by and devoted to this

The Art-Work of the Future

branch of his art. The birth of the true drama would prove the death of the *man-portraying* art of painting, just as it would of Sculpture. But Landscape painting by allying itself with Architecture would produce the *stage* and "picture thereon the warm background of Nature for living, no longer counterfeited, Man."

Having thus traced the decay of the arts of Dance, Tone, and Poetry through their attempts to satisfy their need from their own resources alone, and shown that plastic Art can only prosper in union with Artistic Man as distinguished from the mere Utilitarian, Wagner proceeds to draw his conclusions. Seeing *The Art-Work of the* that any one particular art-variety cannot *Future* flourish in isolation, it follows that the true Art-Work must be *common*, for only then can Artistic Man be *free*, and fully that which he has power to be. The highest conjoint Art-Work is the Drama, and "true Drama is only conceivable as proceeding from a *common urgence of every art* towards the most direct appeal to a *common public*." Architecture and Landscape painting will join hands in preparing a theatre so designed that the spectator shall be able, as it were, to feel himself a part of the scene enacted, a stage so planned as to appear the very semblance of Nature herself. The arts of Sculpture and Historical Painting will reach their perfection in the source from which they sprang—the graceful gestures of the mime, the grouping of colour, the actual human show. When these fail to convey the artist's inner feeling, Poetry will supply by the Word the proclamation of his plain and conscious purpose ; and to Poetry will be added Tone, with all its varied inflections of the human voice, with all the mighty possibilities of emotional expression which Beethoven discovered in the Orchestra.

This will be the Art-Work of the Future ; and this Art-Work can be attained only if " *Life press forward into Art.*" Culture cannot produce true Art, for, as it sprang from regions outside Life, it cannot produce Life out of itself. Community will be essential to this new Art-Work ; for the dramatic Action which will ensure the Drama's *understanding* will be taken from Life itself, and therefore become to Life the picture of Life's own existence. Since the truest fount of Art is the impulse to bring this picture to understanding and acknowledgment as Necessity, it follows that only to a life in common can

The fellow-ship of artists

such a picture appeal, for there can be no Necessity to the egoist. And in this fellowship of artists will the Artist of the Future be found. In every Art-Work each individual participator, in his several degree, whether poet, performer, musician or plastician, will be inspired only by the Life-need which has led to its production—it will be the accomplishment of the Folk. And he " who will endure every sorrow for its sake, and if need should be will even offer up his life—*he, and he alone, belongs to the Folk ;* for he and all his fellows feel a common *Want.*"

This, then, was Wagner's vision of the Art-Work of the Future. If his reasoning is at times difficult to follow —and without doubt it is—the conclusion at which he

Wagner and Beethoven

arrives is sufficiently plain. In our own day it is not easy to imagine what a bombshell this essay was to the art world of Wagner's time. To begin with, the idea of following Art for its own sake, irrespective of monetary gain, was amazing in its boldness to the majority of the artists of the day. But the directness with which the opera of his time was attacked by Wagner made matters worse, and not only were the actual views which he expressed attacked, but he was represented as having said things absolutely opposed to his most cherished convictions. Particularly was he accused of an intention to create a new species of music—the ridicule which formerly attached to the term " Music of the Future " is still fresh in the memory—whereas all that Wagner asked was that what Beethoven had done for absolute music should be done for the music which should form an integral part of the drama of his ideals. He would begin " where Beethoven left off "—the perverted phrase which stuck so badly in the gizzard of his critics ; but only in the sense of pursuing the path which Beethoven's genius had opened up for succeeding musicians to follow.

Wagner saw in Beethoven the emancipator of music, and his attitude was always that of thankfulness that such a great one should have arisen to point out the way in which posterity might go rejoicing. He spoke out plainly, sharply indeed, for he was dominated by the burning desire that the *German race* might be led to see the artistic possibilities that lay ready to their hand. And to do that it was first necessary that error should be

Wagner

swept away, and that in no half-hearted or perfunctory manner; Wagner's motto was ever "thorough." His aim was twofold: to show in what true Art-Work consisted; to do all in his power to elevate the German race into a state capable of producing and receiving it.

Wagner (as has been said previously), in his love for the Fatherland, believed with all his heart and soul that the German race *alone* were capable of being the artists of the future. His article on "Das Judenthum in der Musik"
"Judaism in Music" (Judaism in Music) was entirely prompted by this national feeling. Much has been said and written of the way in which Meyerbeer was attacked in this article, as he undoubtedly was. But a closer examination of the essay will show that it was not against Meyerbeer as a *man* that the keenness of Wagner's satire was directed,
Criticism of Meyerbeer but against him as an *artist*. He saw that Meyerbeer's aim was merely to please the public, not to evolve an artistic creation for its own sake, and he knew from experience that the only form of art which that public appreciated was that in which charlatanism predominated. The public of Wagner's day loved to be dazzled and surprised by novel effects, and Meyerbeer was just the conjurer to provide them.

Wagner's purpose in "Judaism in Music" was to prove that, of necessity, a Jew could not be an artist. Only from the Folk can the artist be born, and the Jew has ever been a wanderer on the face of the earth, with no *national* characteristics about him. Therefore the Jew must inevitably lead an egoistic life, and to the egoist, Wagner held, no artistic production was possible. Wagner was thus pursuing the line of argument he had commenced in " The Art-Work of the Future," and taken together the two essays had resulted, first, in determining that the Drama alone was the true Art-Work, and secondly, that its production was only possible to the Folk—by which Wagner understood the German nation elevated into the higher life to which he believed his fellow-countrymen destined. To complete the investigation upon which he had embarked it was now necessary to determine the nature of this Drama—its most fitting subjects and their method of treatment. This Wagner set himself to accomplish in " Oper und Drama " (Opera and Drama).

CHAPTER VII

"Opera and Drama"—Historical sketch of opera and music—Music, instead of being the *means* of expression in Opera, becomes the *end*—Womanly nature of music—The music of the true Drama must take its origin from the poesy to which it is wedded—Drama derived from (1) Romance, (2) Greek drama —Shakespeare and Racine—The play and its setting—German drama—Goethe—Schiller—The Myth, the poem of a life-view in common—Christian Mythos unsuitable, from the point of view of Art, as a subject for Drama—German Saga—The evolution of Romance—The Romance of Burgher society—The choice of dramatic action—The means for its expression —Tone-speech—Metre and end-rhyme—Melody and harmony —The function of the Orchestra—(a) to supplement gesture— (b) to produce the sense of remembrance—(c) to suggest foreboding—True unity of Drama not one of time or place, but of expression—Wagner's naturalness of expression—His use of the *leit motif*—His influence on music—Melody and declamation—His love of human nature—and of animals—Vegetarianism—The great aim of existence should be man's regeneration.

A GREAT part of "Opera and Drama" consists of the expansion of the historical purview of "The Art-Work of the Future," and, though intensely interesting in itself, must be passed lightly over in the attempt, within such brief limits as are here possible, to trace the evolution of

" Opera and Drama"

118

Richard and Cosima Wagner.

Operatic Melody

Wagner's art theories. The essay is divided into three parts : (i.) Opera and Music ; (ii.) The Play and Poetry ; (iii.) The Drama of the Future.

In the first part he traces at considerable length the history of opera and music down to Beethoven. Starting with the days when the artificial *Historical* aria reigned supreme, he deals with the *sketch of* revolt of Gluck against the mere virtuosity *opera and* which was the *raison d'être* of its exist- *music* ence ; he shows the German Mozart taking the opera of the Italian school as his model, and his would-be imitators mistaking the divinity of his music for a mere form, whereas Mozart had only worked within the limits which alone were possible in the absence of union with a true poet. The essence of the aria was its absolute *musicality ;* the words, without which a tune was an impossibility to the Folk, in the aria became immaterial. Hence arose the school of operatic *melody* with Rossini at its head.

This school Wagner traces through its wanderings into foreign lands for the sake of obtaining relief in local colour and rhythm, and shows that in all its ramifications absolute *music* alone it was which was concerned in the shaping of opera. In Meyerbeer had the culminating point of bombastic musical pretension been reached. But in Weber, Wagner perceived the earnest endeavour to make melody the reflex of emotion, to make it a true explanation of the words to which it was wedded instead of the mere absolute tunefulness of the Rossinian school.

Wagner

Still even he had failed, because he had idealized melody too largely, and had sought to dominate the whole of the operatic fabric thereby.

The history of opera tended to show that music, instead of being the *means* of expression, had become the *end*. And hence music had become barren, for the essence of music's nature is the womanly—she can *Womanly nature of music* bear, but cannot *beget*. The essence of music is *melody*; harmony and rhythm are the shaping organs; but the essence, the spirit of music, is *melody*. The opera composers in their adaptation of the *Folk's melody* to the necessities of the *aria* took heed only of the *form* of that melody. They did not perceive that that very form was evolved out of the Necessity of the words themselves, and that music had merely *borne* the melody which the poetry had generated. But in the mightiest works of Beethoven the truth of the proposition was manifested, for therein he did not as it were assume melody as something ready in advance, but let it be born under our very eyes. And in his final Symphony we see him invoking the aid of poetry, not to add effect to his melody, but to be the begetter of that melody itself. Beethoven succeeded where the opera composer had failed; for he shattered the arbitrary *form* of melody, and proved that from the fragments it was possible to rebuild a perfect whole. (Wagner himself has, to cite no other instance, given us an example of this generation in the "Kaisermarsch," wherein the germs of melody only reach their fullest development at

Sources of Drama

the very end of the work.) And just as the original of all melody, the Folk's melody, was generated by the Folk's poem, and was truly inseparable therefrom, so could Music of herself never bear anything worthy unless fecundated by the poet's Thought. Woman's nature is Love, the Love which manifests itself in surrender; it is the essence of her being. And so must Music surrender herself to the Poet in order that her truest function, the birth of Melody, may be exercised. The Music of the true Drama must therefore *take its origin* from the Poesy to which it is to be wedded.

Dealing next with modern drama, Wagner derives it from two sources—the one, the Romance; the other, misunderstood Greek Drama. The real *Drama de-* kernel lay in the Romance, though for *rived from* variety's sake some poets had more or less (i) *Romance* imitated the Greek Drama. At the head (ii) *Greek* of the dramas sprung directly from Romance *drama* Wagner places the plays of Shakespeare; he finds their diametrical opposite in the *Tragédie* of Racine. Shakespeare translated the narrative Romance into Drama, making his players enact human actions which theretofore had been merely explained by the narrative talk of poesy. He narrowed down both the action and the time-space which had been characteristic of mummers' shows and mystery-plays, but he took from them their action, and joined that action to his own noble poetry. But the *scene* in which that action took place he left to Phantasy. A single board

with its lettered description of the place where the
action was taking place sufficed him ; he had not
deemed the joining hands with as near perfect as
possible an illusion of Nature to be essen-
The play
and its
setting
tial. With Shakespeare "the play's the
thing," the setting immaterial. In French
and Italian stage history the reverse had been
the case ; *Unity of Scene* was deemed the essential condition, with the inevitable result that description and not
action became the business of the player. Hence in the
Tragèdie of Racine the Talk took place on the stage, the
Action *behind* it.

Between these two extremes hovered the Drama of
Wagner's day, the Drama which had been reared on
German soil. Germany had held aloof
German
Drama
from the Renaissance, and the beginnings
of her drama were derived from two
sources—Shakespeare, brought over by English players
and seized upon by the Folk; and Opera, imported
from Italy and cultivated by the rich. The latter
with its wealth of scenic display led to a taste for
elaborate stage mounting, to satisfy which the Shake-
spearian drama in following the prevailing vogue suffered
by the excision of whole scenes to meet the convenience
of the carpenter. Hence the poet, who saw in this state
of affairs the sacrifice of the poetic ideal of Shakespeare
to an incongruous mass of realism, found himself
confronted with two alternatives—the one to confine
himself to purely literary drama, leaving the reader's

Goethe and Schiller

own phantasy to supply the scene ; the other to turn to
the more reflective type of play constructed in accordance
with the so-called Aristotelian rules of unity of time and
place. Thus Goethe, finding that his " full-
blooded " drama " Götz von Berlichingen "
demanded impossible scenic effects, in adapting it for
practical stage purposes was compelled to sacrifice somewhat of the freshness of Romance which it had exhibited
in its original form. In "Egmont" he chose for his
subject one that presented less drawbacks from the standpoint of practical stage management. In "Faust" he
retained only the dramatic mode of expression, the
requirements of the stage being in nowise considered.
And finally, after an experiment in Greek form—
"Iphigenie"—he returned to Romance pure and simple.

Schiller, beginning in the same way as Goethe, found
himself drawn into the domain of History. But here
he was confronted with the impossibility of
adequately portraying the *Surrounding* of the
Individual which alone determines his action. (We have
seen how Wagner himself had come to the same conclusion
four years previously—in 1848, with his study of Friedrich
der Rothbart.) Schiller indeed did not return to Romance,
but having perforce to turn aside from History for absolute dramatic material, we find him hovering between
History and Romance on the one hand, supplying the
true *life* element, and Greek Drama on the other,
replying to his ideal of perfect *form*. And, recognizing
that *our* life could not supply the ideal which was

revealed to him in that perfect Art form, he concluded that Art itself not only was a thing apart from that life, but from Human Life in general, and hence was a thing to be dreamt of, but impossible to attain.

What, then, was the Romance which, taken as the Stuff from which modern Drama had been shaped, had rendered that Drama impotent? The Stuff from which *The Myth* Greek Tragedy derived its being was *Mythos*, which is the result of the grouping by the Folk, in a succinct shape, of the most manifold phenomena. The primal human being, regarding the multiplicity of those surrounding phenomena, and not enabled by the power of Understanding to discover their relation amongst themselves, could only attribute them to the workings of a First Cause which itself was the product of his imagination. That Cause was to him a god. But inasmuch as he was unable to comprehend an essence dissimilar to his own, that god assumed in his imagination the idealized likeness of himself. Hence the Folk recognized their God—their Hero—as a reflex of their own image, and the Myth was the poem of a life-view in common. But reflective Understanding seeing the image, paused to inquire into the nature of what was summed up in it, to analytically dissect a multitude of units where the poetic view had seen but one whole.

With the advent of this method of analysis, the Myth lost much of its force, much of its real nature; but it nevertheless retained sufficient power to materially

Christian Mythos

influence the world. From being the life-expression of one Folk it branched into two channels, the one the Christian mythos, the other the native Saga of new European, and particularly of German, peoples.

In Christian mythos the standard to which all things must ultimately be referred became, instead of *Man*, an *extra-mundane, incomprehensible Being*. The history of the Greeks showed that their idealization of manhood had led to the establishment of the State. But instead of finding therein the realization of their fancied standard, they discovered that the Individual must be opposed to the State, that the human self-will displayed by the latter must ever be antagonistic to the true freedom of the Individual. Consequently the Individual had to look for the appeasement of his longings towards a Being apart from himself, to whom both Law and State were of no moment, insomuch as they were conceived included in his unfathomable will. Only beyond this world was the consummation of the Christian's hopes possible.

The Christian myth saw in the Saviour one who, while in His submission to judgment and death He vindicated Law and State, yet by that voluntary death annulled them both " in favour of *Christian mythos* an inner Necessity, the liberation of the Individual through redemption into God." It followed that the Christian mythos regarded Life as a *longing for Death*, inasmuch as by Death only could perfect bliss be attained. To the Greek, Death revealed itself as the natural termination of Life which *itself* was its

own end; to the Christian, Death was the *object* of life.
Hence, *from the point of view of Art*, the Christian mythos
can never be a well-spring for Drama; for the stress
towards a climax of movement, which is essential to
dramatic Action, necessarily becomes nullified by a belief
which regards existence itself as but an undesirable preliminary to the consummation attainable only by death.

The German Saga had a common origin with the
Christian mythos in the old Pagan myth. The spread

German Saga

of Christianity was, moreover, the cause
of its origin also. The old pagan spirit
had led to the human characterization of
the operations of Nature, characterizations varying in
shape and degree with the poetic intuition of the particular Folk with whom they originated. The rising
and setting of the sun and the other phenomena of
Nature became deified to those old peoples as personal
agents in virtue of their deeds, and in course of time the
Gods that man's fancy had created became humanized
into Heroes. In this manner connection was established
between actual Life and the Myth; and, if a close
examination be made of these old fables, they will all be
found to revolve around one central notion—the religious
notion of Man's relation to Nature. This notion is the
root of the tree of Myth, and it was this which, as has
been shown previously, Christianity necessarily attacked.
But in the case of the Germanic and kindred Sagas the
difference in the effect of Christianity on the original
myth lay in this, that the Folk, having become dissociated

Romance

from the *origin* of myth, applied themselves to the development of its *ramifications*—in other words, they took the *action* which had been the inevitable result of the inner necessity which governed it, and extended and played upon it as though it had been *cause* instead of what it really was—*effect*.

In the multiplying of these actions, the original spirit of Mythos, which regarded all action as the necessary evolution from one great central idea— the relation of Man to Nature—became *The evolu-* finally lost. The action itself, and not its *tion of* reference to its motive, became the main *Romance* consideration. And hence it arrived that instead of Drama, wherein Man dominates his surroundings and the Necessity of his action is demonstrated without reference to aught but the nature of himself, there arose the era of *Romance*, which is the opposite of Drama in that the actions of the central personage can only be explained and vindicated *by reference* to those surroundings.

In Drama the chief actor obeys the promptings of his inner Necessity, and the Drama's ultimate end is to show the effect on his surroundings of the actions which thereby result ; it is the apotheosis of Individuality. In Romance, on the other hand, the writer is compelled to describe his hero's environment with the utmost particularity ; he is constrained to prove that his hero could only have acted as he did because the circumstances in which he was placed irresistibly impelled him to the course he adopted. Romance, at its highest, imitated

Wagner

Mythos in endeavouring to achieve the moulding of types. Just as in Mediæval Romance the generalization of a motley conglomeration of foreign peoples, lands, and climates, had been attempted, so in Historical Romance the endeavour had been made to concentrate in one particular individual the essence of whole historic periods.

But when the impossibility of this generalization had been discovered, Romance, in its desire to present never- *The Ro-* theless the aspects of *life*, had to fall back *mance of* upon Man's social nature, for in the instinc- *Burgher* tive desire of the human being to ally him- *society* self with the remainder of his species lies the origin of all historical and social development. Hence Romance busied itself with the delineation of Burgher-life, for therein the Romancist deemed he might study the Individual—who, although remote from the ken of History, was nevertheless one of its conditioning factors —and study, and depict him also, amongst surroundings accustomed and typical.

In the unloveliness of that Burgher society the poet found his stumbling-block. The more he studied it, the more accentuated did the discrepancy between his ideal of Manhood and Man as he actually existed become. He could not fail to recognize that the depressing conditions of life were the result of the war between the State and the Individual, and that all attempts to satisfy the Individual's need must inevitably entail a struggle against the State—which is the concern not of the Poet but of

The Ideal Community

the *Politician*. In the State-governed community men's actions are conditioned, not by their inner conscience, but by the sense of duty which the State instils into them from their birth ; they act, not because they are impelled by instinctive Need, but because the State decrees that any other course of conduct will be visited with penalties. Hence it must follow that, in such a state of society, human individuality can only be understood by the study of the surroundings which have combined to make that individuality what it is. Only when the community act from an inner religious conscience, an *instinctive* impulse common to all to act in a particular way and in no other, will the ideal society be realized ; only when there is but *one* Religion and *no* State will mankind be truly free. "In the free self-determining of the Individuality lies the basis of the social Religion of the Future."

In such a community as Wagner yearned for, the only restraining influence would be Love. The experience of Age would be able to perceive the characteristic import of the deeds of youth, and in pointing youth towards fresh activity and in beholding that resulting activity, would enrich itself and become the very Life-element of Art. Therein lay the essential difference from the State ; for, in the latter, experience spoke not in the encouraging words of Love, but in the chilling accents of Law. When experience speaks in the words of Law it appeals only to the Understanding ; only when Love is the communicating medium can the Feeling be appealed to. And, as the Feeling can only be reached through the medium of the senses, so only by the presentment of an image akin to itself can it be roused into interest; and that image can prove itself sympathetic to the Feeling of the individual only when it displays itself in an action vindicated by motives akin to those of the individual himself. It follows, from what has been previously postulated, that not in Romance but only in Drama can the experienced one fully exemplify that experience by means of Love. For Love can only appeal to the Feeling; the Feeling can only be reached by allowing the individual to comprehend, through his senses, the action of another inspired by motives similar to his own; and such an action can only be found in the life of the community—the Folk—which can be artistically portrayed in Drama alone.

What then should influence the dramatic poet in the choice of the Action? That action must be one that can be vindicated entirely by the Feeling *The choice* without reference to the Understanding; *of dramatic* it must leave nothing in the nature of a *action* problem for the Intellect to solve; it must be *the realization of its own aim;* it must *itself* present its justification. And, in order that the import of the action may be readily seized, it must be rendered intelligible by the just presentation of its emotional Necessity; for the task of the dramatic poet is not to invent the action itself, but to present and lead up to it in such a manner that its motives may instinctively appeal to the Feeling. An action of itself is necessarily

Tone-speech

unintelligible apart from the motive which prompted it. It therefore follows that, in order to be intelligible, the poet must so limit the moments of his main Action as to leave himself the necessary space for explanation of the motives from which it has sprung. For the same reason he will condense those moments of action, leading up to the stronger ones by weaker ones ; removing everything extraneous to the main action—not by way of arbitrary lopping-off, but in order to clear the way for the development of the motive also condensed into due proportion to the action itself. Thus will be gained one clear, lucid utterance of Nature, condensed by Experience ; a faithful likeness, bringing Man into harmonious union with Nature instead of arbitrarily distorting her image. Such a clear image of Life can best be drawn from the Mythos, the product of Nature's own children—the Folk.

And as with the source of the action and its motive, so with *the means for its expression*—we must go back to the primal source. Just as the former have had to be strengthened, so must the latter be re-invigorated by the expansion of word-speech into *tone*-speech. In man's *The means for its expression* earliest days differentiation of tone was the only means whereby he could convey his emotions ; it was the spontaneous expression of his inner Feeling. With the new necessity of describing objective as well as subjective feelings arose the clothing of the open vowel sounds with varying consonantal prefixes or suffixes, a system

131

which grew until the old necessity for variation of tone to express emotion was supplanted by the ability of word-speech to supply a convention which satisfied the demands of the Understanding. The growth of thought rendered appeal to the Feeling more and more unnecessary. But Poetry which is to appeal to the Feeling *Tone-speech* demands the language of the heart, which is Tone-speech; only by its aid can the poet turn from a mere appeal to the Understanding to intimate communion with that Feeling. As the action and its accompanying motive must be strengthened, so must the means of their expression be lifted above the common everyday life and its habitual means of making known its thoughts. Without Tone, the mother of Speech, the Poetic Aim cannot bear fruit.

In the concluding portion of the essay, Wagner enters into an elaborate technical discussion of the means whereby the Drama of the Future may be fashioned. This portion was written in great haste, and has consequently somewhat suffered in point of clearness; but the main points contended for may be tolerably briefly summarized. In order to impart an emotional significance to the Word-speech which was the medium of his thought, the poet originally employed two devices. The *Metre and end-rhyme* one was the aid of *metre*, derived from rhythm; the other the employment of *end-rhyme*, derived from the sense of melody. But neither could prove entirely satisfactory. For whereas in the former, either the plain sense of the

Poetic Essentials

words was lost (if the verse were declaimed according to its metric accent), or the metre itself rendered non-existent (if the verse were declaimed according to its plain literal meaning) ; so in the latter the whole verse-line degenerated into a mere preparation for the concluding rhyme, to the subversion of all vivifying accent.

With such verse Music could do nothing. If she attempted to follow the metre, she necessarily became stereotyped into phrases which had no alliance with the sense of the words associated therewith ; if she employed herself in mere illustration of the sense, she lost her rhythmic essence and degenerated into mere musical prose. If the Poet would keep touch with Life, he must, to the utmost of his power, win his Expression from the speech of every day. Inasmuch, however, as in the ordinary speech of individuals appeal is made only to the Understanding, and consequently the vital *root* syllables of language which appeal to the Feeling are obscured by the diffuseness of the consonantal combinations which, as before shown, become essential in the evolution of Speech from Tone for the description of objective ideas—so must these excrescences be pared down as much as possible in order that the root syllables may be enabled to make their full appeal to the Feeling upon which Drama must operate. When this has been done, it will be possible to satisfy the requirements of frank emotion, namely to produce a phrase whose significance shall be complete while requiring *one breath* for its enunciation. And as in the rhythmic delivery

Wagner

of verse the ear demands a succession of accents of varying strength corresponding to the crests and hollows of the sea, so the Tone poet will contrive that those crests will be represented by the significant root syllables of the phrase, whereby the union between melodic rhythm and the necessary accent of word-verse will be rendered perfect. As elemental speech was derived from *open* sounds, so the *vowel* is it which appeals to the inner Feeling primarily. The poet will aim at establishing to the Feeling the kinship of these vowel sounds; his diction will be so chosen that those sounds will convey to that Feeling the kinship and continuity of idea which their consonantal clothing will convey to the Understanding. And in this task the consonant itself will come to his assistance. In alliteration (*Stabreim*) the similarity of prefix of two different words calls up an instant association of ideas to the ear. This association may be one of *similar* ideas, as "die Liebe giebt Lust zum Leben" (*Love* gives de*l*ight to *l*iving), or *dissimilar*, as "die Liebe giebt Lust und—Leid" (*Love* gives de*l*ight and—*l*oad); but in each case there is irresistibly brought home to the Feeling the common origin in Love of both "Lust" and "Leid." The kinship between vowel sounds conveying a similar import is obvious. Poetry so conceived will be Word-speech derived absolutely from Tone-speech, and from such only can Melody be born, for Melody is the essence of Tone.

The Orchestra

And as Tone is supplemented and completed in Speech, so is Melody supplemented and completed by Harmony. For the bond of kinship between the moving notes of melody is the relationship between them- *Melody* selves of the notes of the *key* in which *and* that melody lies, which produces in the *Harmony* hearer the sense of homogeneity ; and the power which enables melody to overstep those narrow limits in obedience to the Poet's desire for wider and more emotional expression is Harmony. But the function of that Harmony is independent. The sailor does not build his bark of the water on which he sails ; and even so the verse-melody must float on the sea of Harmony supported by, but not evolved from, the sustaining element. The Harmony will be supplied by the Orchestra ; but the melody of the word- *The func-* verse must not be derived or imitated from *tion of the* the tone-producing capabilities of any *Orchestra* of that Orchestra's members. Thus will the Orchestra be left to fulfil its own function—that of *sustaining* the verse melody. In so doing, three courses will be open to it. *First,* it can supplement gesture ; by the use of appropriate tone-figures and suitable instruments Orchestral melody can intensify and explain the gestures of the actor without the intervention of Word-speech (cf. the first entry of the giants in " Das Rheingold ").

When a particular musical phrase has once been announced in conjunction with Word-speech explaining the phase of emotion which has evolved that musical phrase, it becomes associated in our memory with that particular emotion, and the Orchestra by its repetition can supply, as it were, the sense of thought and bring before us that emotion as a Remembrance; which is its *second* possibility. Closely allied to this is its *third* function, whereby, by similar repetition of the musical phrase, it can produce the sense of Foreboding. (The second device permeates all Wagner's later works; the third is not so common, but a well-known instance occurs in the sinister passage for the trombones at the end of the second Act of "Lohengrin.")

In Drama formed on these lines will be found the true *unity*, which is one, not of time and place, but of *expression*. The key to such Drama will be the Dramatic Situation, which starting with a situation drawn from actual life, and therefore easily recognizable, will by gradual process of concentration keep rising steadily above its surroundings through an ever-connected chain of situations arising from the one primarily exhibited. The poet's verse-melody in the same manner will progress in an ever-ascending scale of emotion, and the whole fabric will be upheld on the waves of the Orchestral harmony with its power of suggesting the actor's very thoughts. Such will be the Drama of the Future.

True unity of Drama

If an apology be needed for what may seem at first sight to be an unduly lengthy exposition of Wagner's artistic views, it may not unreasonably be urged that

His Artistic Ideal

even in the present day there exists no little degree of haziness as to what those views really were. The modern play-goer has become so accustomed to perfection of *ensemble* that Wagner's insistence upon it seems almost superfluous. Except in provincial theatres, perhaps, managers nowadays pride themselves upon casting small parts with as much care as large ones— even acting managers! But to appreciate Wagner's position it must never be forgotten that he uplifted his voice in favour of dramatic balance at a time when he was absolutely alone in his ideas, and that he stuck to his guns for a period of twenty years without hearing a single one of his works performed. He was the strenuous upholder of the natural against the artificial, and therein lies the secret of the enormous influence he has wielded over contemporary art. His Music appeals to the Feeling. His art is the art that conceals art. His Music seems *so natural*. As the dra-   *Wagner's*
matic situation rises in intensity, so the   *natural-*
music seems to lift us on an ever-swelling   *ness of*
flood until we are moved to our very   *expression*
depths, but—*we know not why*. We are conscious of having assisted at something which has lifted us momentarily out of this world into a paradise of intangible emotion, but the proportion of the work is so perfect that it is hard to say which of all the varied scenes has touched us most. It is as though one has walked in a mighty forest, where the sense of the grandeur and completeness of Nature's handiwork has been so

overpowering that the memory is unable to recall the individual outline of any single tree.

It is in this very naturalness that Wagner's genius is so conspicuously demonstrated. Never has genius been *His use of the* Leit motif so completely vindicated by the failure of its would-be imitators. The people who talk so glibly of the importance of the *Leit motif* overlook entirely the fact that in Wagner's hands it is only a *means*, and indeed a comparatively insignificant one, to the great end of his works. The secret of Wagner's power lies, not in the system itself, but in the marvellous power with which he made his *motifs* speak a new language. The very simplicity of them is deceptive, but on a closer examination the feeling instinctively arises that *in no other way* could the particular emotion portrayed have received musical expression. And, consequently, the more one studies Wagner's dramas the more is one impressed by the stupendous power that evinces itself on every page. In studying his writings, while one is confronted on every hand with the influence of his powerful will, the same feeling of absolute conviction does not perhaps arise. Wagner often gives the impression of a man arguing backwards. His processes are almost invariably *inductive*; and this method of reasoning had, no doubt, a great deal to do with the violence with which he was attacked by his enemies. Wagner, in effect, always began by saying, "Now I will show that the *only* solution of the problem I am going to set before you is

His Influence on Music

the regeneration of mankind through the Drama;" a method which, added to the fearlessness he displayed in the enunciation of his ideas, could not fail to arouse the ire of the pedants who could not understand the vital principle for which he fought.

Wagner's influence on modern music has been so potent that there is danger of its being overlooked. It used to be a commonplace of musical criticism, ten or fifteen years ago, to say *His influence on music* that a new composer's orchestration was Wagnerian. There was no help for it, it was bound to be so. Wagner demonstrated the possibilities of new combinations in such a striking manner, that musicians could not but strive to avail themselves of the new tone-world which he opened up for them. Nowadays the sarcasm has ceased to be employed. Everybody employs the Wagnerian orchestra, and will continue to do so until a greater genius arises. But that genius has yet to be born. We have yet to find another melodist who is a musical Tacitus; yet to discover a master who can produce such a musical *atmosphere* as Wagner's orchestration creates. And further, we have yet to unearth the man with the depth of kindly wisdom which Wagner possessed, united at the same time to the wide culture, the creative power, and "the infinite capacity for taking pains" which were exemplified in this marvellous individuality.

Whether Wagner's theories on Art were right still remains to be proved. The mere fact that he himself

Wagner

succeeded with them is no proof of their inherent infallibility. But he has succeeded in breaking down for ever the arbitrary barrier of technical form. He has succeeded in demonstrating once and for all the futility of endeavouring to express human emotion within the limits of a phrase of a prescribed number of bars' length. Wagner has carried on the work of making music an art which shall appeal to the Feeling and not merely to the Understanding. No greater master of musical technique has ever existed—not even Bach. His extraordinary power of combining themes, his unlimited contrapuntal resources, are so universally recognized nowadays that reference to them is superfluous. But the point that is often lost

Melody and declamation sight of is the marvellous wealth of melody that exists in his works. Wagner is too often regarded merely as an orchestral colourist; his hearers are apt to overlook the absolute beauty of his *vocal* melody. Such melodies as the " Prize Song " from the " Meistersinger " obtain their due meed of recognition ; but the wonderful purity and aptness of the setting of declamatory dialogue—such for instance, as Wotan's magnificent soliloquy in the second Act of " Die Walküre "—is often tolerated merely as a somewhat tiresome prelude to the more exciting or more sugary passages to follow. He never let his technical powers or his facility for inventing absolute melody overstep the bounds of giving adequate expression to the dramatic situation on hand. The sense of artistic restraint is nowhere so conspicuous as in

Love of Animals

Wagner's dramas; hence the perfect impression of homogeneity which they produce. He may have been an idealist in his views of the Drama, and the influence it can wield, for the regeneration of mankind. But his whole life was devoted single-heartedly to furthering the regeneration of the human race; and who shall say that Art may not be as potent to that end as—or indeed even more so than—Politics? *His love of human nature*

Wagner had weaknesses—it is useless to attempt to disguise the fact—but his good qualities more than atoned for them. If he loved silks and satins and gorgeous dressing-gowns (as he did), his fondness for animals may well be taken into the other side of the scale as an equipoise to a harmless personal vanity. His letters are full of charming recollections of his dogs and his parrot—the autograph letter on the following page proves, moreover, that his sympathies with the dumb creation were not limited to the circle of his own pets—and one of his most trenchant essays is directed against Vivisection. This essay well illustrates the kindliness of his nature and its impetuousness also, a quality which occasionally upset the generally accurate balance of his views. His argument, for example, attributing human degeneration to flesh-eating, subtle as it is, is scarcely tenable; vegetarianism hardly seems essential to man's regeneration. But with Wagner's presentment of such notions we almost forget their extravagance. The man *And of animals* *Vegetarianism*

Wagner

is so sincere, so earnest, that we see in him the noble
soul which deems no instrument too humble if only the

Man's Regeneration

great goal can be reached ; and, if we cannot hold with conviction to every link in his chain of reasoning, we must at least agree with his final con-clusion—that the great aim of human exist-ence should be man's regeneration. To Wagner much may be forgiven—for he loved much.

Man's re-generation

TRANSLATION OF LETTER ON PRECEDING PAGE.

Under the impression caused by the revolting revelations lately brought to light concerning the cruel treatment that the newly-imposed tax on dogs has occasioned to domestic animals hitherto so highly favoured among us, a Society of Animals' Friends has now been formed, which undertakes the task of mitigating, to the best of its power, this shocking condition of things. With this object, owners of dogs who have decided to destroy the animals in order to escape the tax, are invited to consign them to the care of the Agent of the Society, August Wilhelmj, in order that their purpose may be attained in a humane manner, according to the new legal instructions.

Society for the Prevention of Cruelties caused by the New Dog-tax.

BAYREUTH.

(Translated by Dora I. Beck.)

CHAPTER VIII

WAGNER's earliest efforts in opera were not destined to be great successes. Of " Die Feen " (The Fairies) and " Das Liebesverbot " (Love's Interdict), the former was never performed in his lifetime, and the latter only once. *"Die Feen"* The first performance of " Die Feen " took place at Munich as recently as June the 29th, 1888; "Das Liebesverbot" only saw the footlights on the occasion of Wagner's disastrous benefit at Magdeburg in 1836. A detailed analysis of these immature attempts is hardly called for. There are, however, some characteristic passages in each which are of interest. " Die Feen " was based on a play by Gozzi, entitled " La Donna Serpente." In this play a fairy yearns for mortal love. The only condition, however, upon which this can be attained is that her lover should prove constant under all circumstances. To test his affection she is turned into a snake, but the lover, undaunted, embraces and kisses the hideous reptile, and thereby ensures the fairy's happiness. Wagner works upon similar lines, but he shows an individuality remarkable in one so young (for he was only then twenty), in entirely altering the *dénouement.*

144

" Rienzi "

In the opera the fairy is turned to stone and is awakened by the sweet charm of music—a far more poetic ending. It is characteristic that even at that early age he wrote his own libretto. Turgid though some of it may be, it still contains thoughts remarkable and well expressed, and some of it is even vivid and striking. The overture is regularly constructed out of the themes that acquire importance in the course of the work, and some of the orchestral effects foreshadow those of " Rienzi " in no small degree. The performing rights of " Die Feen " are vested in the Hof-theater of Munich, where the opera is not infrequently performed with success.

As to " Das Liebesverbot," which has never been published, Wagner himself considered it a great advance upon his earlier work. Only manuscript fragments of it now exist. It was based on Shakespeare's " Measure for Measure," the lines of which it, apparently, followed fairly closely.

" Das Liebesverbot"

" Rienzi " was commenced in 1838 and completed in 1840. As has been previously noticed, it was intended for the Parisian stage, and was designed on the avowed lines of spectacular " grand opera." It was first produced at Dresden on the 20th of October, 1842, and was its composer's first emphatic success. On that occasion Tichatschek was the Rienzi, Madame Schröder-Devrient the Adriano, Fräulein Wüst the Irene, Dettmer the Stefano Colonna, and Wächter the Paolo Orsini.

" Rienzi"

The plot is as follows. The first act opens on a street

Wagner

in Rome. The church of St. John Lateran rises in the background, in the foreground is the dwelling of Rienzi. The time is night. Orsini and his attendants enter, and, having placed a ladder against the window of Rienzi's house, attempt the forcible abduction of his sister Irene. Her screams for aid attract the attention of Colonna, the head of the rival faction, and his followers. Adriano, Colonna's son, who has arrived on the scene and who loves Irene, rushes to her protection. A fierce fight commences between the nobles, which the papal legate Raimondo and the people vainly endeavour to end. In the midst of the disturbance Rienzi appears. He bitterly rebukes the nobles for their turbulence, and, passionately recalling the ancient glories of Rome, denounces their rapine and lust. His remarks are received by the patricians with derisive shouts, but they marvel nevertheless at the extraordinary influence Rienzi has over the populace. The rival factions then depart to settle their quarrel without the city gates at break of day. Left with the people and the Cardinal Raimondo, Rienzi is questioned by the latter as to when the fateful signal will be given for the populace to rise and overthrow the tyrannical rule of the nobility. Rienzi asks in return whether the Church will lend him its aid, and, on being assured that every means which will gain success will be hallowed, announces that that very night the signal will be given by the long-drawn note of a trumpet. The people disperse, joyfully anticipating the dawn of freedom, and Rienzi is left alone with Adriano and

146

" Rienzi "

Irene. Rienzi urges Adriano to join the sacred cause of freedom, but the youth shrinks from a movement that must involve him in war with his own kin. Rienzi reminds him that his (Rienzi's) own brother was foully murdered by a Colonna, and Adriano, moved by shame at the cruel deed, promises his help. Leaving his sister to Adriano's protection, the Tribune departs. The lovers sing a passionate duet, at the end of which are heard long-drawn trumpet blasts advancing ever nearer. Day breaks. The notes of the organ peal from the church, soon supplemented by a chorus in praise of freedom. The church doors are thrown open and Rienzi appears, clad in brilliant armour and accompanied by Raimondo and the chief citizens of Rome. He harangues the populace in stirring terms, gives them the watchword of "Rome and Liberty," and the curtain falls on their acclaiming him as their deliverer, and swearing to avenge the crimes of the nobles.

The second Act takes place in a hall in the Capitol overlooking the higher parts of Rome. The "Messengers of Peace" who have been sent out by Rienzi return ; they are clothed in white wrought with silver, they carry tall silver wands in their hands, and are crowned with wreaths. In a melodious chorus they announce to Rienzi, who appears in the dress of a Roman Tribune, that the war is ended and that Freedom reigns o'er all the land. The conquered nobles, Colonna and Orsini, with their followers, then enter and haughtily tender homage to their conqueror. He as proudly receives it, and, after

147

warning them that he will see to it that the law is strictly observed, retires. The nobles, left to themselves, plot to assassinate Rienzi, but are overheard by Adriano, who has entered unperceived. Adriano implores his father to spare Rienzi's life, but is repulsed, and he thereupon vows to save the brother of the woman he loves. The ambassadors of the Lombard cities, Naples, Bohemia, Bavaria, and Hungary, then enter to greet the Tribune, who declares to the assemblage that in future Rome will elect her own king, an announcement which creates great sensation. He then orders the *fêtes* to commence. Adriano hurriedly takes him aside and warns him of the nobles' plot. During the ballet which follows, Orsini endeavours to stab Rienzi, but the weapon glides harmlessly off the shirt of mail which the latter is wearing beneath his toga. The nobles are seized and condemned to death. But Adriano pleads for his father's life, and Rienzi, yielding to his prayers and those of Irene, persuades the people to pardon the would-be assassins on their renewing their vow of allegiance.

The scene of Act III. is a public square in Rome. The people assemble in a state of excitement bordering on frenzy, for news is brought that the nobles, having again broken their oath, are advancing on the city with foot and horse. They clamour wildly for their leader, and Rienzi appears mounted on a splendid charger and accompanied by Irene and the senators. Adriano makes another impassioned appeal to Rienzi to spare

" Rienzi "

the lives of the nobles, but on this occasion his entreaties avail nothing, and the Tribune sets forth to battle, leaving Adriano and Irene alone. News is soon brought of a great victory over the traitorous patricians, and the dead body of Colonna is brought on to the stage. At the sight of it Adriano vows vengeance on Rienzi, and the Act is brought to a conclusion by a thoroughly operatic *ensemble* and procession.

In Act IV. we are transplanted to the Square of St. John Lateran. The Senators Baroncelli and Cecco announce that the ambassadors, incensed by Rienzi's denial of the right of Germany to nominate a king for Rome, have departed in anger, and that Cardinal Raimondo has been recalled. Baroncelli then declares that, in pardoning the nobles, Rienzi was actuated only by the desire to obtain the good offices of Colonna towards alliance with himself through the union of Adriano and Irene. The people demand proof, whereupon Adriano, seeing the opportunity for revenge, comes forward and confirms the story. The people thereupon clamour for their recent idol's death. At this moment Rienzi, accompanied by Irene, appears on his way to the church, where a *Te Deum* is to be celebrated in honour of the victory. He perceives the murmuring of the conspirators, and cowes them with his brave strong words of reproach. But just as he is about to enter the church an ominous chant is heard from within. Awestruck, he pauses, but presently gives the signal for the procession to be re-formed. He ascends the steps; but at that moment the doors are thrown open, and Cardinal Raimondo, appearing, excommunicates the Tribune in the name of Holy Church. The nobles had succeeded in enlisting the aid of the Pope. The people flee from Rienzi in horror. Adriano endeavours to persuade Irene to fly with him, but she prefers to be near her brother in his hour of need. Rienzi, hearing her words, recovers from his stupor, and with his cry "Irene, thou! then Rome is not yet dead," the curtain falls.

Act V. is laid again within the Capitol. Rienzi is discovered kneeling in prayer, and in a noble scene he supplicates Heaven to help his beloved Rome in her hour of need. Irene enters, and he tries to persuade her to seek safety with Adriano, but she resolutely declines to leave him alone with his enemies. He clasps her to his heart, and leaves her, to endeavour once more to waken the people to a sense of their danger. Adriano then enters and passionately implores Irene to escape from the danger which menaces Rienzi, but she remains obdurate. The noise of a furious mob grows nearer and louder outside, and the windows of the apartment are broken by stones. The scene changes to the large square in front of the Capitol. Rienzi, in full armour, but with bared head, appears on the balcony with Irene and tries once more to address the crowd, but with no avail. The maddened populace set fire to the building, and Adriano, rushing into the flames to rescue his beloved, is overwhelmed with the others in the crash of the falling ruins. As the curtain falls, the nobles, once more in the ascendant, are seen butchering the hapless rabble.

"Rienzi" was Wagner's only attempt in the domain of "grand opera," a matter which there is no cause to regret in the light of his later achievements. On his own confession, his only desire in writing the libretto was to produce something effective from a spectacular and operatic point of view, something which provided opportunity for elaborate arias and overwhelming choruses. But in reality, although Wagner regarded it as a "sin" of his artistic youth, and openly said so on one occasion—with the usual result of much misrepresentation—there is much in this same libretto which not only places it far ahead of the majority of contemporary work, but also foreshadows the Wagner of the future. It is interesting to note the sure hand with which the young artist has seized upon the salient points of Rienzi's character, and the certainty with which he has condensed them from the elaborate material of Lytton's novel. There is a distinct foretaste of the great faculty which he afterwards so strikingly evinced for portraying *typical* character. With all the tinsel and glitter of its surroundings, Rienzi's character stands out conspicuously and with a sense of proportion remarkable in a man so young as its delineator then was; for Wagner was only twenty-five when the libretto was written.

As regards the music, it must be criticized entirely from the point of view of ordinary grand opera, and in such surroundings it can very well be left to take care of itself. It abounds in melody of the conventional pattern, the concerted numbers are often marked by distinct originality of thought and expression, and the choruses and orchestration are sonorous enough to satisfy the most exacting taste in such matters. The orchestra indeed is, at times, noisy; Wagner had not yet found out the magical effect of the "soft brass," and lays his colours on with a heavy hand. But there is much real beauty in the work; the well-known "Prayer" is a musical gem, full of dignified and devotional charm, while the "Roman Battle Hymn" is appropriately fiery and impassioned.

Only one remark need be made in conclusion. Wagner has often been accused of following the model of Meyerbeer in this opera, but facts are against this conclusion. At the time it was written it is probable that Wagner had only heard one opera of Meyerbeer's, and that, "Robert le Diable." Wagner himself acknowledges the influence of Spontini, whose "Fernando Cortez" he had heard under its composer's direction shortly before "Rienzi" was conceived. It is far more likely that Meyerbeer was influenced by "Rienzi" in writing "Le Prophète," which was produced in 1849, two years after Wagner had finished "Lohengrin."

CHAPTER IX

" DER FLIEGENDE HOLLÄNDER " (The Flying Dutchman) was written in 1841, in seven weeks ! It was produced at Dresden on the 2nd of January, 1843. Herr Mitterwurzer was the Dutchman, and Mme. Schröder-Devrient the Senta.

"The Flying Dutchman" marks the first stage in Wagner's development, and is an enormous advance upon its immediate predecessor. So much had he thrown off the conventional form of opera, that we find he had actually designed the work to be played without a break, and had originally intended to call it a "dramatic ballad." He considered the ballad sung by Senta in the second act as the pivot of the entire work, which was, so to speak, arranged around it. The legend is so well known that it needs no repetition.

Let us examine Wagner's treatment of it. For the first time he makes use of representative musical phrases. The themes, instead of being merely formal melodies, used once to a particular combination of words, are destined to be constantly employed in connection with a definite personage or idea. The overture, although a formal composition, thus has a story of its own to tell. We are brought into immediate contact with the personality of the hero in the very first bar, and the overture

153

gives in effect a complete *résumé* of the work, so completely does it summarize the leading *motifs* that are subsequently employed. A chapter might easily be written about Wagner's overtures and preludes. In some cases the whole story of the action about to be displayed is musically depicted, whilst in others the composer's sole object has been to create the necessary *atmosphere* in which the commencement of that action might be made. The overture in question belongs, of course, to the former class.

As the curtain rises on Act I. we are confronted with a bay surrounded by cliffs. It is dark, and a violent storm is raging. Daland's ship has cast anchor near the shore, and he himself has landed and ascended a high cliff in order to ascertain, if possible, his whereabouts. The sailors are shouting lustily as they haul at their tackle. Daland finds that he has only just missed being able to make his right harbour, where he would have found his daughter Senta to welcome him. He then bids the sailors retire to their well-earned rest, and himself goes below, leaving the steersman on deck. Left alone, the steersman sings a ballad in praise of his love, but presently, overcome by weariness, falls asleep. Soon there appears in the offing, riding through the now increasing storm, a vessel with black masts and blood-red sails. It is the Flying Dutchman's ship. Its appearance is accompanied by a sinister phrase, which is easily recognizable. With a crash the anchor is dropped ; then in deep silence the sails are furled, and the Dutchman steps ashore. The seven years' term has once more

" Der fliegende Holländer "

expired, and again he is free to roam the earth in the
endeavour to find in a woman's faith release from his
never-ending torture. In a long scena he describes his
wanderings, the way he has risked danger in every form
in the fruitless search for death to put a merciful end to
his sufferings—but all in vain. Only in the crash of
the Day of Judgment dare he expect deliverance from
his pain. A mysterious echo of his last words comes
from the hold of the phantom vessel as the Dutchman
sinks on a rock lost in thought. Daland, who has come
on deck to make observations, perceives the stranger ship,
and hails it. He meets with no response. Seeing the
Dutchman, he attracts his attention, and learns the doleful story of his wanderings. The Dutchman asks shelter
in Daland's home, which is readily granted, for the
wanderer offers to place his whole wealth at Daland's
disposal in return for his hospitality, and orders two of
his sailors to bring a chest of treasure to prove that his
riches are no empty boast. Finding that Daland has a
daughter, the Dutchman begs her as his bride, a request
that the simple sea-captain, dazzled by so much wealth,
readily accedes to. After a somewhat conventional
duet for the two men, Daland returns to his ship,
and, the wind having become more favourable, sets
sail, exacting a promise from the Dutchman to speedily
follow him. The cheery strains of the steersman's song,
now reinforced by the chorus of sailors, are again heard
as the ship gets under weigh, and the curtain falls as the
Dutchman proceeds to board his own vessel.

Wagner

The second Act takes place in Daland's house. Before the curtain rises the steersman's song is again heard in the orchestra, but it soon gives way to a peculiar buzzing of the lower strings, when a number of maidens with Senta's nurse are discovered sitting round the fire and spinning. To the singularly descriptive accompaniment thus provided, the girls sing the well-known Spinning Chorus. Senta herself, however, sits apart, gazing at the portrait of a man dressed in Spanish costume, with pale face and dark beard. The song and chatter jar upon her, for her nurse, Mary, has told her the story of the "Flying Dutchman," and her tender heart has been moved to pity for him. As she will not join in their song, the girls press her to sing one herself, and in compliance she sings the Ballad to which reference has already been made. The first section is wild and passionate; the second, in calmer vein, is in strong contrast to its predecessor, typifying the gentle nature through whose intervention the Dutchman is to gain release.

These two sections are thrice repeated, and after the final repetition Senta ecstatically vows that she will be the woman to save him. She is overheard by a young huntsman, Erik, who loves her and has just arrived with the news that her father's ship is nearing land. Mary and the girls retire to prepare a feast for the home-comers, and Erik, left alone with Senta, endeavours to urge his suit; but in vain, for he finds all her thoughts centred on the doomed mariner, and all her heart filled with pity at his cruel fate. Filled with grief he leaves her, while she,

"Der fliegende Holländer"

still gazing at the picture, softly sings a fragment from the refrain of the Ballad. At this moment Daland enters with the Dutchman. She is spellbound at the sight of the latter, so that she even forgets to welcome her father. He gently chides her, explaining that their guest is a mariner who has undergone great dangers and possesses vast wealth, and has now come to woo her for his bride. She, however, remains as in a dream, with her eyes fixed on the stranger's face. Daland, observing this, discreetly retires, and then ensues a long and finely impassioned duet in which Senta and the Dutchman pledge their troth. A short trio, completed by Daland, brings the Act to a close.

The scene of the third Act is a rocky bay close to Daland's house, which lies on one side in the foreground. The two ships are anchored close together in the background under a starry sky; but while all is life and merriment on the Norwegian vessel, an unnatural darkness is spread about the Dutchman's ship, and a death-like stillness reigns on board. As the curtain rises the Norwegian sailors are singing a lively ditty, which also plays a part of some importance in the overture. A group of maidens presently arrives with baskets of food and wine. They hail the phantom ship, but get no answer; the Norwegian sailors add their entreaties, but with no avail. Suddenly the sea becomes agitated in the neighbourhood of the Dutch vessel, though perfect calm reigns everywhere else. The wind whistles through her rigging, she rocks and heaves in the tempest, and a dark blue flame plays about the masthead like a watch fire. The crew, seemingly summoned into life by the mysterious fire, appear on deck and in a fiendish chorus taunt their absent captain on his ill-luck in winning a bride. The Norwegians, terrified, endeavour to drown the hideous chorus with their own singing, but, failing in the attempt, make the sign of the cross and hurriedly go below. The Dutch sailors, seeing this, give vent to a shrill, discordant laugh, and instantly the storm subsides, and their vessel is shrouded in silence and gloom as before. The effect is finely conceived and eerie in the extreme; unfortunately, the stage management is not always equal to the production of the appropriately mysterious suggestion. At this moment Senta leaves the house hurriedly, followed by Erik. He implores her to listen to him, reminds her of the days when they stood watching her father sail away, and when he believed he saw signs that his love was returned. The Dutchman overhears, and in fearful excitement bids her farewell, believing that she has but played with his love. He reminds her that death and damnation are the fate of those who have played him false, but she will be spared this doom, because she has not yet plighted her troth before the Eternal One. Pointing to his ship, where the blood-red sails are already being set, he reveals himself as the terror of the seas—the Flying Dutchman—and, tearing himself from her, goes on board. Senta, rushing after him, cries with all her strength that she is still true to him, and plunges headlong into the sea. As she does

" Der fliegende Holländer "

so the phantom ship sinks with all hands, and in the light of the rising sun the glorified figures of the Dutchman and his devoted bride are seen rising heavenwards from the bosom of the ocean.

This opera has often been linked with " Rienzi," and spoken of in the same breath with it. To a certain extent there is justification for this procedure, but there is perhaps even more to be said against it. "The Flying Dutchman" occupies a place quite unique in Wagner's work, whether looked at from the dramatic or musical point of view; and, except in point of time, the connection with its predecessor is remote. Looked at superficially, the numerous set arias, duets, and choruses savour of the form which Wagner was destined to revolutionize; but if we examine the score more carefully, the difference shown in Wagner's treatment of them is enormous. There is a far greater feeling of continuity; the set forms are led up to and connected by episodes which grow naturally from the main melodic material employed; and the representative themes constantly arrest the attention at the crucial moments of the drama's action. These *leit motifs* are, it is true, introduced with the directest simplicity—there is, as yet, no anticipation of the polyphonic structure which is so important in the later works; but they play no inconsiderable part in welding the musical structure into a homogeneous whole. The "Dutchman" marks the commencement of Wagner's symphonic treatment of the orchestra.

CHAPTER X

" TANNHÄUSER " was commenced in 1842 and finished in 1844. It was first performed in Dresden on the 19th of October, 1845. Tichatschek was the Tannhäuser, Mme. Schröder-Devrient the Venus, Johanna Wagner (the composer's niece) the Elizabeth, and Mitterwurzer the Wolfram.

The overture commences with the solemn strains of the Pilgrims' Chorus softly intoned by the wood wind. Rising in intensity it is ultimately thundered forth with all the power of the orchestra, and then gradually dies away as though the pious throng had receded into the distance. Its cadence is interrupted by the tumult of the Venusberg music, which in its turn gives way to the theme of the exultant song of Tannhäuser. This again is succeeded by the seductive song of Venus. The orchestral tumult now increases. Tannhäuser's song reappears in even more jubilant form, the Venusberg music grows madder and madder, until with a mighty rush of the strings a climax is reached. After a long decrescendo the air seems to be filled with the echo of the unhallowed

160

revelry, through which there grows ever clearer the solemn strain of the Pilgrims' Chorus, which, at last, in its full glory proclaims Tannhäuser's salvation. (It will be remembered that in the version which Wagner prepared for Paris in 1861 the final repetition of the Pilgrims' Chorus is omitted, and the music passes without a break into that of the first Act.)

The curtain rises on a wide cave in the Hill of Venus. Naiads are bathing in a pool dimly seen in the background; sirens recline upon its undulating banks. In the foreground Venus is lying on a magnificent couch, Tannhäuser reclining at her feet, his head on her knees. The whole cave is illuminated by a rosy light. Nymphs and bacchantes dance with wild abandon, while ever and anon an invisible chorus of sirens is heard chanting an exquisite little phrase of the most seductive character. When the dance is at its height mists descend and shroud the dancers from view, and Tannhäuser and Venus are left alone. Tannhäuser seems to wake from a dream; the reminiscences of his life on earth come over him. He fancies he has heard the bells; longing for the sky and woods and flowers comes over him, and he begs Venus to let him depart. She endeavours to calm him, and then, finding her efforts fruitless, threatens. In vain. Not to her does he look for salvation; his hope is fixed on the Virgin Mary! With a terrible crash the grotto vanishes, and Tannhäuser, who has not moved from his rapt attitude (Wagner insisted very particularly on this point), finds himself in the midst of a beautiful

valley. The sun is shining, and the tinkling of sheep-
bells and the song of a young shepherd are heard from
the heights. Slowly down the mountain winds a procession of pilgrims, chanting as they go. Deeply affected,
Tannhäuser sinks on his knees and vows to atone for his
sin by penitential suffering. The sounds of hunting-
horns are then heard, and the Landgrave and his minstrel
knights appear on their way home from the chase. Wolfram, one of the knights, recognizes the kneeling man
as their old companion, and tries to persuade him to
rejoin their band. Tannhäuser hesitates, bent on being
faithful to his newly made vow; but Wolfram tells him
that the Landgrave's niece, Elizabeth, loves him, and he
then resolves to return with his old companions, the act
ending with a fine septett.

In the second Act the stage represents the Hall of
Song in the Landgrave's palace. Elizabeth, entering,
joyfully hails it, for soon she will meet the man she loves,
and who has been absent seven long years. Presently he
appears with Wolfram and casts himself at her feet. She
is unable to keep her secret from him, and while they sing
an impassioned duet, Wolfram, who has remained in the
background, recognizes that the love he has so long felt
for the maiden can never be requited. The two knights
withdraw together, and the Landgrave, entering, rejoices
to see his niece again resolved to be present at the
tourney of song, a scene she has lately avoided, and
present the prize to the victor. He tries to get her to
reveal her secret, but she tells him he must read it in

her eyes, and he desists from further questioning.
The guests then commence to arrive, and are ushered
to their places to the strains of the famous " March,"
to which they presently add their voices in a chorus
of honour to the Hall of Song and loyalty to their
prince. The contending minstrels then make a dignified entry, and take their places opposite the daïs on
which the Landgrave and his niece are seated. The
former then announces that the tourney is held to
commemorate Tannhäuser's return amongst them, suggests that the minstrels shall take Love as their theme,
and hints that the victor may claim the hand of Elizabeth
as his guerdon. The lot falls on Wolfram to commence.
He sings of Love as something holy, almost beyond
human ken, something which he would hardly dare to
sully with his touch. Against this view Tannhäuser
vigorously protests; Love to him must be something
more fiery, more passionate. The other minstrels
protest against Tannhäuser's more sensual views; the
discussion waxes hot, and Wolfram invokes Heaven's aid
to preserve his pure ideal. Maddened at this, Tannhäuser
springs up and bursts into his song in praise of Venus.
A cry of horror bursts from all at this unholy confession;
the assembly is broken up in confusion, and the Landgrave, with his knights, rushes upon the offender sword
in hand. Elizabeth, however, throws herself between
them and passionately pleads for pity, for even for such as
he the Saviour died. The chorus which accompanies
this scene is truly inspired. Elizabeth's prayers prevail.

Wagner

The nobles sheath their swords, and the Landgrave
advises the repentant Tannhäuser to join the band of
pilgrims now about to proceed to Rome, and there obtain
pardon for his sin. The pilgrims are heard approaching,
and, filled with eager hope, Tannhäuser rushes forth to
join them.

The third Act is preceded by a most impressive
prelude principally based on phrases previously heard, to
which is added another, the *motif* of "Pardon," which
plays an important part later on in the scene of
Tannhäuser's pilgrimage. The scene is the same peaceful valley as that in which the latter half of the first Act
is laid, but it is now autumn. Elizabeth kneels in silent
prayer before the image of the Virgin. The chant of
the returning pilgrims is heard in the distance; they
cross the scene telling of pardon gained, and their voices
gradually fade away into silence. Elizabeth fails to
recognize her lover amongst them, and then sings the
beautiful Prayer for his pardon, which is familiar to
opera and concert goers alike. At its conclusion she
slowly retires towards the Wartburg, while the orchestra
reminds us of the presence of Wolfram, who is watching
her, by a reminiscence of his song in the second Act.
He would fain accompany her, but by an affectionate
gesture she gives him to understand that her only hope
now lies in Heaven. Wolfram sadly takes his harp, and
sings the touching " Romance to the Evening Star,"
which now shines brightly overhead, beseeching it to bear
the saintly maiden from the troubles of earth to the

" Tannhäuser "

pure joys above. As he lingers, lost in contemplation, Tannhäuser, ragged, pale, and worn, enters leaning heavily on his staff. The orchestra accompanies his entrance with a sinister motive, indicating that he is still unpardoned.

Then follows a scene which, when the opera was first produced, spelt its ruin, but is now generally recognized as the finest in the work—the story of the wretched man's pilgrimage. To him alone the Pope refused pardon, saying that, before such a thing could be, the staff he carried would rather bring forth leaves. In his despair Tannhäuser calls upon Venus to come to his aid. The goddess appears, but just as he is about to throw himself into her arms, Wolfram checks him with the mention of the name of Elizabeth. Tannhäuser stands rooted to the ground, and Venus disappears in a cloud of mist. Voices are heard in the distance praying for the repose of the soul of the pure girl who is now dead, and presently a funeral procession is seen winding slowly down the hill. At a sign from Wolfram the bearers place the bier on the ground, and Tannhäuser, sinking on his knees by the side of his dead love, dies, with his last breath imploring her to pray for him. The funeral train invert their torches and extinguish them. The sun rises and floods the scene with light, and another band of pilgrims arrive with the news that the miracle has taken place, and Tannhäuser has been pardoned. All then unite in a triumphal hymn of thanksgiving, and the curtain falls.

Wagner

If the "Flying Dutchman" proved Wagner's advancing power as a musician, "Tannhäuser" certainly showed his added strength as a dramatist. The two works both depend on the same motive—the redeeming power of woman's love; but whereas in the former (as Wagner himself admits) the outline only is broadly sketched, and the development of the motive is inadequately presented, in the latter the *dénouement* is worked up to with unerring certainty and completeness. In the former work Wagner was still hampered by conventional form, and, although his genius was equal to the task of illuminating that form with a light such as had never previously been thrown upon it, the very formality of the design prevented his developing his theme, *as a drama*, in the way in which he developed the underlying motive of "Tannhäuser." Convention there is in "Tannhäuser" as in its predecessor. But the dramatic side of the work is insisted on with a far firmer hand, and, in the last Act particularly, the scheme is conceived more from the dramatic than the purely musical standpoint. Even at this early stage, too, Wagner's treatment of the old Sagas is striking. He has laid his finger on the essential dramatic point of the rune—the pure saintly love of Elizabeth—and has grouped his incidents around it with a singular sense of proportion. The variety of those incidents, moreover, strengthens the main motive, and does not divert attention from it. One never finds " padding " in Wagner's dramas, from the " Dutchman " downwards—and even in the earlier works

"Tannhauser"

the underplot is duly kept under. But "Tannhäuser" affords abundant evidence that he had
already been led intuitively to the practice, which
he afterwards elucidated with such pains in his
literary writings, of making the whole of the
action evolve itself naturally from motives
derived in themselves from the main
motive of the work. The
variety of that action came
by itself with' his in-
creased facility in
handling his
subject.

CHAPTER XI

" LOHENGRIN " was commenced in 1846 and finished in 1848. It was first produced at Weimar, under Liszt, on August the 28th, 1850.

The scene of the first Act is laid in a meadow near Antwerp; the period is the early half of the tenth century. Discarding a formal overture, Wagner prefaces the action by a prelude of singular beauty. It is based on a single theme which is used throughout the drama as typical of the Holy Grail.

Commencing in the highest register of the strings, this theme produces one of the most ethereal effects in music. Gradually it descends in the scale, the orchestration becoming fuller and richer with each repetition, until a magnificent climax is reached ; then the process is reversed, and at last the music seems to die away in the infinite. It is as though the holy vessel had been borne on angels' wings from heaven for the comfort of poor mortals travailing on earth, and, its mission accomplished, had been carried back by the heavenly host into the ethereal blue. When the curtain rises King Henry the Fowler of Germany is discovered sitting beneath a

" Lohengrin "

mighty oak tree surrounded by the Saxon and Thuringian nobles. He has summoned the nobles of Brabant to do fealty, and to bid them prepare for the defence of the country against invaders from Hungary. Frederic, Count of Telramund, and his wife Ortrud, a descendant of the former rulers of the country, are standing hard by during this scene. At the conclusion of his speech to the nobles, the king calls upon Frederic to explain the nature of the discord which, he has been told, exists in Brabant. Thus adjured, Frederic declares that the late Duke of Brabant, when on his death-bed, confided to his care his boy and girl children, Gottfried and Elsa. Elsa one day came back from a walk in the forest without her brother, who had accompanied her on starting, and suspicion has fallen upon her as his murderess, since no trace of him has ever been found. This suspicion has more readily gained credence from the fact that Elsa's demeanour has led to the belief that she has a secret lover with whom she wishes to share the dukedom. Under these circumstances Telramund has renounced the right to claim Elsa's hand in marriage given him by her dying father, and has married Ortrud. He concludes by claiming the kingdom in right of his descent from a former Duke, and demanding Elsa's punishment for her unnatural crime. The king summons Elsa to his presence. Clad in virgin white and accompanied by her maidens similarly attired, she appears and advances as one in a trance. She is almost unconscious of the king's questioning, but refers to a dream wherein a gallant knight, in silver armour, came to her side and whispered words of comfort in her troubled ear.

The king is touched by her innocence and purity, but Telramund demands that if her champion be real he shall come forward and confront him in wager of battle. Elsa, strong in the belief that her dream will prove true, consents, and promises to wed her champion should he prove successful. The king proclaims reference to the judgment of God, and bids the heralds summon the unknown champion. There is no answer. Again, at Elsa's urgent prayer, the summons rings out. Again silence. Suddenly those of the people who are nearest the river's bank perceive a wondrous sight. In the far distance there appears a boat drawn by a beautiful white swan, and in the boat a knight in shining silver armour stands leaning on his sword. Amidst feverish excitement, which culminates in a triumphant burst of the "Lohengrin" *motif*, the boat reaches the bank. The knight alights and in touching phrases bids the faithful swan return to the land whence it has brought him on his mission. Of the simplest character, this little melody is one of the most lovely in all Wagner's works; at its close a *motif* indicative of the swan appears, which those who are curious may find repeated in "Parsifal."

The swan slowly turns and floats back up the stream. Proudly advancing, the knight advances and declares his readiness to champion Elsa's cause. He then asks her if she will become his bride if he succeeds in defeating her traducer; she rapturously consents. One condition, however, he must impose; she must never ask his name, nor whence he comes. To these words is wedded an important *motif*, twice repeated (the second time a semi-tone higher), as if to insist on the mystery. The champions then measure swords, and after a fierce conflict Telramund is worsted. The stranger generously spares his adversary's life, and the curtain falls on a scene of mingled excitement and rejoicing.

The second Act takes place outside the fortress of Antwerp. It is night. In the background rises the Pallas, or residence of the knights, with its windows brilliantly illuminated; in the foreground the Kemenate, or residence of the ladies, lies on one side, the Minster on the other. Frederic and Ortrud are seated gloomily on the steps of the latter. Two new and important *motifs* make their appearance in a prelude which, in its gloomy and sinister effect, faithfully reflects the thoughts of the two conspirators, the one typifying their evil plots, the other the doubt which is to poison the happiness of Elsa and her lover. These are significantly intermingled with the "mystery of the name," the bursts of joyous fanfares from the Pallas accentuating the gloom that reigns without. A highly dramatic scene now ensues. Telramund vehemently reproaches his wife. She it was who had declared that she saw Elsa drown her brother in a pool in the wood; who had predicted that the future ruler of Brabant would come from her own line, and thereby induced him to wed

herself instead of Elsa. Ortrud then declares that by
magic she has learned that the stranger will lose all his
Heaven-sent strength if once his name or the place
whence he comes be revealed; nay, further, that the loss
of even a finger-joint will reduce him to the level of an
ordinary mortal. The miscreants then resolve that
Ortrud shall endeavour to poison Elsa's mind, while her
accomplice shall denounce the knight as a sorcerer, or,
failing the success of that device, shall even descend to
murder. Elsa now appears on the balcony of the
Kemenate and sings of her love and happiness. Ortrud
craftily works upon the girl's sense of pity, and is taken
by her indoors, thus gaining the opportunity for instilling
the insidious poison of mistrust into her ear. The *motifs*
of "mystery" and "doubt" suggest in a way impossible
to attain by any other means the cruel design that is
masked by the sorceress's pseudo-humiliation.

Day breaks, and the scene rapidly fills with groups of
people in holiday attire. A herald presently announces
the outlawry of Telramund, and proclaims Elsa's future
bridegroom as ruler of Brabant. Elsa's bridal procession
now appears, Ortrud, gorgeously dressed, being amongst
the number. Just as the procession reaches the steps,
Ortrud rushes forward and, confronting Elsa, denounces
her lover as a sorcerer and darkly hints that it is for
that reason that he conceals his name and origin. The
dispute is temporarily stopped by the arrival of the
bridegroom and the king, but Telramund now appears
and in stronger terms denounces the stranger. In

" Lohengrin "

the confusion which ensues, he manages to whisper to Elsa that the loss of even a finger-joint will keep her lover for ever at her side ; but he is thrust aside, and amidst the imposing sound of organ, chorus, orchestra, and wedding bells, the procession passes into the minster. Just as the curtain falls the sinister *motif* of "mystery" is thundered forth with almost terrible effect.

After a brilliant orchestral introduction the curtain rises for the third Act on the bridal chamber. The bridal procession enters and sings the well-known Bridal Chorus, and then departs, leaving the newly wedded pair alone. Then ensues a beautiful duet in which the lovers breathe their mutual happiness. But Elsa has become completely unnerved by the exciting events of the day. She imagines she sees the swan approaching to take her husband from her ; Telramund's hint that she will only be able to keep him by her side by magic arts has done its work; and in a frenzy of fear she demands his name and origin. At this moment Frederic rushes in, hoping to catch his rival unarmed, but Elsa gives the latter his sword and with one blow Telramund is struck dead. Sorrowfully the stranger bids the accomplices, who have entered with Telramund to assist in his evil mission, carry the body to the king. He himself will follow, and then reveal his name and the place whence he has come. He leaves the weeping Elsa to her attendants and sadly departs, the solemn notes of "mystery" sounding like a knell. The scene changes to the flowery mead of the first Act. The nobles

173

and king arrive, and the dead body of Telramund is brought in on a bier. Elsa appears, soon followed by her husband. He is acclaimed by the nobles as their leader, but replies that this cannot be. Then, uncovering the bier, he relates the story of Frederic's treachery, and his slaying of the miserable man is held to be completely justified. He then tells the awe-struck assemblage that his wife has broken her vow and asked his name. One of the Knights of Montsalvat he is, they who guard the Holy Grail. Part of their mission is to succour the innocent and oppressed, but if their identity be once disclosed they must return to Montsalvat. His father is Parzival, the king of the brotherhood; his own name is Lohengrin. Turning sadly to Elsa, he bids her farewell. The swan is seen slowly returning, and Lohengrin gives Elsa his sword, horn, and ring, so that she may give them to her brother, if he should ever return. Ortrud then suddenly appears, and with fiendish exultation declares that by magic she changed Gottfried into a swan, that she recognizes the chain by which the swan is attached to the boat, and that that very bird is the long-lost heir; and she taunts Elsa by saying that, if she could have kept Lohengrin by her side only for one year, her brother would have been restored to her. Lohengrin, hearing this, falls on his knees in prayer. Presently the white dove of the Grail is seen hovering over the boat. With a joyful expression Lohengrin springs up and removes the chain from the swan's neck. It instantly disappears, and in its place there rises into view poor Elsa's long-lost brother. The dove seizes the chain and gently draws away the boat, and Elsa, as she sees her lover gradually disappear, falls fainting into her brother's arms, while a pathetic touch is given to the situation by the recurrence in the orchestra of the " Lohengrin " *motif*, now in the minor.

Of all Wagner's works " Lohengrin " is undoubtedly the most *popular*, and the reason is not far to seek. The melodic element prevails to an extent perhaps greater than in any of his other compositions, and such parts of the second Act as are more purely dramatic in expression are very generally sacrificed in representation. This practice of "cutting" calls for vehement protest. Wagner's plots do not depend so much on incident as on the working out of motives, and such excision as is too often ruthlessly pursued is fatal to the logical development of the drama. Consequently, owing to the very wealth of pure melody which " Lohengrin " contains, it has very frequently been mutilated to the point almost of stultification. So much so has this been the case that the character of Elsa has often been completely misunderstood. She has been represented as a mere inquisitive woman, whose natural curiosity gets the better of her. And, unless the second Act be treated with the respect which is its due, such a misunderstanding is not unnatural. Elsa's real nature is that of a true, loving woman, with a sincerity and affection almost dog-like in its devotion. She hails the unknown knight as her deliverer, her hero, for whom she would gladly die. It is no curiosity which

Wagner

leads her to ask the fatal question, but the frenzy of fear
of losing her lover, which has been instilled into her by
the devilish promptings of Ortrud and her mean accomplice, and which temporarily unhinges her reason.
It is her very love which works her woe, and in
Wagner's poem the end is arrived at by means painful in their certainty and humanity. The figure of
the noble Lohengrin is no less pathetic. The tragedy
of the wreck of his dream of happiness is the
most poignant situation in Wagner's dramas.
The ending is the saddest of them all.
No ray of hope pierces the gloom,
for not even in the restoration
of Gottfried to life and
joy can we forget the
sacrifice by which
it has been
attained.

CHAPTER XII

"TRISTAN UND ISOLDE" did not, of course, come next to "Lohengrin" in point of time. Meanwhile "Das Rheingold," "Die Walküre," and the greater part of "Siegfried" had been written. But, as it will be more convenient to deal with the "Ring" as a whole, the departure from strict chronological order may, perhaps, be forgiven. "Tristan" was commenced in 1857 and finished in 1859. It was first performed at Munich on the 10th of June, 1865, under Von Bülow, Ludwig Schnorr being the Tristan and his wife the Isolde.

The prelude to this great drama of Life and Death comprises some of the chief *motifs* of the work, and the system which Wagner laid down in "Opera and Drama" had been so elaborated by him at this period, that the whole score is a very network of *motifs*, all having a definite connection and meaning. By a succession of pregnant phrases, Wagner presents us with a tone picture almost unique even for him. The *motifs* as used in the drama are all connected with different phases of Tristan and Isolde's love, and the similarity, and yet withal the difference, between them cannot fail to be noticed. More perhaps in " Tristan " than in any other of Wagner's works does he let us see the birth of his melodies with our own eyes. The whole of the varying emotions of the lovers, in their musical shape, seem to grow naturally out of the simple phrase which opens the prelude, and the additional force which the tonal expression of these emotions consequently gains is enormous. The different phases are perfectly defined, and yet the connecting link spreads a subtle influence over them all.

The prelude leads without a break into the first Act. The scene is laid on the deck of a ship in which Isolde is being brought from Ireland to Cornwall by Tristan in order that she may become the bride of King Mark. As the curtain rises, a young sailor is heard singing at the masthead. Part of his song contains a *motif* of which considerable use is made, and has especial reference to the sea. Isolde lies on a couch beneath a pavilion which has been erected on the deck, her face buried in the cushions. Brangäne, her maid, stands looking through the curtains, and, in answer to her mistress's questions, announces that the ship is nearing her destination. Isolde, in a wild frenzy, calls upon the wind and tempest to overset the vessel ; half-fainting she cries for air, and Brangäne opens wide the curtains, disclosing the fore part of the vessel. Tristan is seen with folded arms, standing apart from the sailors and warriors of his retinue, gazing thoughtfully out to sea ; his faithful henchman Kurwenal lies at his feet. Isolde sees Tristan, and gazes

"Tristan und Isolde"

stonily upon him; she loved him once, but now she is destined to be the bride of another. She calls him coward for shunning her glance, and bids Brangäne not entreat, but order him to come to her presence. The message is given, whereupon Kurwenal angrily interrupts. Tristan is a hero-knight, not to be addressed in that manner, he reminds her. When Sir Morold came from Ireland to levy a tax on the Cornish, Tristan slew him, and sent back his head to his own country— the only tax ever obtained from English hands.

Brangäne returns, and Isolde then tells her of her love for Morold. His head had been brought to her, and in it there was embedded a fragment of sword-blade which she kept. Tristan had been wounded in the conflict, and, as Morold's weapon was poisoned, the wound would not heal. In despair he bethought him of the Irish princess whose medicinal skill was famous over all the world, and, under the assumed name of Tantris, he sought her out, and was healed by her. She grew to love the stranger. But one day she observed a gap in the edge of his sword ; the piece of steel she had found in Morold's skull fitted the notch. The man to whom her heart had gone out was revealed as the slayer of her dead lover. Nevertheless, she could not resist the pleading look in Tristan's eyes; the sword with which she would have avenged Morold's death dropped from her nerveless fingers, and she let him depart with a thousand protestations of truth and love on his lips. And now this man, with his splendid retinue, has come to bring her to another

for bride. She loves him still, and his neglect of her is
torture. Brangäne tries to comfort her mistress, and
hints that magic may avail to bring Tristan to her side.
Isolde bids her bring the casket of magic drugs which
her mother has bequeathed to her. Brangäne does so,
and taking out a vial containing the love-philtre, points
to it as relief from the heart-break that is killing the
unhappy woman. But Isolde seizes another flask, and
triumphantly points to it. " The draught of death ! "
exclaims Brangäne in horror. A touch of Wagner's
marvellous genius reveals itself here. The theme of the
"death-potion" is united with that of "desire," indicating
the tumult that is raging in the bosom of the wretched
Isolde. At this moment the voices of the sailors are
heard shouting to each other to shorten sail ; they are
nearing land. Kurwenal boisterously enters, and bids
the ladies prepare to disembark. Isolde declares she will
not make ready until Tristan has asked forgiveness for
his base conduct, and orders Kurwenal to deliver her
message. She then bids Brangäne prepare the death-
draught for Tristan. Brangäne, horror-struck, remon-
strates.

The hero slowly approaches. He asks Isolde what
she desires of him. She bitterly reproaches him for what
he has done, and reminds him that she has vowed
vengeance for Morold's death. He offers her his sword ;
she declines it, but motions Brangäne to give her the cup.
Tristan seizes it eagerly. He loves Isolde no less passionately than she him, but his honour forbids his revealing

"Tristan und Isolde"

his love to the woman whom he is bringing for bride to his king. Death will be a welcome friend. He seizes the cup and drinks, but, ere he has finished the draught, Isolde snatches it from him and drains it to the dregs. The two gaze into each other's eyes with ever-growing longing. Love surges over them in a full tide of passion. Tristan, bewildered, heeds not the shouts of the seamen announcing the arrival of the ship. In a frenzy of terror Brangäne confesses that the cup has contained the love-philtre instead of the death-potion, and the curtain falls on a scene of bustle and excitement as the king, with his retinue, boards the ship.

The scene of the second Act is a garden in front of Isolde's chamber, which lies at one side and is approached by steps. It is a genial summer night. A burning torch is fixed near the open door, and the sounds of hunting horns are heard as the curtain rises. Brangäne stands on the steps anxiously watching the retreating hunters. Isolde comes from the chamber and impatiently awaits the last echoes of the horns, so that, by extinguishing the torch, she may give Tristan the signal to come to her. Brangäne warns her that Tristan's friend, Melot, who has divined the secret and has arranged the night hunt ostensibly in Tristan's interest, may prove a traitor. But Isolde, blinded by love, refuses to listen. She dashes the torch to the ground and extinguishes it. Tristan appears, and then begins the longest and most perfect love duet in all music. In tenderest tones they sing of Night, the friend of lovers, and the purity both of the diction and its musical expression is unsurpassable. Breaking in upon this *ensemble* the voice of Brangäne is heard from the watch-tower warning the lovers of the approach of day; words are powerless to express the witching effect of the accompanying orchestration.

Following immediately upon this there occurs a new *motif* expressive of "Felicity." The duo grows more and more passionate until the magnificent "Song of Death" is reached, in which the lovers ardently desire death as the end of their sufferings. It is interrupted by the hasty entrance of Kurwenal warning his master of danger. The king, Melot, and the retainers come swiftly up the avenue, while Brangäne hastens to Isolde's side. The king sadly, but with no trace of anger, upbraids Tristan for his perfidy. Tristan, scarcely comprehending the position, tenderly asks Isolde if she will accompany him to the far-off land whither he must now go, and gently kisses her. Melot then rushes forward with drawn sword. Tristan also draws, but, on the onslaught of Melot, drops his guard and sinks wounded into Kurwenal's arms as the curtain falls.

The third Act takes us to Brittany. We see the castle garden of Tristan's ancestral home. It is a wild, rugged spot, built on the cliffs and wearing a neglected aspect. The prelude admirably attunes the mind to what is to follow, with its mournful and pathetic harmonies. In the centre of the stage is a huge lime tree whereunder, on a rude couch, lies the unconscious Tristan with Kurwenal watching at his head. As the

" Tristan und Isolde "

curtain rises, the mournful sound of a shepherd's pipe is heard. Kurwenal has sent for Isolde, and the dolorous tune is the agreed sign that no ship is yet in sight. Tristan presently opens his eyes, and asks where he is. Kurwenal, overjoyed, tells him he is in his own Kareol, to which his faithful servant has brought him, carrying him in his own arms to the ship.

As he lies weak and helpless, the hapless knight deliriously recalls the past events of his life, and is immeasurably excited by Kurwenal's news that Isolde is coming to him. In his delirium he fancies he sees the ship, falls back fainting into Kurwenal's arms, and is only with difficulty again aroused. At this moment the shepherd is heard playing a cheerful melody outside. It is the agreed signal of Isolde's arrival. Kurwenal becomes wild with excitement, and Tristan, staggering to his feet, in frenzy tears the bandages from his wound. His blood bursts forth afresh, and just as Isolde rushes in he falls and dies, murmuring her name with his last breath. His prayer has been answered; Death the deliverer has come at last. Isolde falls in a swoon on his body. The clash of arms is heard. The shepherd announces the arrival of another ship. Kurwenal fears the arrival of the king with hostile intent, and recognizing Melot who is about to enter over the drawbridge, attacks and kills him, being himself mortally wounded in the conflict. But the noble king, who has only recently learned Brangäne's fatal secret, has in reality come to pardon the unhappy lovers. No anger is there in his heart; nothing but supreme love and pity. But Isolde hears him not. Her heart has gone out to Tristan. Slowly, as in a trance, she rises, supported by the repentant Brangäne, and, with ever-increasing ecstasy, pictures herself and the noble dead wafted away through the billowy ether into endless space. The superb "Song of Death" rises to its complete climax, and, as it softly dies away, Isolde gently sinks down and follows her lover into the realms of Eternity. And as the curtain slowly falls, the four notes of the *motif* heard at the very commencement of the prelude are heard— thus *must* it have been, they seem to say; in death the faithful pair have attained the bliss which was denied them on earth.

In no other drama does Wagner exhibit such a completely satisfactory vindication of his theories, such a perfect example of the action evolved "from within." The economy of incident is extraordinary, and yet the emotion is sustained at a pitch which is at times well-nigh overwhelming. When compared with the old legends from which the story of "Tristan" was derived, another point of great importance presents itself, namely, the singular power of selection which Wagner possessed. The various forms of the old Saga are nothing more than the story of a vulgar amour. But in Wagner's poem all the superfluous and degrading detail vanishes as if by magic, and nothing is left but the grand epic of Love itself. Tristan becomes a noble hero who values his honour more highly than anything else that the world can

"Tristan und Isolde"

offer. He grasps at death with exultation as a happy ending to the torment which the struggle between love and that honour rouses within him. Isolde is transformed into a woman who would rather die with her lover than live a hopeless life without him. And the irresistible power of Love is symbolized in the potion which the lovers drink; Love is stronger than death. "Tristan" is a psychological study couched in dramatic form, and every incident is evolved from the development of the inner workings of the lovers' hearts. No extraneous circumstances intervene; the drama proceeds along lines which we recognize as inevitable from the very outset, because—and here lies the secret—they are the embodiment of the tragedy of Humanity. "Tristan" is the most human of all Wagner's works, and in its simple majesty complements, as Wagner destined it should, the great world-allegory which is presented in the "Ring." As to the music, nothing but an exhaustive analysis of nearly every bar would suffice to connect the meaning of the surging masses of sound with the emotions they depict. The whole score, almost, seems to be derived from the simple chromatic progression which begins the prelude. "Tristan," in fact, abounds with similar progressions, with the result that a feeling of unrest is produced which sympathizes intimately with the nature of the poem. No finer expression of the most intense human emotion has yet been written.

CHAPTER XIII

"DIE MEISTERSINGER," which was sketched as early as 1845, was begun in actual earnest in 1861 and finished in 1867. It was first performed at Munich under Von Bülow on the 21st June, 1868. On this occasion Betz was the Hans Sachs, Nachbaur the Walther, Schlosser the David, Bausewein the Pogner, Hölzel the Beckmesser, Fräulein Mallinger the Eva, and Frau Dietz the Magdalena.

In this work Wagner, for the last time, indulged in a full-blown overture. This overture has become so familiarized by concert performances as to have become almost a household word. As played in the theatre, it passes, without a break, into the opening notes of the first Act.

The scene is the interior of the Church of St. Katharine in Nuremberg at the beginning of the sixteenth century. The congregation are singing a stately chorale. Leaning against a pillar is a young knight, Walther von Stolzing, who is earnestly watching a maiden seated hard by. It is Eva, the daughter of Pogner, the rich goldsmith, who is accompanied by her nurse, Magdalena. It is the old

" Die Meistersinger "

story ; Walther loves the maiden and she timidly returns
his love. His tender glances fill her with confusion, but
she cannot resist turning loving looks on him in response.
As the congregation departs he steps to her side, and she
demurely sends her nurse back, first on one pretext and
then on another, while she talks to her lover, who tries to
glean some words of promise that his suit will be successful. To his alarm he hears that she is practically pledged
to another. Her father has promised her hand to whom-
soever the Meistersinger shall, on the morrow, pronounce
to be the best singer at the festival ; but Eva will nevertheless be free to refuse him if he should be distasteful to
her ; and she promises her lover that, come what may, she
will wed him and no other. She departs with her nurse,
and David, Hans Sachs' apprentice, begins bustling about,
making preparations for the assembly of the Meistersinger
which is shortly to take place.

Walther questions him as to how admission may be
gained into this select band. He learns it is no easy matter.
He must first learn all the various modes, of which David
reels off a string with the most fantastic names, and be
able to recognize them at once, before he can become a
singer. Then he must be able to compose words in any
of these outlandish metres before he can become a *poet*.
Finally, he must be able to compose both a poem and
accompanying music without breaking more than seven
of the rules before he can become a full member of the
august body. Walther, nothing daunted, resolves to aspire
to the highest honours at once. The apprentices, who

187

during this scene have been continually teasing David, now bring forward the "marker's" box, and arrange the curtains around it. Here, David explains, sits the judge, who marks on his slate the errors committed. Having completed their work, the young urchins break into a merry chorus, but retire discreetly as the Meistersinger approach. The young knight is welcomed by Pogner, who admires his pluck, but is looked upon with disfavour by Beckmesser, a crabbed, vain old man, who aspires to Eva's hand himself, and consequently regards a possible rival with malevolence. Unfortunately for Walther this personage is the "marker." In a dignified address Pogner announces that on the morrow, the feast of St. John, he will endeavour to do honour to German art by presenting his daughter as a prize to the best singer. This announcement is greeted with great enthusiasm, albeit a certain amount of animated criticism.

Quiet having eventually been restored, Pogner presents Walther to the assembly. He is asked where he learnt poetry and music. He replies that he gained the former by the hearth in winter evenings, conning the poems of the Minnesinger ; the latter he studied in Nature, in the murmurs of the woods, the songs of the birds. After an animated discussion, in which the quarrelsome nature of Beckmesser is humorously portrayed by the orchestra, it is resolved that Walther shall be allowed to try and establish his claim to be admitted into the Meistersinger's ranks. But his song violates every one of their fossilized rules : Beckmesser shows his slate covered on both sides

" Die Meistersinger "

with " bad marks." Hans Sachs, the old cobbler, alone perceives the genius of the singer. He is only one, however, and Walther is rejected amidst great confusion. As the curtain falls, Hans Sachs is left alone on the stage mutely expressing his disgust at the decision.

A bright, merry prelude ushers us into a street in old Nuremberg. On one side is Pogner's house, on the other the humble shop of Hans Sachs. The day is slowly drawing to a close, and David and the other apprentices are putting up the shutters of their masters' shops. The apprentices have perceived David telling his sweetheart Magdalena the unfavourable result of Walther's essay before the Meistersinger, and begin rallying him on his own love affairs. David, very irate, endeavours to chastise them, until Sachs comes out and ends the noise by packing the youth off to bed. As the youngsters retire, Pogner and his daughter come down the street. Pogner would fain visit his old friend, but the shop is closed, and Eva persuades him to go indoors. Dallying on the steps, she learns from Magdalena of Walther's non-success, and resolves to return to Sachs later on and obtain from his lips a fuller version of what has happened. As she retires into the house, David sets Sachs' bench in front of the shop, and the dear old cobbler seats himself at it. He tries to work; but the charm of Walther's singing is too strong for him, and in an exquisite monologue he recalls the events of the day. Eva then comes to him to learn more about the morning's disaster. In his heart of hearts Sachs loves the sweet maiden, but by a little artful cross-questioning he soon discovers her secret. Eva cannot repress her annoyance at the pedantic conduct of the Meistersinger, and departs in dudgeon. Sachs observes her whispering with Magdalena, and heroically sacrificing his own love, resolves to watch over her with all his tenderest care. He goes back into his shop suspecting that something is afoot, and resolves to keep watch. His suspicions are soon justified, for Walther appears and proposes that Eva shall fly with him. The horn of the watchman is heard, and the lovers hide behind the trees in front of Pogner's house to escape observation. This alarm passed, Eva retires into the house, and presently emerges disguised in her nurse's clothes. But Sachs now opens his window, thereby throwing a strong light into the street, and for a second time Walther's scheme is frustrated. To make matters worse, Beckmesser appears on the scene with his lute, having already sent a message to Eva announcing his intention of singing to her beforehand the Serenade by which he hopes to win her hand on the morrow. To Beckmesser's great disgust, Sachs now carries his bench into the street, and commences a jovial song concerning Eve's discomfort before she wore shoes.

This highly incenses Beckmesser, who cannot make himself heard for the noise. He implores Sachs to desist; the latter retorts that he has Beckmesser's own shoes to finish for to-morrow. Eventually a compromise is arrived at. Sachs will cease singing if he is allowed to "mark" Beckmesser's mistakes by hammering on his

"Die Meistersinger"

shoes. The conceited personage readily assents, anticipating complete silence. He then commences a ludi-
crously inharmonious effusion, accompanying himself
on his cracked lute. But the cobbler's strokes fall thick
and fast. Finally, amidst a tornado of hammering,
Beckmesser gives up the attempt in despair, whereupon
Sachs sarcastically thanks him for having committed so
many errors that he has made the finishing of the shoes
an easy task. A female figure in Eva's dress has meanwhile appeared on the balcony ; it is Magdalena, engaged
in furthering her mistress's little plot. David, however,
who in common with the other sleepers has been aroused
by the noise, recognizes his sweetheart, and forthwith
belabours the unfortunate Beckmesser, breaking his lute
on his own head. The occupiers of the whole street,
now thoroughly aroused, join in the row. Women pour
water from the windows on the combatants' heads, and
in the confusion Eva escapes into the house. With an
admirable touch of humour, the chief theme on which
this wonderful shindy is based is the *motif* of Beckmesser's
serenade. When the tumult is at its height the watchman's horn is heard. As if by magic the stage is suddenly
cleared. The old watchman totters across intoning
his time-honoured formula, and, as the sound of his horn
dies away in the distance, the orchestra returns to the
beautiful *motif* illustrative of the peace of the summer
night, which has accompanied the loves of Walther and
Eva earlier in the act, and the curtain descends upon
an absolutely empty stage. And yet it has been

solemnly asserted that Wagner had no sense of dramatic effect !

The third Act is introduced by a prelude of the most touching beauty, admirably allusive to the noble character of the cobbler poet. The scene opens in his room, bathed in the warm light of a summer morning. Sachs is sitting meditatively reading a huge volume. David enters in trepidation, fearing his master's anger on account of his share in the events of the preceding night. But he is graciously received, and, after singing his candidature song, is dismissed with a kindly word, not before he has expressed the hope that his beloved master will succeed in winning for himself the sweet prize which the approaching contest offers. Left to himself, Sachs meditates thoughtfully on the passions of human nature. He is recalled to himself by the thought of his self-imposed mission to make the young lovers happy, and by the entrance of Walther, who has been his guest for the night. Walther relates a wonderful dream he has just had, and, at Sachs' suggestion and with his advice and assistance, puts it into metrical shape as his test song, Sachs noting the words on paper as the young knight sings them. This done, they retire to prepare for the festival. The miserable Beckmesser, very lame from his drubbing, now enters by the window, the orchestra humorously illustrating his terror and uneasiness. He discovers Sachs' notes of the song. Here is a prize indeed ! Hearing footsteps, he hastily thrusts the manuscript into his pocket. Sachs enters,

and ironically inquires if the shoes are a success. But
shoes are not uppermost in Beckmesser's thoughts at the
moment. He thirsts for revenge, and, pulling the verses
from their hiding-place, accuses Sachs of treacherously
trying to win Eva for himself. Sachs laughs at him,
and tells him that he may keep them, and moreover
that he, Sachs, will never proclaim himself as their
author. The contemptible fellow's attitude then
changes to one of fawning flattery, and he departs with
the conviction that the prize is as good as won.
Scarcely has he vanished when Eva enters. She says
one of her shoes hurts her, but the excellent cobbler
plainly sees through the ruse, and notes her start of joy
as Walther enters in brave array. He suggests that music
would help him in his work, and Walther, seeing the
kindly motive, sings the song he has just composed. To
conceal his own aching heart, Sachs jestingly puts aside
their thanks, recalling the old story of Tristan and
Isolde, and saying he could never be a King Mark.
(These allusions are pointed by musical quotations from
"Tristan.") To aid in stifling his own emotion he calls
in Magdalena and David, on the latter of whom he
bestows the Companionship of the Meistersinger by
means of a traditional hearty box on the ear; and the
scene finishes with an exquisite quintet in honour of the
new song.

The scene now changes to a beautiful meadow where
the contest of song is to take place. All is gaiety,
animation, and holiday attire. The various guilds enter

with their banners, the apprentices join the girls in a merry dance, and all is bustle and gaiety until the Meistersinger make a dignified entry and the serious business of the day commences. The uprising of Sachs to address the people is hailed with delight. He is loved by them all, and in his honour their voices unite in singing his own chorale. Silence being restored, he reminds them that only those who have a stainless past may strive to win the beautiful maiden whose hand is the prize. To all such the invitation to compete is extended. Beckmesser, full of vanity, thereupon ascends the mound upon which the competing singers have to stand. But the verses he relies upon will not fit in with his ridiculous tune, and, to make matters worse, he forgets the words and enunciates a miserable parody of them. His voice is eventually drowned in the laughter of the assembly, and then, in a fit of rage, he tears up the manuscript and denounces Sachs as the real author, who has endeavoured to play a scurvy trick upon him. Sachs, however, picks up the pieces and says that the poem is not his but Walther's, and calls upon the young knight to prove his statement by singing the words to their appropriate music. Walther then sings the Prize Song in its complete form, and is loudly acclaimed as the victor. Eva, radiantly happy, places the victor's crown upon his brow, but he indignantly refuses the gold chain and image of King David which is the badge of the guild of the Meistersinger. Hans Sachs, however, gently rebukes him for his discourtesy to those who have placed his supreme happiness within his grasp, and then utters a warm pæan of praise of national art. The populace break into loud demonstrations of approval of their favourite; Eva takes the wreath from Walther's brow to place it on that of Sachs; and the curtain falls on a scene of general homage to the noble, kindly-hearted cobbler of Nuremberg.

In its richly varied incident " Die Meistersinger " presents a strong contrast to its predecessor with its studiously severe simplicity. Its genial humour, its keen satire on artistic pedantry, its bustling panorama of mediæval times, all belong to the comedy of life. But underlying all these incidents, and shaping their course, is the tragedy of Hans Sachs. He loves Eva with a fond and holy passion, a love so true that, by its help, he is enabled to conquer his sorrow and make her happiness the object of his tenderest solicitude, although his action involves the destruction of his own hopes. There is something infinitely pathetic in his noble self-sacrifice, in his serene resignation to the inevitable, and his whole nature brims over with kindly broad sympathy. A truly lovable character is Hans Sachs. His importance to the dramatic scheme is nevertheless often lost sight of, owing in a great measure to the blue pencil of those who imagine they know more of dramatic construction and balance than Wagner did, with the result that Walther becomes elevated to a pedestal which he was never intended to occupy. In reality Walther's importance is merely *musical*, and, presumably for the reason that in the old form of Italian opera the hero appropriated all the vocal tit-bits, Walther has often been mistaken for the pivot around which all the other characters revolve by those with whom the music outweighs the drama.

As in " Lohengrin," Wagner has, in a sense, only himself to thank for the mutilation his work has suffered at the hands of stage-managers. Its very wealth of melody has led to the excision of passages in which dramatic necessity has demanded methods of less suavity. But, under any circumstances, the certainty of Wagner's method is made apparent in every phrase. The power of characterization is extraordinary. The meditative calm of Sachs, the acid vanity of the chattering Beckmesser, the pompous mannerisms of Kothner and his associates, the gentle sweetness of Eva, the dignity of Pogner, the boisterous spirits of the apprentices—all are touched with unfailing happiness and dexterity; and Walther's " Prize Song " will remain for all time as one of the most perfect examples of pure melody in existence. In his choice of keys Wagner is no less felicitous; all are selected with appropriate feeling for joyous expressiveness. And whereas in "Tristan " the strenuous emotions of the actors find their counterpart in the chromatic harmonies and melodic intervals which pervade the score, so in " Die Meistersinger " the prevailing *feeling* of the music is diatonic, with a consequent effect of cheerfulness and repose. There is hardly a bar in which some masterly stroke may not be discovered; humorous and human touches abound.

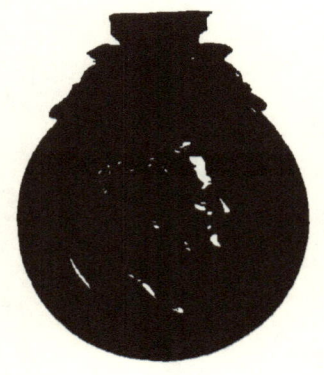

THE BAYREUTH MEDAL.

CHAPTER XIV

THE gigantic tetralogy of "Der Ring des Nibelungen" was projected as early as 1848. The music was not, however, commenced until 1853, and not completed till 1874. It was first performed on August the 13th, 14th, 16th and 17th, 1876, at Bayreuth. The cast is of such length that it will be more convenient to give it in the Appendix.

"Das Rheingold," which forms the Prologue to the trilogy proper, was completed in 1854, and contains the key of the entire tragedy. The prelude is perhaps the most original of all Wagner's preludes. No less than 136 consecutive bars are based upon a pedal point. Starting with a single E flat sounded in the bottommost depths of the orchestra, an undulating theme gradually swells louder and louder above it till the air becomes flooded with sound. It is the musical picture of the mighty Rhine, and as the curtain rises (or rather *parts*— for Wagner set his face steadfastly against the traditional drop-curtain) we are transported to the lowest depths of the river where the three Rhine-maidens are disporting themselves in the waters. Presently appears Alberich,

197

Wagner

the chief of the Nibelungs, a race of dwarfs who inhabit
the bowels of the earth. Ugly and malicious is he,
cruel and crafty to boot. Clumsily he tries to make
amorous advances to the maidens, but they easily escape
his clutches as he slides about on the slippery rocks. The
light has been gradually growing brighter, and suddenly
a sunbeam strikes upon the point of one of the submerged
rocks and the depths are illuminated by a golden glow.
It is the Rhein-gold, the treasure of the Rhine-maidens.
Gaily they swim around it, chanting its praises, while the
orchestra supplies an accompaniment whose glitter can
almost be seen. They foolishly tell the dwarf that
whoso possesses the gold may by its power become
ruler of the world, but he must first renounce Love.
Alberich's cupidity is excited beyond measure. With
frantic haste he scales the rock, curses and for ever
renounces love, and, clutching the glittering metal,
disappears into the depths below. Darkness once more
falls, and the voices of the maidens are heard disconso-
lately lamenting their loss. Gradually the darkness gives
way to a vaporous mist, and, as it disperses, a rocky region
is revealed. At the back, on a high eminence, stands
a mighty castle, its turrets glistening in the rising sun ;
in the foreground the god Wotan and Fricka, his spouse,
lie sleeping on a grassy mound. The Rhine flows at
the bottom of the valley that separates the foreground
and background. They awake, and gaze on the castle.
It is Walhalla, the palace that Wotan has commissioned
the giants Fafnir and Fasolt to build for him. But, now

"Das Rheingold"

that the work is completed, the price that has to be paid weighs heavily on Fricka's mind. At the instigation of Loki, the embodiment of shiftiness and craft, Wotan has promised to the giants Freia, the goddess of youth and beauty, Fricka's sister. Fricka had herself persuaded Wotan to build Walhalla; she hoped thereby to keep the roving god more closely to her side, marital constancy not having been one of his strongest characteristics. But she has been no party to the agreement to surrender Freia, and she bitterly upbraids her lord for what he has done. The hapless Freia now rushes in in tears, pursued by the two giants, who demand their reward. Wotan endeavours to temporize, but the giants are obdurate.

At this juncture the advent of Loki is hailed by Wotan with delight. He has been deputed to search the earth for some equivalent which will satisfy the giants, but nowhere has he found anything to equal woman's matchless worth. He has, however, learned from the Rhine-maidens the story of Alberich's rape of the gold. The giants, hearing the conversation, agree to accept this in exchange for Freia if Wotan can procure it, and depart, taking the goddess with them as hostage. After she has gone the gods feel a curious sense of age stealing over them. It is because Freia alone knew the secret of growing the golden apples which brought eternal youth. Wotan resolves that he will seek out Alberich, and take the gold from him by force. Loki readily falls in with the scheme, and the two disappear through a cleft in the rock that leads to the underground kingdom of the gnomes.

As they enter, a thick vapour arises from the cleft and darkens the whole stage. The clanging of anvils is heard, and, when the mist clears away, a subterranean cavern is seen, narrow passages leading off from it in all directions. Alberich enters, dragging after him the shrieking elf Mime, whom, as being a skilful smith, he has charged to make him a helmet. Mime, who has intended to keep it for himself, reluctantly hands it to his persecutor, suspecting that it possesses magic properties. Alberich, placing it on his own head, to the accompaniment of eerie sounds in the orchestra, immediately becomes invisible, and gives the wretched Mime a merciless thrashing. Wotan and Loki, attracted by the luckless dwarf's shrieks, enter. They learn from Mime that Alberich has forged the gold into a ring, and by its magic has obtained complete mastery over all the dwarfs, so that now they have to labour to heap up wealth to satisfy his insatiable greed. In confirmation of this story Alberich appears, driving before him with his whip a throng of Nibelungs bearing gold and silver ornaments, which he makes them pile up into a hoard. Seeing the two gods, Alberich pours out his hate of their race in unmeasured terms, and vows vengeance upon them. Wotan's anger is checked by Loki, who craftily persuades Alberich to give them practical demonstration of the powers of the Ring and the magic helmet. Alberich's vanity is excited. He changes himself first into a huge serpent, and then

" Das Rheingold "

into a toad. In this guise Wotan puts his foot on him, and they wrench the helmet from his head. Alberich immediately resumes his ordinary shape, whereupon the gods bind him hand and foot, and drag him up the passage by which they descended. The stage is again filled with murky vapour, and when it clears away the rocky pass whence Wotan and Loki descended into the Nibelungs' cavern is again revealed ; the background is, however, now veiled in mist.

The gods enter from the cleft, dragging the bound Alberich with them. After compelling him to summon his slaves and deliver up his treasure, they take the Ring from him also, by force. They then loose his bonds, and he, after pronouncing a terrible curse on all into whose possession the Ring shall come, disappears down the cleft. The giants now enter with Freia to claim the treasure that has been promised them. They ask for as much gold as will hide Freia completely from sight. The hoard is piled round her, but the glint of her hair is visible ; the magic helm is then added. Fasolt, however, declares he can still see her eyes through a chink. Nothing but the Ring is now left, and that Wotan obstinately declines to relinquish. The giants seize Freia to drag her away, when suddenly a bluish light breaks from a neighbouring cavern, and Erda, the Earth-mother, appears. Solemnly she warns Wotan to give up the Ring, which will bring doom to him and all his race. Deeply moved by her words, Wotan adds the Ring to the pile. Its evil influence is at once apparent.

Wagner

The giants quarrel over the division of the spoil, and Fafnir slays his brother with his staff. A shudder goes through the onlookers, and Donner, springing up, invokes the aid of the storm to dispel the gloomy mists which hide the new abode of the gods from view. A terrific thunderstorm bursts overhead, and, as it clears, a rainbow bridge is seen leading over the valley to Walhalla. Amidst the pomp of the majestic Walhalla *motif*, the gods pass over it to their new abode, and the curtain slowly closes, but not before the plaintive voices of the Rhine-maidens have been heard from the river beneath, sadly bewailing their loss.

" Die Walküre " was begun in 1854 and finished in 1856.

The prelude to this section is wild and stormy. The soughing of the wind, the pattering of hail, the hoarse growl of the thunder, are suggested. The storm rises to a climax, but, ere the curtain parts, passes away in distant rumblings. The scene is a large hut, rudely furnished. In the centre there rises through the roof the trunk of a mighty ash tree ; on one side the hearth is illumined by a flickering glimmer of light from the slowly dying embers ; on the other are steps leading to the bedchamber. A rough table and stools stand at the foot of the tree. A man, weaponless and dishevelled, staggers in through the door at the back, and falls exhausted on the hearth. The mistress of the dwelling, Sieglinde, enters, and regards the intruder with astonishment, which is turned to compassion when she perceives his pitiable plight. She gives

" Die Walküre "

him drink, and learns that he is fleeing from his enemies, his weapons having treacherously broken in his hand. Their conversation is interrupted by the entrance of Hunding, Sieglinde's husband, a rough, uncouth fellow, who regards the pair with suspicion. But, learning that the stranger has come to his roof seeking shelter, he bids him join himself and his wife at their evening meal and relate his history. The wanderer then recounts the events of his life. His infancy was a happy one. He lived in the woods with his father, mother, and twin-sister; their life knew no care. But one day, on returning with his father from the chase, they found that in their absence the race of the Neidungs had burnt their homestead, slain his mother, and carried off his sister. His father soon after, pursued by his relentless enemies, had been compelled to flee; and he alone was now left, a child of misfortune. Hence he was named " Woeful," an outcast, homeless and wretched. That very day, in defence of a helpless maiden, he had been overpowered by numbers, and in danger of his life. Hunding then recognizes in his visitor the man whom his tribe have called upon him to help exterminate. The laws of hospitality will save him for the night, but on the morrow let him look to himself. The gentle Sieglinde throws a glance full of meaning at the ash tree; but Hunding, who has perceived a strange resemblance between his wife and the stranger, observes it, and roughly orders her to prepare his evening draught, and accompany him to their chamber. Left to himself, the unfortunate man becomes the prey of bitter thoughts. Would that he could now handle the sword that his father once promised him—a weapon nothing could withstand! The dying embers flare momentarily into a blaze, and illuminate what is seen to be a sword-hilt embedded in the tree; but the stranger sees it not. Worn out and weary, he thinks of Sieglinde's beauty, and sinks down on the hearth. Sieglinde then enters clad in a white robe. She has drugged her husband's drink, and now returns to bid the guest flee while he may. She has it in her power to procure his safety. She then tells him that she loathes Hunding. He obtained her by purchase from those who tore her from her home.

At the wedding feast there appeared a stranger, wearing a large hat to conceal a lost eye, who, thrusting a mighty sword into the ash trunk, declared that it should belong to the hero who could draw it thence. Many warriors have tried and failed, and the sword still remains fast in its living sheath. The stranger at these words is seized with a premonition that this is the weapon of which his father has spoken to him. He passionately embraces Sieglinde, and at this moment the door opens of its own accord. The warmth and light of a beautiful spring morning glint through the opened portal, and, lost to the world, the lovers sing a duet of extraordinary beauty and passion. Sieglinde then perceives in her lover's eyes a light which shines in none other than those of the Wälsung race. Is not his name Siegmund? She has guessed rightly, and she is his long-lost sister. Now he

knows that this is the sword which his father, who is
Wotan himself, has promised him in his hour of need.
With a mighty effort he wrenches it from the tree, and,
as they throw themselves into each other's arms, the
curtain closes quickly.

The second Act is laid in a wild, rugged mountain
gorge, a chaos of rocks towering in the background.
An equally wild prelude, in which the bounding *motif*
of the " Walküre " plays an important part, precedes the
parting of the curtain. Wotan is discovered with his
favourite daughter Brünnhilde, the chief of the Walküre,
to whom he confides the care of Siegmund in his
approaching conflict with the pursuing Hunding. As
Brünnhilde, delighted with her mission, departs, she
announces the approach of Fricka, who enters in a
chariot drawn by two rams. Fricka, the protectress of
marriage vows, deems the protection which Wotan
would afford to the unholy love of Siegmund and Sieglinde an outrage to herself. Their very existence she
deems an insult to her wifehood, seeing that they are
the living evidence of his inconstancy to her. Wotan,
abashed and reluctantly compelled to acknowledge the
justice of her charges, is forced to promise that his protection shall be withdrawn. Brünnhilde returns as Fricka
triumphantly departs, and tries to comfort her sorrowful
parent. But in vain ; the greyness of twilight is closing
round him. In a monologue, unsurpassed both in point
of length and dramatic force, he gives his beloved child
the reason of his tribulation. He tells her the story of

the Rhinegold, now jealously guarded by Fafnir in the guise of a dragon. Powerfully moved by the warning of Erda, given when he was bargaining with the giants, he sought her out, and became, by her, the father of Brünnhilde and her eight sister Walküre. He has learned from her the doom that awaits the gods, and to try and fight against it has commissioned the warrior maidens to bring to Walhalla the heroes who are slain in battle to people his kingdom withal. For had not Alberich threatened to bring all his forces against him? But all his precautions will be vain if Alberich can once more gain possession of the Ring, and to that end the Nibelung ever watches Fafnir's cave. Wotan himself cannot make the attempt because he is bound by his treaty with Fafnir; what he has once given he cannot take back. His only hope is that a hero shall undertake the task voluntarily and of his own free will. To that end has he endeavoured to shape Siegmund's life. He has inured him to hardship; he has kept him from the delights of life in the hope that the lust of power may tempt him to the quest; he has provided him with an invincible sword. But what avail these now that he has been compelled by Fricka to withdraw his protecting ægis from the man whom he had hoped to hail as a deliverer? He rages at the thought of having to abandon him he loves. He prays for the End —the annihilation of the gods.

And that end is in view. Erda has prophesied that it will come when a son is born to Alberich, and Alberich's former riches won him a loveless mate, who

" Die Walküre "

even now bears that son in her womb. Brünnhilde vainly tries to move him, but he sternly bids her remember and respect his vow to Fricka. As she slowly and sorrowfully wends her way up the rocks, Siegmund and Sieglinde enter, and she remains a short while watching them ere she finally disappears. Worn out with fatigue, the unhappy Sieglinde is almost hysterical with fear. She fancies she sees the dogs of the pursuing Hunding rending her beloved Siegmund in pieces, and falls fainting on the ground. While Siegmund tenderly caresses her, Brünnhilde gravely advances, and warns him that in the ensuing combat with Hunding he must die ; he must prepare to follow her to Walhalla. He, finding in answer to his questions that his beloved Sieglinde may not accompany him thither, would plunge his sword into her. Brünnhilde reminds him that in so doing he would destroy two lives, for Sieglinde bears within her the pledge of their love. He refuses to hearken, and is about to plunge the steel into the swooning woman's breast, when Brünnhilde, moved to pity by his distress, resolves to break her promise to her father, and tells Siegmund she will save him. Siegmund, overjoyed, places the sleeping Sieglinde in a sheltered nook, and disappears amidst the thunder-clouds now rapidly form-ing on the mountain-top in search of Hunding, whose defiant challenge is heard drawing nearer. A flash of lightning reveals him fighting with his enemy, while Brünnhilde hovers overhead protecting him with her sword. Suddenly Wotan appears in a blaze of fire. He strikes Siegmund's sword with his spear; it shivers in pieces, and Hunding, taking advantage of the opportunity, runs his adversary through. Darkness falls on the scene as Brünnhilde rushes to the senseless Sieglinde, places her on her horse, and rapidly disappears. Wotan gazes in sorrow on the dead body of his son. With a contemptuous wave of the hand he bids Hunding tell Fricka that her will has been accomplished, and Hunding falls dead at his feet. Disappearing amidst thunder and lightning, the god vows a terrible vengeance on Brünnhilde for her disobedience, and the Act closes.

The scene of the third Act is a bleak mountain-top. Here and there solitary pine trees accentuate the loneliness of the situation. Heavy mists ever and anon roll up from the valleys, and temporarily obscure the distant peaks. Hither arrive the eight Walküre, each carrying the corpse of a dead warrior across her saddle, amidst the strepitous rhythm of the "Ride of the Valkyries." Brünnhilde alone is absent. She, too, presently appears, bearing the senseless Sieglinde. Her sisters eagerly question her, and she relates the story of the combat and her father's anger. She begs them to help her save the unhappy woman she has so far rescued; but they, fearful of the god's terrible anger, refuse. Sieglinde implores Brünnhilde to kill her and end her misery, but the latter comforts her by the assurance that in due time a hero will be borne by her. She must, however, hide herself from Wotan's wrath. Hard by lies a wood wherein dwells Fafnir the guardian of the Ring. Thither

the god will never pursue her; there she will be safe.
Brünnhilde then gives her the pieces of Siegmund's
sword which she has carefully collected. Reunited
they shall form the hero's weapon; Siegfried shall be that
hero's name. Sieglinde in an ecstasy of gratitude pours
forth her grateful thanks to the divine maiden, and
hastens away as the rapidly increasing storm heralds
Wotan's approach.

In all Wagner's works there will probably be found
no finer instance than this of the dramatic use of the
leit motif. The beautiful phrase in which Sieglinde
testifies her gratitude to the noble unselfishness of
Brünnhilde's loving nature does not occur again till the
very end of the tetralogy, when it appears as typical of
the overwhelming love that inspires the divine self-
sacrifice whereby this grand type of womanhood secures
the redemption of the world. No more poetic idea than
this could well be imagined.

To resume our story. Wotan appears. The Walküre
fail to shelter their sister from his piercing gaze. In
vain she pleads that what she has done has been but
what his inmost soul secretly desired. His oath is all
he dares remember. He dare not trust himself to listen
to her. Punishment must follow on her disobedience.
Her divinity will be reft from her; she will become a
spinner of flax, a mere woman. Whatever mortal shall
wake her from the deep sleep into which he is about to
cast her may claim her as his bride. Since she has
allowed herself to be influenced by love, the love of a

mortal shall be her master. Affrighted, the Walküre flee
from the god's terrible anger, and Wotan is left alone
with his daughter. Then ensues a touching scene. The
unhappy Walkür pleads piteously for remission of her
dreadful doom, but her father is obdurate. At last she
begs that, at any rate, he will raise such a barrier round
her that only a hero shall be able to wake her from her
slumber. Deeply touched by his child's undaunted
courage, Wotan consents. In an exquisite page he bids
her a tender farewell. With one long kiss he takes
away her immortality. Then, gently laying her down
on a grassy couch, he closes her helm, covers her with
her shield, and places her spear beside her; and, calling
to his aid Loki, the god of fire, raises round her a
barrier of fire that scintillates and glows in ever-increasing majesty. The curtain slowly closes as he departs
with many a longing look after the noble maiden
whose punishment is forced on him by an inexorable
fate. The web of destiny is slowly but surely closing
round him also.

Wagner commenced "Siegfried" in 1857, but,
laid aside as it was for the composition of "Tristan"
and "Die Meistersinger," it was not completed till
1869.

"Siegfried" is a drama of youth and love to him who
looks casually upon the surface of things. The adventures of the young hero lend colour to this view; but
"Siegfried" is only a part of the gigantic scheme of the
"Ring," and, viewed in this light, its very brightness and

" Siegfried "

buoyancy are freighted with tragic import. The scene
of the first Act is laid in a cavern in the woods, where
Mime has established himself. Mime discovered Sieglinde dying in giving birth to Siegfried, and took the
babe under his care. But the high-spirited youth has
proved a sore trial to him, and as the curtain rises he is
heard lamenting his inability to forge a sword that shall
satisfy his *protégé's* demands. Notwithstanding all his
skill as a smith, Siegfried smashes all the blades he
gives him. Mime laments bitterly his inability to reunite
the fragments of the sword which Sieglinde gave him—
her babe's only heritage. He is now trying to fashion
another weapon, and with little hope of success. He
curses his misfortune, for his desire is that Siegfried may
overcome Fafnir, who, in the shape of a dragon, guards
in a cave hard by the wonder-working Ring. That
accomplished, Mime anticipates for himself power and
riches, for by his craft he will reap the reward of Siegfried's bravery. But he cannot manufacture a sword
which Siegfried cannot break. Whilst he rages at this
fact, and petulantly hammers on his anvil, Siegfried
appears, leading by a rope a bear which he has cap-
tured in the woods. He sets it at Mime, laughing up-
roariously at the miserable dwarf's terror. He releases
it, and it joyously returns to the freedom of the woods.
Then he demands of Mime his new sword. The dwarf
produces it, but with one stroke of Siegfried's brawny
arm, it is shivered in pieces. Siegfried petulantly casts
himself on a couch of skins, and spurns the dwarf's

offers of food. He questions Mime as to his origin ; he cannot believe that he is the offspring of the hideous imp who stands before him, although Mime has always endeavoured to pose as his father. Gradually he extorts from Mime the story of his birth, and learns that the dwarf possesses the fragments of his father's sword. In a rage Siegfried bids him at once reunite them, and, with threats of vengeance if he does not succeed, plunges again into the forest. Mime is left in a state of doleful perplexity. He knows not how to fashion the sword, and he feels his influence on Siegfried rapidly slipping away. Whilst he is occupied with these disquieting thoughts a stranger enters. He is wrapped in a dark cloak, and his large hat partially conceals his features. He declines to reveal his identity, merely stating that he is a Wanderer, and demands rest and shelter. He tells Mime that those who entertain him hospitably may invariably learn from him secrets which they are eager to know, and he offers to pledge his head that the dwarf will be no exception to the rule.

Three questions he will allow him. Mime asks them. "What people dwell in the depths of the earth?" He is answered, the Nibelungs, whom Alberich reduced to submission through the power of the Ring. "What people, then, inhabit the earth?" The race of giants, he is told, of whom Fafnir, in the guise of a dragon, guards the treasure that has been wrested from Alberich. "And who dwell in the cloudy heights?" The gods, of whom their king, Wotan, has conquered the world by

" Siegfried "

the power of his spear on which the sacred runes are
engraved. With these words the stranger smites the
ground with his staff, and a peal of thunder is heard.
Mime then recognizes his visitor as none other than
Wotan, the All-Father himself. He would fain get rid
of him, but the god demands that Mime shall in his turn
answer three questions, his head to be forfeit if he fails.
" What race does Wotan persecute despite his love for
them?" "The Wälsungs," replies Mime. "What
sword is it which, wielded by Siegfried, is to bring death
to the dragon, and make Mime, if his plans succeed, the
master of the world?" Greatly excited, Mime declares
it must be Nothung—the Needful—the weapon that
now lies before him in pieces. "Who, then, is the smith
who will reunite those fragments?" Terror-struck,
Mime cannot answer, and the god tells him that only
he who has never known fear will be able to accomplish
this. His head he has forfeited by his inability to
answer this last question, and Wotan departs, bequeathing
it to the fearless one. Siegfried returns to find Mime
rolling on the ground in abject fright. He sees now
that it is to Siegfried, who has never known fear, that
Wotan has bequeathed his head. He tries to implant
the unknown sensation in the young hero's breast,
telling him that his mother's wish was that he should
not roam forth into the world before he had learned what
fear was. He draws a moving picture of the mysterious horrors of the forest at night, and the quaking
and shuddering at heart it causes him; Siegfried has

never known that feeling. Mime then pictures the horrible dragon in his gruesome cave. The recital only makes Siegfried wishful to meet him face to face, and he calls once more for his sword that he may go forth and do battle with the monster. Mime has to confess his inability to mend it, and Siegfried, snatching the pieces from him, thereupon proceeds to file them to powder. Then, singing the joyous "Song of the Sword," he forges hammers and shapes it, while Mime, who perceives that all his plots will be foiled, gloomily watches him. Suddenly a thought strikes him. Siegfried shall slay the dragon, and then, when he is exhausted after the fight, his faithful Mime will give him a refreshing draught. He will mingle a sleeping potion with it, and, while the youth lies unconscious, he will possess himself of the treasure. With trembling fingers he proceeds to compound the hellish brew. But Siegfried's task nears completion. He fits the blade into the haft, and, with a gleeful shout, splits the anvil in halves with one stroke.

The second Act takes place in the heart of the forest. At the back is the entrance to the cave of the dragon; in the foreground a mighty tree, whose spreading roots form a natural couch. It is night, and the form of Alberich, keeping watch outside the cave, is at first hardly visible. Accompanied by a clap of thunder, the Wanderer arrives. Alberich becomes infuriated. He knows that Siegfried is on his way to attack the dragon, and suspects Wotan of having come to his aid. But the god will take no

part in the fight. He tells Alberich that the only person
from whom he need fear danger is Mime; Mime knows
the secret of the Ring, but Siegfried does not. Wotan
himself will have nothing to do with it. In proof of his
words he calls to the dragon, and tells him that if he
will give the Ring to Alberich his life will be spared and
his treasure also. The dragon hoarsely declines. Let his
antagonist hasten; he is hungry. With mocking laughter
Wotan departs, while Alberich curses the race of the
gods, and swears to slake his vengeance by their exter-
mination. As the day breaks he hides himself amongst
the rocks. Mime then appears with Siegfried and points
out the cave. Siegfried listens impatiently to his
foster-father's twaddling chatter, and bids him begone.
Left to himself, he throws himself at full length beneath
the shade of the huge tree, and indulges in a day-dream
of anticipatory delight in freedom from the trammels of
the hideous dwarf. Tenderly he thinks of his mother,
and wonders what she was like. Poor boy, he has never
known a woman's love.

As he lies thinking, the forest wakes into life 'neath
the caress of the dawning day; the air gradually fills
with the hum of life, until it becomes one pulsating
harmony. Nothing more exquisite exists in music than
this scene. A beautiful bird perches itself above Siegfried's head, its little throat bursting with song. What
can the pretty songster be saying? he wonders. Cutting
a reed he tries to fashion a pipe and answer the bird's
melody, but the sounds he produces are harsh and

discordant. Flinging it away in disgust, he takes his horn and winds a joyous call. The unaccustomed sound wakens the sleeping dragon. He comes forth from his lair, a terrible apparition, breathing fire and venom. Siegfried, so far from showing fear, laughs at and defies him. Drawing his sword he advances; the dragon's wiles are powerless against the young hero, who soon buries Nothung in his heart. With his dying breath the dragon reveals himself to his destroyer in his true light of Fafnir, the keeper of the hoard, the last of the giants, and warns him against treachery from Mime. Siegfried then withdraws his sword from the dragon's body. In so doing the fiery blood gushes over his fingers. Instinctively he thrusts them into his mouth.

What miracle is this? He seems to understand the song of the birds. His little favourite sings to him again, and now he learns that within the cave he will find the magic Ring and Helmet. He plunges into the gloomy recess. Mime now issues from his hiding-place and, seeing the monster dead, is about to enter the cave, but finds his way barred by Alberich. A bitter wrangle ensues as to who shall possess the spoil, but it is interrupted by the appearance of Siegfried, who now has the Tarnhelm slung from his girdle, and wears the Ring on his finger. Again the voice of the bird is heard, this time warning him, as did the dragon, against the falseness of his pretended friend Mime. The crafty dwarf now proffers a draught to Siegfried, accompanying his action with what he believes to be fair words. But in the new understanding that Siegfried has acquired through tasting the dragon's blood, they stand out in all their black treachery, and he divines that the cup is poisoned, that Mime desires the Ring and the Tarnhelm for himself and would steal them from him as he lies still in death. Utterly disgusted, Siegfried slays the perfidious imp, and rolls his body, along with the dragon's, into the cave to silently guard Fafnir's ill-gotten hoard. Exhausted, the youth again flings himself down in the friendly shade of the tree. The music of the forest recommences with added beauty, and the bird tells Siegfried the story of Brünnhilde sleeping amidst the protecting fire. Only he who knows not fear will be able to rescue her. Overjoyed, he springs to his feet. He it must be who is destined to rescue the maiden. In a frenzy of excitement he bids the bird lead him to the enchanted rock, and rushes forth to his new quest as the curtain closes.

A wild rocky gorge veiled in semi-obscurity confronts us as the scene of the first part of the last Act. Hither comes Wotan to consult with Erda, the fount of wisdom, regarding the future. She slowly appears in a cleft of the rocks in response to his summons, but her wisdom forsakes her when she wakes from her eternal sleep, and she is powerless to answer his questions. She bids him ask her daughters the Norns, who spin the thread of destiny. If not them, why not question her and Wotan's own daughter, the far-seeing Brünnhilde? That, he says, is impossible, since he has doomed her to eternal sleep and taken her divinity from her. Erda is troubled; she is unwilling to help one so changeable, who perjures himself to keep his oaths. She begs him to let her return to her long sleep. Wotan, perceiving that all hope of averting destiny is at an end, consents. He foresees in Siegfried the one who will conquer Alberich, and win the power of the universe; in Brünnhilde, who will be awakened by this hero, he foresees the saviour of the world. Let, then, the doom of the gods come quickly, since only by that means can deliverance from the curse of the gold be won. As Erda vanishes, he remains in silent contemplation. The day begins to break. The bird comes flying upon the scene, but, frightened by Wotan's two ravens, disappears. Siegfried following is confronted by Wotan, and relates the events that have happened. Now he is endeavouring to reach the rock where a beauteous maiden lies sleeping. Wotan makes one more effort to avert the doom which the meeting will render inevitable, and stretches forth his spear to bar the way. But it splinters into fragments before the stroke of Nothung. The stage is filled with fire, and, blowing a merry blast on his horn, Siegfried plunges into it and becomes lost to sight. The hissing and roar of the flames are marvellously depicted as the sound of the horn becomes fainter and fainter in the distance.

The scene now changes to the rock on which Brünnhilde lies sleeping. Siegfried enters, but, instead of the

" Siegfried "

maiden he expected to find, discovers a war-horse and what seems to be a sleeping warrior. He raises the shield, and cuts away the cuirass to give the sleeper more air. With a start of surprise he then perceives that it is no warrior, but a beautiful woman dressed in a long white robe. A new emotion steals over his senses. Can it be that at last he knows fear? At any cost he must waken the sleeper. He imprints a long kiss on her lips; gradually the heavy eyes open, and Brünnhilde once more looks upon the glorious sun, which she hails in ecstasy. Her gaze then lights upon Siegfried, and she knows it is he who has waked her from her long oblivion. She eagerly asks his name. Siegfried? Then it is he who even before his birth she watched over. Siegfried, misled by these words, imagines he has met with his mother; but Brünnhilde smilingly tells him that her meaning is that she saved his mother from Wotan's pursuing rage. As the remembrance of her lost immortality floods over her memory, she shrinks terrified from Siegfried's caresses. She now recognizes that her godlike attributes have vanished for ever, and that she has become a mere woman. But in vain are her struggles. Love overmasters her. Let the gods perish; she has found her destiny in Siegfried's love, and in an impassioned duet the lovers plight their vows of eternal affection.

"Die Götterdämmerung" (The Twilight of the Gods) was commenced in 1870 and finished at the end of 1874, and consists of three Acts and a Prologue.

Wagner

The scene is still Brünnhilde's rock, but it is now quite dark save for the fitful glimmer of the guardian fire in the distance. The three Norns, the prophetess daughters of Erda, sit spinning the golden cord of destiny, tossing the thread from one to the other as they utter their rede. The first recalls the days when Wotan came to the World-Ash tree to drink of the fountain of wisdom which flowed at its foot. He paid the penalty inexorably exacted, the loss of one of his eyes, and, when he departed, he stripped a mighty branch from the tree to fashion himself a spear. Thereafter the tree died and the fountain became dry. The second relates that, when the spear was shattered by the young Siegfried, Wotan gathered his warriors around him and cut down the world-ash. What happened then ? The third says that, splintering it into faggots, they erected a pyre around Walhalla, and there sits now the god in gloomy silence awaiting the end, when the wood shall take fire and destroy the fateful palace. As they question when that end will be, the cord snaps ; their power of prophecy is gone, and, tying themselves together with the broken thread, they sink into the earth to join their mother in unending sleep. As the darkness gives way to day, Siegfried and Brünnhilde approach. She has taught Siegfried much of her divine wisdom, and now urges him forth to do the work of a hero in the world. All she asks in return is his constancy and love. This he swears, and gives her the Ring as a pledge of his affection. She, in return, gives him her steed Grani, and he sets forth in search of adventure. As he departs the orchestra commences a long interlude, in which themes peculiarly connected with Siegfried gradually give place to those representative of the Rhine; and when the curtain, which closes soon after his exit, again opens upon the first Act proper, the great hall of the castle of the Gibichungs is disclosed, a view of the mighty river being obtainable through the openings at the back. Seated at a table are Gunther, Gutrune, and Hagen.

The first-named is the chief of the Gibichung tribe; Gutrune is his sister; while Hagen is his half-brother, his mother being the same as Gunther's, but his father none other than the dwarf Alberich. In Hagen all Alberich's hopes of regaining his lost power are centred, and the dark-hearted villain has hatched an evil plot to obtain his ends. He pretends that it grieves him to see his relatives both unwedded. Gunther should be united to Brünnhilde. Hagen knows that Siegfried is approaching, and suggests the following scheme. Under pretence of friendship they will give him a love-potion. He will then become so enamoured of Gutrune that he will forget the past, and all that Gunther will have to do will be to make a condition that before Siegfried can wed Gutrune he must first pass through the fire and win Brünnhilde for Gunther's bride. The conspirators hail the plot with delight. Almost immediately Siegfried's horn is heard in the distance, and the hero, with Grani, are soon observed approaching down the river in a boat. Siegfried, having landed, declares that he has heard of the fame of Gunther, and offers him his choice between battle and friendship. Gunther accepts the latter alternative. The stranger is led on to talk of his adventures, and Hagen questions him as to what has become of the Nibelung's treasure. Siegfried contemptuously replies that he left it in the cave; he has no use for such things. But he did bring away a helmet and a ring? The former he wears at his side, the latter he has given to the woman he loves; he takes little interest in Hagen's recital of the magic attributes of the Tarnhelm. Gutrune then enters in response to Hagen's summons, and offers a drinking-horn to the guest. As he gazes at her he thinks of Brünnhilde, and vows to be true to the woman he has left on the fire-girt rock.

But the potion begins its fell work. Gradually the past becomes blotted from his memory, and an over-mastering passion for Gutrune seizes him. Gunther then unfolds his dastardly plot. Siegfried enthusiastically gives promise of help. With the aid of the magic helm he will assume the shape of Gunther and win Brünnhilde for him. The two men pledge each other from the same cup, in which they mingle drops of their own blood, and, having sworn a bond of eternal brotherhood, forthwith enter the boat and set sail. Hagen, who is left in charge of the castle, gloats over the irony of fate which has placed these tools in his hands. The scene changes to Brünnhilde's rock. She sits silent and thoughtful, gazing at Siegfried's ring. Presently a

"Die Götterdämmerung"

familiar sound strikes upon her ear; it is the gallop of one of her sisters' horses. Perhaps her father has forgiven her. She greets Waltraute, who hurriedly enters, in feverish anticipation. But Waltraute has no such reassuring message to bring; she has come in defiance even of the god's commands. She recounts to Brünnhilde the preparations he has made for the end which the Norns have already made us acquainted with. Silent and moody he sits, and in answer to Waltraute's caresses, has only uttered the enigmatic prophecy that if Brünnhilde would only surrender the Ring to the Rhine-maidens, its curse would be lifted from the gods and the world. But Brünnhilde remains deaf to her sister's entreaties to cast the foul thing into the flood. The Ring is the symbol of her Siegfried's love, and only to him would she resign it. Waltraute sorrowfully departs, and night slowly falls. Suddenly the sound of a horn is heard, and a man emerges from the flames. It is Siegfried, but in the guise of Gunther. The terrified Brünnhilde tries to fly. He seizes her, and she madly struggles to regain her liberty. She shrieks to Wotan for assistance; is this a further part of her punishment? Her cries are unanswered; her captor tears the Ring from her finger, and, her strength reft with it, she can resist no longer. She obeys the command to go into the grotto, and the disguised Siegfried, calling his sword to witness that he will be true to his new friend Gunther, follows her, and the curtain closes.

The second Act brings us back to the home of the

Wagner

Gibichungs, but the scene is now transferred to the river bank outside their palace which rises on one side of the stage. It is dark, but the moonbeams fall on the figure of Hagen, who, fully armed, sits at the foot of a pillar seemingly in a trance. At his feet kneels Alberich, gazing steadfastly into his son's face. With urgent insistence he beseeches him to obtain possession of the Ring ere Siegfried, who either knows not its power, or despises it, and therefore is exempt from its curse, can through Brünnhilde's influence be induced to restore it to its rightful owners. Hagen dreamily gives the required promise, and the gnome slinks away. Siegfried, transported back by the magic power of the helm, now appears in his own guise, and is joyfully greeted by Gutrune, to whom he announces the speedy arrival of Gunther with the bride he has won for him. The grim Hagen now summons the vassals and bids them prepare for feasting in honour of the approaching bridals, not forgetting appropriate sacrifices to the gods. The warriors, in savage chorus, vow to protect their coming queen, and amidst general rejoicing the boat bearing Gunther and Brünnhilde comes into sight. The unfortunate woman, when she sees Siegfried, is struck dumb with astonishment and indignation. Nearly fainting with emotion, she perceives the Ring on his finger, and fiercely demands an explanation of its coming into his possession since it was taken from her by Gunther. Encouraged by the crafty Hagen, she denounces Siegfried as a traitor, and declares that he, and not Gunther, is her lawful husband. A

"Die Götterdämmerung"

scene of intense excitement follows. Siegfried, still under the influence of the magic draught, is bewildered. But seizing Hagen's spear, he swears, under penalty of death by that self-same weapon, that her story is false. Brünnhilde, beside herself with grief, seizes the spear, and, as Siegfried departs into the castle with Gutrune, calls down the vengeance of heaven upon his perjured head. Hagen then proffers his aid in wreaking her vengeance, but she scornfully derides him. How could he vanquish the hero whom she herself has rendered invulnerable? There is only one chance to inflict a fatal blow. Knowing that Siegfried would never turn his back on a foe, she has left that spot unprotected. Hagen then draws Gunther on one side, confides to him his plot to murder Siegfried, and tries to wave aside his scruples with hints of the power that the Ring will bring him. Gunther hesitates, swayed by repugnance at the thought of betraying one to whom he has sworn the bond of brotherhood, and fear of Gutrune's grief. At the sound of Gutrune's name Brünnhilde's fury bursts out afresh, and she join her entreaties to those of the hateful Hagen. Gunther at last consents to lend his aid. It is resolved to carry out the vile deed while on a hunting expedition, and then to tell Gutrune that her Siegfried has been killed by a wild boar. Siegfried and Gutrune with their attendants then enter in nuptial attire and form a procession towards the palace; Gunther takes Brünnhilde's hand and joins it, while the vassals depart up the mountain paths to sacrifice to the gods and deck their altars with flowers, leaving Hagen triumphantly anticipating the successful issue of his plot.

The scene of the first portion of the concluding Act of the tragedy is a beautiful landscape on the banks of the Rhine, in whose limpid waters the three Rhine-maidens are disporting themselves. Sorrowfully they lament the loss of their beloved Rhine-gold and wish that its possessor would restore it to them. As if in answer to their prayer, the sound of Siegfried's horn is heard, and the hero, who has become separated from his companions in the pursuit of a bear, appears. The nixies try to wheedle him into giving up the Ring, and he is almost tempted into parting with that to which he attaches no value, when they change their tone and warn him of the power and also the curse which attach to it. If he persists in his resolve to keep it he will meet with death that very day. But he laughs at their threats; fear is powerless to influence him. Gunther, Hagen, and their followers then rejoin their companion, and the elves vanish. The midday meal is spread, and Hagen presses Siegfried to tell them of the days when it was said he could understand the language of the birds. Siegfried, however, retorts that he now prefers the words of a woman to those of birds, and has forgotten the old days. At last, nevertheless, he consents and relates his history up to the time when he slew the dragon and learned the message of his feathered friend. At this point Hagen cunningly mingles with his drink an antidote to the philtre of oblivion, and as his memory gradually returns the hero triumphantly narrates

" Die Götterdämmerung "

his conquest of Brünnhilde and pays ecstatic tribute to her glorious love. A light seems to break in upon Gunther's understanding. At this instant two ravens fly out from a thicket and circle round Siegfried's head, and, as he turns to look at them, the cowardly Hagen thrusts his spear into his back, and the great-hearted hero dies, uttering with his last breath the name of her he so fondly loved and so innocently wronged. Gunther is overwhelmed with horror at the cruel deed, and the body is taken reverently up and placed upon a litter of boughs. Sorrowfully the men lift up the corpse, and bear it slowly up the rocky heights amidst the sounds of funeral music, which for solemnity and sweet sadness knows no equal in the realms of sound. The one who can witness this scene unmoved must be callous indeed. As the mournful procession recedes from sight, a thick mist comes down and envelops the scene. When it rises, the interior of Gunther's castle is again disclosed, but it is now enveloped in darkness except at the back where the waters of the Rhine shine silver in the moonlight. Gutrune emerges filled with vague forebodings of disaster, and the voice of Hagen sets her shuddering. "Where is Siegfried?" she asks. Hagen evades the question and tells her to prepare for his return, but at last brutally tells her he is dead, slain by a boar in the forest.

The funeral procession enters, and servants bearing torches press around. The body is placed in the centre of the hall, and Gutrune falls fainting upon it. Recovering herself, she accuses Gunther of murdering her beloved, and he then in holy anger reveals Hagen as the author of the accursed wrong, and calls down the vengeance of Heaven upon his head. The villain, unabashed, advances and admits his deed, and claims the Ring as his by right of conquest. Gunther forbids him to touch it, whereupon Hagen slays him also, and turning to the corpse endeavours to wrench the glittering circlet from its finger. But the dead man's clenched hand lifts itself menacingly, and the women shriek at the awful sight. Then the wronged Brünnhilde solemnly enters and stills the tumult. Gently silencing the unhappy Gutrune, she proclaims herself as Siegfried's true wife; and Gutrune, now realizing the part that Hagen has made her play with the love-philtre, heaps bitter curses upon his head and falls swooning upon her brother's body. Hagen stands gloomily and defiantly apart. Gazing lovingly upon the valiant dead, Brünnhilde orders the vassals to prepare a funeral pyre on the river's bank, and sends for her steed Grani, who shall share in the honours to be paid to the noble hero. She now understands everything; she sees that through her it is that Wotan's sin must be expiated— but at what frightful cost to herself! Still, cost what it may, she will make the sacrifice, and as she sees the god's ravens circling overhead she bids them fly to him and announce the fulfilment of destiny—" Rest thee, thou god !" Meanwhile the pyre has been built and the body of the murdered hero placed upon it, but not before she has lovingly removed the Ring and placed it upon

" Die Götterdämmerung "

her own finger. Amidst her ashes the Rhine-maidens shall find their own again. Then, approaching the pyre, and seizing a torch, she bids the ravens fly back to Wotan with her message, and tell Loki, who still guards the rock where she slept, to betake himself to Walhalla, and there accomplish his mission; for the Twilight of the Gods is at hand. The pyre kindles from the brand she casts into it. Turning once more to the awe-struck assemblage, she gives them her last message. The race of the gods may die, but Love will remain triumphant to the end. Then, springing upon her noble steed, with one bound she plunges into the flames. The pyre flares into a mighty conflagration, and then dies down, leaving a heavy cloud of smoke hanging over it like a pall. As this clears away the Rhine is seen to be rising, with the Rhine-maidens swimming on the top of the cresting waves. With a desperate cry Hagen flings himself into the advancing flood in one last effort to gain the object of his greed, but he is dragged down and engulfed as Flosshilde appears holding aloft the Ring, regained at last. A great glow appears in the sky, and, as the curtain closes, Walhalla is seen engulfed, as it were, in an ocean of fire; while there seems to float over earth from the topmost heights of the ether the magic beauty of the *motif* of Brünnhilde's sacrifice—" the redemption of the world by Love."

The gradual disappearance of Wotan from the action of this tremendous drama is one of its most striking features. And yet, when we come to closely examine the work, the dramatic necessity for this disappearance becomes convincing. The tragedy arises from Wotan's fatal greed. In his desire for power he stoops to a mean theft, and thereby incurs the curse attaching to the gold which Alberich has stolen. But, whereas Alberich, in his lust of dominion, was willing to pay the price for its acquisition—the renunciation of Love—Wotan would fain hold the one without resigning the other. But he is ever confronted with the baleful curse. He is compelled to abandon Siegmund, whom he regarded as his chosen instrument to free him from the bane, and with his death he has perforce to abandon the hope of ever actively influencing the course of the events on which his own destiny hangs. Siegfried must fight his battle himself, and when the god's spear is shattered by the fearless one's unconquerable sword—the weapon which he himself has designed for his own protection— he recognizes that his power is broken. There is nothing more left for him but the End—the destruction of the race of the gods—the negation of the will to live. And the pathos of the "Götterdämmerung" is marvellously accentuated by the mental vision of the silent brooding figure, the origin of this world-tragedy, sitting in lonely silence awaiting the final catastrophe; although invisible, Wotan pervades the whole of the concluding portion of the drama. Against this lurid background the figures of Siegfried and Brünnhilde stand out in sharp relief. He is the incarnation of free, untrammelled Manhood; she the type of true, unselfish Love. Both are the victims

" Die Götterdämmerung "

of fate ; but while Siegfried's tragedy is brought about solely through his connection with Wotan, Brünnhilde's character and fate are rendered infinitely more touching by her connection with both sources of disaster. Wotan's child and Siegfried's lover, her final act of renunciation becomes the culminating point of the great myth as Wagner presents it, and embodies the whole philosophy of life.

The music provides no less striking an example of evolution from one central idea. From the first simple phrase which conveys the notion of the primitive element in which the gold, the fount of evil, reposes, there proceeds an infinitude of *motifs*, all distinct and yet all connected. Note how the phrase associated with the Ring itself is a species of minor variation of the *motif* of the Walhalla which it has purchased. And this is only one instance out of many. Wagner's system of orchestration, also, is nowhere better illustrated than in this marvellous score. By completing and at times supplementing the various families of the orchestra as he found it, he obtained effects which even the greatest modern composers have not succeeded in surpassing. The six harps used in the third Act of the " Götterdämmerung " produce an aural impression attainable by no other means ; and instances of his employment of additional brass and wood wind-instruments for the production, not of extra noise, but of specific tone-colour, might be multiplied *ad infinitum*. The metamorphosis of themes, too, is very conspicuous. To take only one

Wagner

instance, and that one of the most familiar, namely the occurrence in the Funeral March in " Die Götterdämmerung " of Siegfried's well-known horn-call, in the minor. Associated as it is with the funeral pageant of the murdered hero, it appeals to the feeling with results such as oceans of rhetoric would fail to produce.   And, as in
the poem the action all seems to converge in the pure
soul of Brünnhilde when the drama draws to its
conclusion, so the music draws together
the threads of the emotion it so elo-
quently expresses, and, after the
turmoil of lust and hate,
subsides into the calm
regions of tran-
quillity and
peace.

"WAHNFRIED."

CHAPTER XV

" PARSIFAL " was commenced in 1877, and finished in 1882. It was first performed at Bayreuth on the 26th July, 1882. For cast, see Appendix E.

The reader's time will be saved if a portion of the events prior to the commencement of the action, which are related in narrative form during the drama, are dealt with before an analysis of the plot is attempted. In the remote hills of Spain was situated the Castle of Monsalvat, the abode of the Knights of the Grail. It was built by Titurel, the first king of the order, and the knights' holy mission is to guard the Grail, which is the sacred cup with which the Saviour celebrated the Last Supper, and which afterwards received His life-blood when His side was pierced as He hung on the Cross. The Grail possesses the miraculous power of giving new life and strength to those who gaze upon it, and every year a white dove descends from celestial regions and renews its life-giving properties.

Hard by the castle is the abode of a pagan knight, Klingsor by name. He once aspired to belong to the number of the Grail's guardians, but was rejected on account of his impure heart. Self-mutilation failed to

233

attain his object, and in revenge he summoned round him a bevy of beautiful daughters of evil, and by their instrumentality wrought the ruin of many a noble knight. Foremost amongst his miserable tools is Kundry. She, in a former state of existence, was none other than Herodias, who laughed at the sufferings of Christ, and for her sin has been doomed to the curse of harsh, baleful laughter, and to wander over the earth until she can find one to redeem her by his love. In ordinary guise she is a wild object, but under the spell of Klingsor she becomes a woman of devilish beauty. In course of time Titurel became too old and feeble to reign longer, and resigned his crown to his son Amfortas. The latter, with pious zeal, visited the enchanted palace to rescue his miserable companions enslaved therein. But he, too, fell a victim to the wiles of the arch-temptress, and worse misfortune overtook him. For Klingsor, snatching away the sacred spear, which had pierced the Saviour, from the infatuated king, wounded him grievously in the side. The wound refuses to heal, and whenever Amfortas has to exercise his kingly office and unveil the holy vessel, his tortures are renewed. Kindly death is denied him.

The prelude to the drama itself consists almost entirely of a mere statement of the principal themes which occur in the work, but they are so imbued with sacred mysticism as to hold the hearer almost spell-bound. The curtain parts on a glade in the woods that surround Montsalvat, at the back being a lake. Gurnemanz, an old and faithful knight of the Grail, with two young esquires, is discovered sleeping under a tree. Distant trumpets are heard from the castle as the day breaks, and the three, awaking, kneel in silent prayer. Gurnemanz bids the young men prepare the bath in the waters of the sacred lake which brings Amfortas temporary relief from his anguish, and inquires from two knights who come down from the castle if there is any improvement in the king's condition. The negative answer he receives, although it grieves, does not surprise him. Kundry is then perceived approaching. When she is not under the magic influence of Klingsor, she devotes her life to trying to atone for some of the evil she is forced by the magician's baleful mesmerism to work. She has now returned from the uttermost parts of Arabia, bringing a balm which she hopes may alleviate the sufferings of Amfortas, and, after giving the phial to Gurnemanz, sinks exhausted on the ground. The king is now borne in on his litter on his way to the sacred lake. He prays for death, or else that the " pure fool " may come and end his sufferings—for while bent in fervent prayer one day before the holy vessel, a message came from Heaven that he would obtain relief when "the pure fool, by pity enlightened" should come to his aid. Gurnemanz gives him Kundry's balsam, but she takes little notice of his thanks.

When the procession has departed on its way to the lake, the esquires bitterly reproach the wild-looking woman with endeavouring to harm their king with

hurtful drugs; but Gurnemanz reminds them of the zeal
with which she has tried to do good service to the knights.
She was found by Titurel in the woods asleep when he
selected the spot as the site for the castle, and is always
found there after her long absences. Still the fact remains
that those absences have invariably coincided with the
happening of evil to the knights. It was so when Amfortas was wounded; why was she not then at hand to
aid him? She is silent, and then Gurnemanz explains
to the listening esquires the history of the king's misfortune, which he supplements by recounting at length
the history of the Grail, and the promise of help from
the "pure fool" so miraculously given. At this instant
the whiz of an arrow is heard, and a swan falls to the
ground in dying agonies. Parsifal, for he is the author
of the cruel deed, is brought to Gurnemanz. He is a
youth who seems more proud of his prowess in archery
than conscious of having committed an act of wanton
cruelty; but beneath Gurnemanz' grave rebuke a change
comes over him, and he snaps his bow in pieces. Questioned who he is, he is unable to answer; all he remembers
is that his mother's name was Herzeleide (Broken Heart).
But Kundry can supplement this; his father Gamuret
was slain in battle, and his mother, to keep him from a
like fate, has brought him up in wild fastnesses far from
the haunts of men.

Parsifal then relates that one day, attracted by the
glitter of their arms, he followed some mounted warriors
and lost his way. Since then he has been a wanderer,

" Parsifal "

and obliged to defend himself against both men and
beasts. Kundry then tells him of the death of his
mother. Parsifal would strangle the bearer of these ill
tidings, but is prevented by Gurnemanz, and Kundry
shows her forgiveness by bringing water and reviving
the strange boy, in whom revulsion of feeling has well-
nigh brought on a fit. Kundry now feels the magic
spell of Klingsor coming over her. A hideous drowsiness
which she knows only too well seizes on her brain. Her
efforts to shake it off are fruitless, and she succumbs,
dragging herself into the neighbouring thicket. The returning litter of Amfortas is now seen. A thought has
struck Gurnemanz. Perchance this youth is the " pure
fool " of the prophecy. He resolves to take him to the
castle, and let him witness the sufferings of Amfortas as
he celebrates the mystic function of the Grail. Supporting
the youth's faltering steps, he sets out towards the castle.

The scene panoramically changes as they proceed,
while the sound of great bells and trumpets seems to draw
nearer and nearer. At last they enter a door, and,
proceeding through underground passages, eventually
arrive in a large hall to which light is admitted only
through the high domed roof. In stately procession the
knights enter and take their places at two long tables.
Amfortas is also brought in on his litter, which is set
down near the shrine whereon the holy vessel is placed.
The wretched man's torment increases. In vain he
pleads that his terrible trial may be spared him. The
voice of the aged Titurel is heard from the darkness of

the adjoining chapel solemnly adjuring him to fulfil his mission. Amfortas, with a supreme effort, bows his head in fervent prayer : a thick cloud descends, and through it a ray of heavenly light falls upon the sacred cup which glows with a purple light. With transfigured mien the suffering king elevates the glowing Grail, before which all present humbly kneel, and when the darkness has cleared away, the cups on the long tables are seen to be filled with wine and a piece of bread lies by each. The knights then solemnly celebrate the mystic supper, and Amfortas, whose sufferings have now returned with redoubled anguish, is borne away half fainting. Parsifal during this scene has remained motionless, as if transfixed. He ignores the invitation of Gurnemanz to sit beside him ; and seems perfectly untouched by the moving events he has witnessed. The knights then slowly quit the hall, and, as the voices of the choir of boys peal down from the topmost heights of the dome, Gurnemanz roughly shakes Parsifal out of his reverie, and bids him begone as one unworthy to share in the holy mysteries.

The second Act opens in a roofless tower in the magician Klingsor's palace. The instruments of magic are scattered about, and deep gloom pervades the scene. Klingsor has recognized in Parsifal the being who is destined to fulfil the prophecy, and determined to employ his arts to the full to accomplish the youth's ruin. He kindles a magic fire, and in response to his incantations Kundry, whom he destines as the means for Parsifal's destruction, appears enveloped in a sort of violet light.

" Parsifal "

The sorcerer mocks at her devotion to the cause of the Knights of the Grail, and reminds her that beneath his spell she has been their arch-temptress. In vain the wretched woman tries to rebel against his hateful spells. Her agony is intensified when she learns that Parsifal is destined to be her next victim. But resistance is useless; she *must* obey. Parsifal has now been attracted to the castle by Klingsor's magic acts, and puts to flight the knights there held in thrall who rush at him. The tower sinks into the earth and in its place appears a beautiful garden of flowers, to which the enchanted castle forms a background. Parsifal, who appears on the castle wall, beholds the scene unfolded before him in wonder. Groups of beautiful maidens assail with alluring glances the young hero. They exercise all the fascinating enticements at their command; they deck themselves with flowers till they become like living flowers themselves; but to no purpose. Parsifal's first innocent amusement at their gambols gives way to feelings of repulsion. Suddenly a voice is heard softly calling his name. He thinks it is his mother's voice. The flower maidens reluctantly leave him, and turning he sees a wondrously beautiful woman half hidden in a bed of flowers. It is Kundry, thus equipped by the sorcerer for her errand of destruction. The snare is cunningly laid. She works on his emotions by telling him of his mother, her love for him, her sad and untimely death. Then she hints that only by love can the remorse which has sprung up in his heart be quenched. She draws him to her and imprints a long burning kiss on his lips. Horror-struck he recoils. A pain seizes his heart. And then the memory of the suffering Amfortas rushes over him like a flood—the self-reproach of the unhappy king, his piteous appeals for mercy.

In vain the temptress tries another wile. She tells him of the curse that hangs over her as a punishment for her impious gibes at the suffering Saviour; if only Parsifal will give her his love he may enable her to obtain redemption. But he remains firm. He now perceives that his mission is to help the king; Kundry must work out her own redemption by aiding him in his mission and showing him the mysterious passages which lead to the abode of Amfortas. She breaks into harsh laughter at this, and tells him that only by yielding to her love will he gain what he desires, otherwise the fate of Amfortas will be his and by the same holy Spear. Her renewed caresses meet with no further success, and she then bitterly curses him, vowing that he shall never reach Montsalvat. Klingsor, who is attracted by the sound of Kundry's angry exclamations, rushes in and hurls the lance at Parsifal. But it remains suspended in the air above the pure youth's head, and, taking it in his hand, he makes the sign of the cross. Instantly the castle falls in ruins; the flowers lie in withered heaps, and the flower maidens share the same fate. And, as Parsifal mounts the wall to depart, he turns to Kundry, who lies swooning on the ground, and reminds her that she knows where alone their next meeting can be.

" Parsifal "

The third Act opens in a beautiful flowery mead adjoining Montsalvat, but on the other side to that to which the first Act introduced the spectator. A rude hut, now the dwelling-place of the aged Gurnemanz, stands on one side 'neath the shelter of a rock. The old knight, who has heard low moaning sounds, comes out to ascertain their cause. He finds they emanate from Kundry, who, again in the guise of " wild woman," lies seemingly half dead in the neighbouring undergrowth. He reanimates her, and she at once begins occupying herself with a servant's duties, scarcely vouchsafing him a word of thanks for his care. But the service she offers is not needed now; the castle is wrapped in gloom, and no one goes out or comes in. A knight dressed in black armour, his vizor down, is now seen drawing near with weary steps. Exhausted, he sits down to rest. Gurnemanz approaches him and tells him that it is an unseemly thing to appear armed in such a place, on such a day. For he is within the holy grounds of Montsalvat and it is Good Friday. The knight replies that his error has been made in ignorance, and, doffing his casque, sword, and buckler, kneels long in silent prayer. The two watchers then perceive that Parsifal has come back to them, and that he carries the holy Spear. Parsifal now tells them of the sufferings he has undergone, his privations, and his desperate conflicts in his endeavour to reach Montsalvat once more; but through all he has kept the sacred Lance from profanation. Gurnemanz in return tells him of the sad history of the castle. Amfortas, hoping for death, now refuses to celebrate the mysteries of the Grail, and the knights grow faint from lack of its support; while the aged Titurel has already succumbed, the victim of his son's selfishness. On hearing this, Parsifal reproaches himself with not having succeeded earlier in his quest, and well-nigh faints with emotion. He is revived by the water which Kundry brings, and then the three proceed to the side of the lake. Here Kundry bathes the wanderer's feet, and he learns from Gurnemanz that Amfortas has consented to once more perform the sacred rites that very day. Still, both he and Gurnemanz feel that from henceforth another than Amfortas must guard the Grail's mysteries, and that Parsifal himself is the one appointed for the task. Gurnemanz thereupon solemnly baptizes Parsifal and anoints him king and priest of the Grail, pouring oil upon his head from the golden vial which Kundry gives him. Parsifal in turn baptizes the kneeling woman, who hails her pardon with silent tears of joy, and amidst the heavenly strains of the "Charfreitagszauber" (Good Friday Spell) Gurnemanz tells Parsifal the reason why the Day of Atonement is held in such reverence in that holy place—it is the symbol of new life through the Redeemer. He then clothes his new king with the armour and cloak of the knights, and they set out for the castle. Another panoramic change gradually takes place, and again the great hall is reached. Two processions enter, the one bearing the litter of Amfortas, the other the bier of Titurel. As they advance they chant the sorrows that the cowardice of Amfortas has caused. The wretched king shrinks in terror from his task. The celebration of the mystery only brings him new life and new torture. Tearing the bandages from his frightful wound, he implores the knights to plunge their weapons therein and end his awful torment. Parsifal, hitherto unobserved, then approaches, and touching the wound with the sacred Lance, brings the long desired relief and healing, the spear-point meanwhile glowing with sacred light. Then, announcing himself as the chosen priest of the holy vessel, he takes it, again glowing with heavenly radiance, in his hands, and makes the sign of the cross. Even the dead Titurel momentarily comes under its reviving influence, and blesses the assembly, while the white dove descends and hovers over the head of him whose purity and pity have wrought the wondrous miracle. Kundry sinks at Parsifal's feet; Amfortas and Gurnemanz kneel in homage before him; and the air is filled with a subdued adoring chant of thanksgiving.

Such was the crown of Richard Wagner's work. As the " Ring " is the embodiment of human Love, so is " Parsifal " the expression of the Love Divine. "Parsifal," in truth, is not a drama—it is a religious ceremony. It is one of those works from which the cold lance of criticism glances without piercing. That it came at the end of Wagner's life was, in some measure, an accident; the idea occurred to him when he abandoned his sketch of " Jesus von Nazareth." But it is probably safe to say that it owes its perfection of truth and fervour to the fact that it came as the climax to his work. Beautiful as are his earlier conceptions, they pale before the supreme grandeur of the central idea of " Parsifal," and we may be well content to let this sublime drama speak for itself, without attempting to pry into the mysteries of the skeleton which is hidden by its outward living loveliness.

The only critical remark that is at all called for is the one necessary to refute the erroneous statement, which is occasionally even still made, that Wagner in his age saw the wrongheadedness of his earlier ideas, and therefore introduced choruses into " Parsifal." The slightest examination of the poem ought to be sufficient to prove that these choruses are the outcome of *dramatic*, and not musical, necessity. The so-called criticism carries its own refutation ; for it surely must be obvious that if a representative body of persons sharing the same emotion (as is undoubtedly the case here) are to express that emotion at all, they must do so collectively. " Parsifal " cannot be dissected in this manner. It is more seemly to regard it as the last message to his fellow-creatures of a man who laboured with all his strength to propagate the noble truth—Love is of God. As such let us honour both it and its author.

APPENDICES

APPENDIX A

CHRONOLOGICAL LIST OF WAGNER'S COMPOSITIONS

COMPOSITION.	INSTRUMENTS, ETC.	COMPOSED.
Sonata, Quartet, and Aria		1829
Overture in B flat	Orchestra	1830
Arrangement of Beethoven's 9th Symphony	Pianoforte	1830
Sonata in B flat	Pianoforte	1831
Polonaise in D major	Pianoforte (4 hands)	1831
Overture in D minor	Orchestra	1831
Concert Overture and Fugue in C major	Orchestra	1831
" *Die Hochzeit*," portion of an opera (Introduction, chorus, and septet)	Orchestra etc.	1831
Fantasie in F sharp minor	Pianoforte	1831
Symphony in C	Orchestra	1832

Wagner

COMPOSITION.	INSTRUMENTS, ETC.	COMPOSED.
Seven compositions for Goethe's "Faust"— (1) Soldier's Song (2) Peasants under the lime tree (3) Brander's Song (4) Song of Mephistopheles ("Es war einmal") (5) Song of Mephistopheles ("Was mach'st du mir") (6) Gretchen's Song ("Meine Ruh ist hin") (7) Gretchen's Melodrama ("Ach neige du Schmerzensreiche")	Voice, etc.	1832
Overture to the tragedy "*King Enzio*"	Orchestra	1832
"*Die Feen*," Romantische Opfer (in 3 acts)	Orchestra, etc.	1833
Allegro in F minor (zu der Arie in dem Vampyr von Marschner)	Voice and Orchestra	1833
Symphony in E (unfinished)	Orchestra	1834
Festspiel für den Neujahrstag, 1835 (New Year's Cantata)	Orchestra, Chorus, etc.	1835
"*Columbus*," Overture	Orchestra	1835
"*Das Liebesverbot*" (or "Die Novize von Palermo"), Opera	Orchestra, Chorus, etc.	1835-6

Appendix A

COMPOSITION.	INSTRUMENTS, ETC.	COMPOSED.
Overture (" *Rule Britannia* ")	Orchestra	1836
Overture (" *Polonia* ") in C major	Orchestra	1836
Incidental music to a " Zauberposse " by Gleich	Orchestra and Voice	1836
Romance in G	Voice and Orchestra	1837
Hymn of the people on the Emperor Nicholas ascending the throne	Voices and Orchestra	1837
3 *Romanzen—* (1) Dors mon enfant (2) Mignonne (3) Attente	Voice and pianoforte	1839–40
" *Die beiden Grenadiere* " (Song)	Voice and pianoforte	1839–40
" *A Faust Overture* "	Orchestra	1840, Re-written 1855
" *Der Tannenbaum* " (Song)	Voice and pianoforte	1840
" *Rienzi der Letzte der Tribunen* " (Grand Opera in 5 acts)	Orchestra, Chorus, etc.	1840
" *Der fliegende Holländer* " (Romantic Opera in 3 acts)	Orchestra, Chorus, etc.	1841
Arrangement of Halévy's " La Reine de Chypre"	Pianoforte	1841
Arrangement of Halévy's "'Le Guittarero "	Pianoforte	1841
Arrangement of Donizetti's Opera, " La Favorita "	Pianoforte	1841

Wagner

COMPOSITION.	INSTRUMENTS, ETC.	COMPOSED.
Arrangement of Donizetti's "L'Elisir d'Amore "	Pianoforte	1841
Gelegentreits cantate (composed for the unveiling of the statue of King Frederick Augustus)	Orchestra, Chorus, etc.	1843
"*Das Liebesmahl der Apostel*" (Eine biblische Scene)	Full orchestra and male voices	1843
"*Gruss an den König*" (On the return from England of King Frederick Augustus)	Orchestra and male voices	1844
Trauermarsch (An Weber's Grabe) on a theme from "Euryanthe "	Orchestra (wind instruments)	1844
" An Weber's Grabe "	Double quartet for voices	1844
"*Tannhäuser*" (Romantic Opera in 3 acts)	Orchestra, Chorus, etc.	1844–5
Arrangement of ending to Overture to Gluck's " Iphigenia in Aulis "	Orchestra	1847
"*Lohengrin*" (Romantic Opera in 3 acts)	Orchestra, Chorus, etc.	1847
Arrangement of portions of Mozart's " Don Giovanni"	Orchestra, etc.	1850
Album Sonata in E flat	Pianoforte	1853
"*Das Rheingold*; " part I. of "Der Ring des Nibelungen"	Orchestra, etc.	Commenced 1848, completed May, 1854

Appendix A

COMPOSITION.	INSTRUMENTS, ETC.	COMPOSED.
"*Die Walküre*;" part II. of "Der Ring"	Orchestra, etc.	Commenced 1854, completed 1856
"*Tristan und Isolde*" (Opera in 3 acts)	Orchestra, etc.	Commenced 1857, completed 1859
"*Albumblatt*" in C	Pianoforte	Composed 1861
Fünf Gedichte— (1) Der Engel (2) Stehe still (3) Im Treibhaus (4) Schmerzen (5) Träume	Pianoforte and female voice	1862
Huldigungsmarsch	Orchestra (originally scored for a military band)	1864
"*Die Meistersinger von Nürnberg*" (Opera in 3 acts)	Orchestra, Chorus, etc.	Commenced 1862, completed 1867
"*Siegfried*;" part III. of "Der Ring," in 3 acts	Orchestra, Chorus, etc.	Commenced 1857, completed 1869
Siegfried Idyll	Orchestra	1870
Kaisermarsch in B flat	Orchestra and Chorus *ad lib*.	1871
"*Die Götterdämmerung*;" part IV. of "Der Ring" (Vorspiel and 3 acts)	Orchestra, Chorus, etc.	Commenced 1870, completed 1874
Albumblatt in E flat	Pianoforte	1875

Wagner

Composition.	Instruments, etc.	Composed.
Grosser Festsmarsch (for the Centennial Exhibition at Philadelphia)	Orchestra	1876
Arrangement of Palestrina's " Stabat Mater "	Orchestra, etc.	1877
" *Parsifal* " (Bühnenweihfest-spiel in 3 acts)	Orchestra, Chorus, etc.	Commenced 1877, completed 1882, (the Charfreitagszauber in 1857)

APPENDIX B

Literary Works

An das deutsche Heer vor Paris. 1871.
Autobiographische Skizze. 1842.
Bayreuther Blätter, eight articles in the. 1878–1882.
Beethoven. 1870.
Bemerkungen zur Aufführung der Oper "Der fliegende Holländer."
   1852.
Bericht an Seine Majestät den König Ludwig II. von Bayern, etc.
   1865.
Bericht über die Aufführung des "Tannhaüser" in Paris. 1861.
Bericht über die Aufführung der neunten Symphonie von Beethoven.
   1846.
Bericht über die Heimbringung der sterblichen Uberreste Karl
   Maria von Weber's ans London nach Dresden. Rede an
   Weber's letzter Ruhestätte. Gesang nach der Bestattung.
   1844.
Bericht über eine neue Pariser Oper ("La Reine de Chypre") von
   Halévy. 1840–1.
Bericht über die wieder Aufführung eines Jugendwerkes. 1882.
Brief an Hector Berlioz. 1860.
Brief an H. v. Stein. 1883.
Brief an H. v. Wolzogen. 1882.
Bühnenfestspiel in Bayreuth, 1882.
Censuren : (1) W. H. Riehl, (2) Ferdinand Hiller, (3) Eine
   Erinnerung an Rossini, (4) Edward Devrient, (5) Aufklärun-
   gen über "Das Judenthum in der Musik." 1868–9.
Das Judenthum in der Musik. 1850.
Das Künstlerthum der Zukunft (a fragment). 1849.
Das Kunstwerk der Zukunft. 1849.
Das Liebesverbot. Bericht über eine erste Opernaufführung. 1836.
Das Publikum in Zeit und Raum. 1878.

Wagner

Das Wiener Hof-Operntheater. 1863.
Dem Königlichen Freunde. Gedicht. 1864.
Der Freischütz (two articles). 1841.
Der Nibelungen Mythus. 1848.
Deutsche Kunst und deutsche Politik. 1865.
Die Glückliche Bärenfamilie. 1838.
Die Hohe Braut (sketches). 1836.
Die Kunst und die Revolution. 1849.
Die Sarazenin. 1843.
Die Sieger. 1856.
Die Wibelungen. (Weltgeschichte aus der Sage.) 1848.
Drei Gedichte: (1) Rheingold, (2) Bei der Vollendung des
    " Siegfried," (3) Zum 25th August, 1870. 1869–70.
Ein deutscher Musiker in Paris (a series of seven articles). 1840–1.
Ein Rückblick auf die Bühnenfestspiele des Jahres, 1876. 1878.
Ein Theater in Zurich. 1851.
Eine Kapitulation. 1870–1.
Eine Mittheilung an meine Freunde. 1851.
Entwurf (concerning the projected Bayreuth School). 1877.
Entwurf zur Organisation eines deutschen National Theaters für
    das Königreich Sachsen. 1848.
Epilogischer Bericht über die Umstände und Schicksale, etc. 1863.
Erinnerungen an Auber. 1871.
Erinnerungen an Spontini. 1851.
Erkenne dich selbst. 1881.
Friedrich der Rothbart. 1848.
Gluck's Ouvertüre zu "Iphigenia in Aulis." 1854.
Heldenthum und Christiantum. 1881.
Jesus von Nazareth. 1848.
Kunst und Klima. 1850.
Lebenserinnerungen. (A privately printed autobiography).
Meine Erinnerungen an Ludwig Schnorr von Carolsfeld. 1868.
Modern. 1878.
Nachruf an L. Spohr und Chordirektor W. Fischer. 1860.
Offenes Schreiben an Herrn Ernst von Weber. 1879.
Offenes Schreiben an Herrn Friedrich Schön in Worms. 1882.
Oper und Drama (3 parts). 1851.
Programmatische Erläuterungen. (Eroica Symphony and Coriolan
    Overture of Beethoven.) 1852. (Overtures to Der fliegende

Appendix B

Holländer, Tannhäuser, and Lohengrin.) 1853. Beethoven's
C Sharp minor Quartet (posthumous).
Publikum und Popularität. 1878.
Religion und Kunst. 1880.
Sacrificial scene and invocation (for a play, unknown). 1837.
Schlussbericht über die Umstände und Schicksale, etc. 1873.
Sendschreiben und Kleinere Aufsätze (7 articles). 1872–3.
Siegfried's Tod. 1848.
Trinkspruch am Gedenkstage des 300 jährigen Bestchens der
Königlichen, etc., Capelle in Dresden. 1848.
Ueber das Dichten und Komponiren. 1879.
Ueber das Dirigiren. 1869.
Ueber das Opern Dichten und Komponiren im Besonderen. 1879.
Ueber das Weibliche in Menschlichen. 1883.
Ueber die Anwendung der Musik auf das Drama. 1879.
Ueber die Aufführung des " Tannhäuser." 1852.
Ueber die Bestimmung der Oper. 1871.
Ueber die " Goethestiftung." 1851.
Ueber die Ouvertüre. 1840–1.
Ueber eine Aufführung von Spohr's " Jessonda." 1874.
Ueber Franz Liszt's symphonische Dichtungen. 1857.
Ueber musikalische Kritik. 1852.
Ueber Schauspieler und Sänger. 1872.
Ueber Staat und Religion. 1864.
Was ist deutsch ? 1878.
Was nützt diese Erkenntnis ? 1880.
Wieland der Schmied. 1849.
Wollen wir hoffen ? 1879.
Zukunftsmusik. 1860.
Zum Vorspiel von Act III. der Meistersinger (posthumous).
Zum Vorspiel von Parsifal (posthumous).
Zum Vorspiel von Tristan und Isolde (posthumous).
Zum Vortrag der neunten Symphonie Beethoven's. 1873.
Zur Widmung der zweiten Auflage von " Oper und Drama." 1863.

N.B. This list does not include the texts of his Dramas or his
voluminous correspondence with Liszt, Uhlig, and others.

APPENDIX C

Principal Events in the Life of Wagner

1813, May 22 ... Born at Leipzig, in the Brühl (now No. 88).

1822, Dec. ... Commenced his studies at the Kreuzschule, Leipzig, and remained there until autumn of 1827.

1828 ... ... Continued his education at the Nicolaischule, Leipzig. Commenced studying thorough-bass and composition, and became pupil of Gottlieb Müller (afterwards Organist at Altenburg).

1829–1830 ... Attended the Thomasschule. His overture in B flat played at the Theatre—a fiasco.

1830 ... ... Matriculated at Leipzig University and became the pupil of Theodor Weinlig, Cantor at the Thomasschule, who thoroughly taught him composition, thoroughbass, etc.

1832 ... ... Visited Vienna.

1833 ... ... His symphony in C played at Gewandhaus Concert at Leipzig. In this year he commenced his musical career in earnest. Became Chorus-master under his brother Albert, at the Theatre at Würzburg. Composed his opera "Die Feen."

1834 ... ... Returned to Leipzig. In the autumn of this year was appointed Musik-director at the Magdeburg Theatre. The company became bankrupt and Wagner returned to Leipzig. Visited Berlin, and from there went to Königsberg and obtained the appointment of Conductor of the Theatre there.

256

Appendix C

1836, Nov. 24 ...	Married Fräulein Planer, daughter of Gothilf Planer of Dresden. The Director of the Königsberg Theatre became insolvent.
1838	On the recommendation of Dorn, Wagner obtains the post of First Musikdirector of the Theatre at Riga.
1839, July ...	His contract at Riga having terminated, he sailed, with his wife, for London en route for Paris. Stayed eight days in London. Met Meyerbeer at Boulogne, and stayed with him for one month. Meyerbeer gave him letters of introduction to Schlesinger (the publisher and proprietor of the *Revue et Gazette Musicale*), to M. Gouin, his agent, and to the Directors of the Opéra and the Théâtre de la Renaissance.
1839, Sept. ...	Arrived in Paris (where he resided until the 7th April, 1842).
1842	Left Paris for Dresden—made a trip to the mountains of Bohemia, and finished (at Teplitz) his sketches for Tannhäuser.
1843, Jan. ...	Appointed Hofcapellmeister at Dresden at a salary of 1500 thalers (£225), and was installed on February 2nd.
1849	Became involved in political troubles, and (orders having been issued for his arrest) removed to Weimar. In June, 1849, went to Zurich, where he was joined by his wife, and in October of the same year became a citizen of that town.
1850, Aug. 28	First performance of " Lohengrin " at Weimar, under the direction of Liszt.
1855, Jan. ...	Invited by Mr. Anderson (a Director of the Philharmonic Society of London) to take the *bâton* at the forthcoming season's concerts, which offer he accepted and arrived in London in February.

Wagner

1859	Took up his abode at Venice, with the sanction of the Austrian officials, and from thence moved to Lyons. In September of this year (1859) he again went to Paris. Tannhäuser performed there, through the influence of Madame de Metternich, and as a further result of her exertions on his behalf permission was given him to re-enter German states (except Saxony).
1861	Returned to Germany.
1863	Gave concerts in Germany and Russia.
1864	King Ludwig II. of Bavaria invited him to Munich, and allowed him a salary from the Privy purse of about £100.
1865, Dec. ...	In consequence of the conspiracies and cabals formed against him in Munich he went to Vevey and Geneva, where he remained until his departure for Bayreuth in 1872.
1866, Jan. 25 ...	His first wife, Minna Wagner (*née* Planer), died.
1870, Aug. 25	Married Cosima von Bülow (*née* Liszt).
1872, April ...	Removed to Bayreuth, and in May founded his Theatre there.
1876	The entire work of " Der Ring des Nibelungen " performed at Bayreuth.
1877, May ...	Wagner Festival at the Albert Hall, London.
1879–1882 ...	In consequence of attacks of erysipelas he decided to go to Italy, and took up his residence at Palermo in January, 1882 ; and afterwards removed to Venice.
1882, July ...	First performance of " Parsifal " at Bayreuth.
1883, Feb. 13 ...	Died in the afternoon of this day, and was interred on the 18th February at Bayreuth.

APPENDIX D

Cast of First Performance of "Der Ring des Nibelungen"

Conductor—HANS RICHTER.

Leader of Orchestra—AUGUST WILHELMJ.

"Das Rheingold"

Wotan	. Franz Betz.	*Fafnir*	. Franz von Reichen-berg.
Donner	. Eugen Gura.		
Froh .	. Georg Unger.	*Fricka*	. Friederike Grün.
Loge .	. Heinrich Vogl.	*Freia*	. Marie Haupt.
Alberich	. Carl Hill.	*Erda*	. Luise Jaïde.
Mime	. Carl Schlosser.	*The*	Lilli Lehmann.
Fasolt	. Albert Eilers.	*Rhine*	Marie Lehmann.
		Daughters	Minna Lammert.

"Die Walküre"

Siegmund .	Albert Niemann.	*Ortlinde*	. Marie Lehmann.
Hunding	. Joseph Niering.	*Waltraute*	. Luise Jaïde.
Wotan .	. Franz Betz.	*Siegrune*	. Antonie Amann.
Sieglinde	. Joséphine Schefzky.	*Rossweisse*	Minna Lammert.
Brünnhilde	Amalie Materna.	*Grimgerde*	. Hedwig Reicher-Kindermann.
Fricka	. Friederike Grün.		
Gerhilde	. Marie Haupt.	*Schmertleite*	Johanna Jachmann-Wagner.
Helmwige .	Lilli Lehmann.		

259

Wagner

Siegfried	. Georg Unger.	*Fafnir*	. Franz von Reichen-berg.
Mime	. Carl Schlosser.		
The Wan-derer	Franz Betz.	*Erda*	. Luise Jaïde.
		Brünnhilde	Amalie Materna.
Alberich	. Carl Hill.	*The Bird*	. Marie Haupt.

" DIE GÖTTERDÄMMERUNG "

Siegfried	. Georg Unger.		⎰ Johanna Jachmann-Wagner
Gunther	. Eugen Gura.	*The*	
Hagen	. Gustav Siehr.	*Norns*	Joséphine Schefzky.
Alberich	. Carl Hill.		⎱ Friederike Grün.
Brünnhilde	Amalie Materna.	*The*	⎰ Lilli Lehmann.
Gutrune	. Mathilde Weckerlin.	*Rhine*	Marie Lehmann.
Waltraute	. Luise Jaïde.	*Daughters*	⎱ Minna Lammert.

APPENDIX E

Cast of First Performances of "Parsifal"

Conductors : Hermann Levi, Franz Fischer.

Amfortas	{ Reichmann.	*1st Esquire*	Keil.
	Fuchs.	*2nd Esquire*	Galfy.
Titurel	. Kindermann.	*3rd Esquire*	Hubbenet.
Gurnemanz	{ Scaria.	*4th Esquire*	Mikorey.
	Siehr.	*Kundry*	{ Materna.
Parsifal	{ Gudehus.		Malten.
	Winkelmann.		Horson.
	Jaeger.		Meta.
Klingsor	. Hill.	*Flower*	Keil.
1st Knight	Fuchs.	*Maidens*	Andre.
2nd Knight	Stumpf.		Belce.
			Galfy.

Chorus : 46 men, 36 women, 45 children.

Index

Index

Index

Wagner

THE END

LONDON : PRINTED BY WILLIAM CLOWES AND SONS, LIMITED,
STAMFORD STREET AND CHARING CROSS.